IMPRACTICAL MAGIC

MYRTLEWOOD MYSTERIES BOOK 9

IRIS BEAGLEHOLE

Copyright © 2024 by Iris Beaglehole

All rights reserved.

No part of this book may be reproduced in any form or by any electronic or mechanical means, including information storage and retrieval systems, without written permission from the author, except for the use of brief quotations in a book review.

DEAREST READERS...

I'm thrilled that you've come along with me on the Myrtlewood Mysteries journey this far. At the time of writing it has been a little while since Rosemary and Athena have been my main characters and it was wonderful to spend time with them. This story is a little longer than most of their books and goes into some challenges, for Athena especially. She's had a rough time, as we all do from time to time. I write fairly intuitively and this was the story the characters and I needed to tell. I want to let you know that there are some themes of coping with mental health challenges, and that the main characters will all be okay. It's still a cosy read, and sometimes it's only in going through the darkness that we find our light again.

Blessed be xx

Iris

MAGICAL GIFTS FROM IRIS

Hey lovelies. I have a special gift for you including bonus scenes and other magical goodies, when you sign up to my newsletter!

The Keys to Myrtlewood include:
🗝Accidental Magic alternative perspective scene (Perseus Burk meeting Rosemary for the first time)
🗝Accidental Magic Tarot Spread
🗝Seasonal Ritual Mini Guide
🗝Quest of the Dreamcharmer (Dreamrealm Mysteries prequel)

Subscribe to the Myrtlewood Coven newsletter and get instant access to this fabulous selection of special Myrtlewood content: irisbeaglehole.com/newsletter

1
ATHENA

"So good to see you. I missed you so much." Rosemary wrapped her arms around her daughter. The afternoon sun streamed through the stained glass windows surrounding the front door, catching the red and copper tones in their hair.

"It's only been a week, Mum. You're acting like you haven't seen me for a whole year," Athena replied, but she squeezed back just as tightly.

"It feels that way," said Rosemary. She stepped back, drinking in the sight of her daughter. "Look at you." A newfound grace clung to Athena's movements, a subtle reminder of her time in the fae realm. "You're looking really well. I'm so glad."

The sentient house hummed with contentment at Athena's return, the floorboards creaking softly beneath their feet as they made their way to the kitchen.

"Turns out a trip to the fae realm was just what I needed to lift my spirits," said Athena. There was a tightness in her voice that suggested there was something more to it.

"How was everything with your other family?" Rosemary asked, trying to keep her tone light despite the worry gnawing at her insides.

"Actually, fabulous," said Athena. "The queen is...odd as usual."

"It is strange how you call her 'the queen' when she's your grandmother."

"You mean when she looks younger than you?" Athena quipped, her green eyes sparkling with mischief.

Rosemary elbowed her daughter playfully. "You're right. She's a gorgeous creature."

Athena smiled. "You're gorgeous too. Even with your wrinkles."

"I'm glad to hear it," said Rosemary, putting the kettle on for tea, "though I'm not sure what Burk will think of my wrinkles in the next few decades, given that he probably has exactly the same number he had a thousand years ago."

"That's what you get for shacking up with a vampire," Athena teased.

"Speaking of him..." said Rosemary, looking out towards the late morning sun in the back garden. "Let's go have a look."

They walked towards the French doors that led out to the back garden, the house seeming to guide them with a gentle shift in the air.

The trees surrounding the back lawn had started to grow fresh green baby leaves and gentle blossoms, so early for the season – a sign of the magic that permeated Myrtlewood. The herbs and shrubs by the back door released a heady mix of scents: rosemary, thyme, and daphne lingering in the air.

Burk stood barefoot on the grass, eyes closed, face tilted towards the sun. His skin shimmered like black diamonds in the warm light, an otherworldly quality that took Rosemary's breath away, even though she'd seen this sparkly vampire before. She felt both wonder and concern as she watched him, marvelling at the magic and mayhem of the Winter Solstice when he'd first gained the ability to withstand sunlight through her own attempt to save him.

"Do you think he's going to start a cult?" Athena asked, breaking the spell. "Isn't that what ultra shiny people do?"

"Perhaps. Want to join?" Rosemary winked.

They both giggled, the sound causing a nearby windchime to tinkle softly in response. "He's been doing this a lot?" Athena asked.

Rosemary shrugged. "Well, at first, after the solstice, when you were still here, he didn't dare go outside just in case it had worn off. But more recently, he got braver. He started experimenting with going near the open windows, exposing himself to more and more sunlight, even in the middle of the day. And now, well, he's been doing this every day. He seems to enjoy himself, so I suppose it's fine."

"Until he bursts into flames," Athena said dryly.

"That's what I've been worried about," Rosemary admitted, "but he's close enough to the house that he could come back in at any moment. Plus, I've got a protective charm ready, just in case." She pointed to a bucket of water near the door.

Athena chuckled. "Trust you to put a protective charm in a bucket of water."

"I thought it would be more fun that way," said Rosemary. "And also more intuitive, you know…I always want a bucket of water to hand when I set things on fire."

Athena shook her head, bemused. "It's still weird to see a vampire sunbathing."

"Do you want to keep watching?" Rosemary asked.

"Maybe over a cup of tea," Athena suggested.

Rosemary gasped and looked horrified as the kettle began to whistle. "Tea! You've been here a full five minutes and I haven't made any. All right. We'd better remedy that situation forthwith." She put her arm around her daughter, and together they went back to the kitchen.

Rosemary reached for their favourite teacups – hers was a deep forest green at the moment, Athena's a swirling pattern of purple and silver that seemed to shift in the light. The familiar weight and warmth of the porcelain in her hands was comforting.

They carried the tea tray to the lounge.

"Let's sit by the windows so we can keep an eye on Mr Sparkles," said Athena.

"Good idea," Rosemary said. "How are Finnegan and Cedar and your dad?" Rosemary asked as she sipped the strong Earl Grey that was their regular blend.

"The boys are enjoying married bliss," said Athena. "But Dad seems a little bored, I think."

"Oh, no," said Rosemary. "A restless Dain is never good news."

"No, well, he's never been that interested in fae politics. And now that Finnegan and Cedar are settled into their new roles, I think Dad's getting a bit antsy."

"Perhaps we should cook up some new scheme for him to pursue," Rosemary suggested. "Something to keep him occupied. He needs novelty, that one."

"You're right," said Athena, "but I can't think of anything that would keep him entertained for more than five minutes."

"Well, Imbolc is coming up soon," Rosemary said, glancing at the calendar on the wall where the upcoming celebration was circled in red. "Perhaps you could ask him to come back and be on the lookout for mischief. He could bring some fae soldiers. I'm sure something will happen. If there's anything to be said about the seasonal festivals in Myrtlewood, it's that they're full of unexpected twists."

Athena sighed. "And here you were hoping for a nice, quiet life."

Rosemary sighed. "You know, I think I've mostly hoped for a nice, quiet life because I get overwhelmed and burnt out easily. I'm not the best at relaxing, even with the lovely hammock you got me. I probably need a new project too."

"Maybe you and Dad can work on one together," Athena suggested.

"Maybe," said Rosemary. "Though I doubt we could work together without driving each other batty. But I agree with your point. Perhaps, if we occupy ourselves enough with some new challenge, the chaos that this town insists on throwing our way won't be such a big deal."

"Unless you get way in over your head."

"Can you figure out what the stars and planets are doing so we can work with the tensions rather than against them?" Rosemary asked. "Isn't that what you're always telling me to do?"

"It's a good point," said Athena. "It might help me catch up on my schoolwork too. I'm so behind, even on Astrology class."

Rosemary felt the chill of dread. Athena was seventeen, which was magically "of age". She was in her last school year, which meant that she had to become a proper adult at some point, or at least a fledgling adult.

The last few months – in fact, the whole last year – had been so intense that Rosemary hadn't wanted to broach the subject of Athena's plans too much. The future hovered over them like dark looming clouds, or perhaps more like a net ready to ensnare them into some tricky situations at any moment.

Pushing aside her worries, Rosemary took another sip of tea before speaking again. "Only a few more months of school," she said, smiling at her daughter.

"Yeah," said Athena. She replied with a smile, but she looked down at her cup, nervous.

"Worried?" Rosemary asked softly.

"Just don't know what I'm going to do," said Athena, her voice low, almost a whisper. "I'm worried I've messed up my grades, and I don't really understand the magical education system or what the options are."

"I'm sure there's somebody at school you can talk to about it," said Rosemary, reaching out to squeeze Athena's hand. "And don't worry, most people don't know what they want to do when they're seventeen years old, or eighteen, or twenty-one, or forty for that matter."

"You figured it out when you were about thirty-nine, so good for you," Athena retorted.

"It's true, I have the shop," said Rosemary, "but that doesn't mean I'm not going to do anything else with my life."

"What else are you going to do?" said Athena. "Maybe you really do need a new project. Everything's going too smoothly for you. As much as you wouldn't want to admit it, you totally thrive on chaos."

Rosemary smirked and gently nudged Athena with her elbow.

A thudding sound drew their attention. Two small creatures burst into the room, one scampering across the floor and the other bounding in with impossible grace for its size.

"Serpentine Fuzzball and Nugget!" said Athena.

"The familiars certainly know how to make an entrance." Rosemary smiled, watching as the fuzzy black cat leapt onto the window seat beside her, clearly anticipating ear scratches. Meanwhile, Nugget, the mischievous golden squirrel, scrambled up Athena's legs to perch on her shoulder. "They've missed you."

Athena cooed and patted both of the familiars, Nugget chittering excitedly on her shoulder while Fuzzball purred loudly enough to make the cushions tremble. "I missed you too, my darlings," she said to the magical creatures. "It's good to be home, even if I don't know what I'm doing with my life."

"Well, the funny thing about life," said Rosemary, absently stroking Fuzzball's soft fur, "is that you never do completely know. And that's half the fun."

Athena rolled her eyes. "Sure it is."

Nugget, as if sensing her mood, nuzzled against her cheek, his fluffy tail tickling her ear.

"Just be gentle with yourself," said Rosemary, her tone becoming somewhat uncomfortable. "You weren't feeling too good before you went away to the fae realm. Do you want to talk about it?"

Athena shrugged. "There's nothing to talk about. Everything was lovely in the fae realm." As she spoke, Nugget scampered down her arm and onto the windowsill, his bright eyes fixed on something in the garden.

Rosemary patted her daughter on the shoulder. "It'll be okay, I promise you. Things will get better in time." Fuzzball padded over to Athena and butted her head against the girl's hand, as if offering comfort.

"You know what? At first, I suppose I was still high on the adrenaline from everything that happened. It was quite an intense Winter Solstice," Athena admitted, scratching Fuzzball behind the ears.

"Exactly," said Rosemary. "Then things get back to reality and that becomes less fun."

"Exactly," said Athena. "But I'll be back to school tomorrow, and it'll be nice to see my friends again and at least have an excuse to be busy. I've got so much to catch up on."

"You can throw in a little research on Imbolc while you're at it," said Rosemary. "I'm sure it'll come in handy."

Athena groaned. "More distractions. Yay!" At her words, Nugget chittered what sounded suspiciously like a laugh, drawing an amused glance from both witches.

"Oh, come on," said Rosemary. "There'll be plenty more distractions in our future." As if in agreement, Thorn Manor creaked softly, and a warm breeze wafted through the room, carrying the scent of early spring blossoms. Fuzzball's ears perked up at the sound, while Nugget's tail twitched in anticipation of new adventures to come.

Rosemary gazed out to where Burk was still basking in the sunlight. She felt a surge of love for her unconventional family and this bizarre and beautiful life they were creating together, but something told her to prepare for the unexpected. There were always more surprises in Myrtlewood.

2

THE DEVOURER

The afternoon was slowly bleeding into the night. A man stood at the edge of the forest, his head tilted downwards, occasionally glancing towards Thorn Manor and then across towards the township of Myrtlewood. There was only one thought in his mind: revenge. His clothing was tattered now, where it used to be lush, plush, and awesome velvet. The brushed down jacket was stolen from a washing line he passed on his journey. He could see lights on in Thorn Manor; Rosemary would be there with her entourage. They would probably be full of smugness over their own victories, caring little for the damage they caused to so many lives, especially his own. He would get revenge. He would reclaim the town.

He turned and headed off towards one of the worn paths through the forest. But as he proceeded, he heard a shuffling sound. The man froze and looked around him. There was nothing. He took a cautious step and then another. It wasn't long before he was back to his regular pace, assuming that it had just been a squirrel, an owl, or some other night time animal. His thoughts returned to plotting revenge, and the hunger to inflict pain on those that he believed had wronged him resumed total control of his mind.

Another sound broke through the silence: a cracking branch. A figure stumbled towards him, limping along. His initial reaction of fear subsided as he saw it was only an old man with a weathered-looking hat, a few branches and sticks protruding from the rags he wore. As the man limped closer, his eyes wide and bloodshot, he reached out. "So hungry," he said with a croaky voice. "Is there any food?"

"Don't be ridiculous," the man scoffed. "I only have what I need for myself."

"Please," the old man pleaded.

"Shove off with you," the man said, pushing the wretched figure away as he continued on his path.

The tugging in his belly alerted him to his own hunger. He reached into his knapsack and began to quickly sift through his meagre supplies. It should have been enough to last several days. Perhaps he could have even shared with that man, if there was something in it for him. And yet, quickly, he demolished all the food he carried, still ignoring the remaining thirst and hunger as he moved on through the forest, searching for something that could satisfy him.

3

ROSEMARY

As they gathered around the dinner table, Rosemary smiled and felt a well of deep appreciation for the wonderful people in her life that she couldn't quite find the words to express, although she had made them a delicious chocolate tart for dessert. Marjie had also made the dinner, a casserole prepared with chicken, potatoes, and other vegetables in a tomato gravy with spices.

Burk inhaled deeply. "It smells fantastic," he said.

"It does," Rosemary agreed.

Athena shot Burk a puzzled look. "Do you usually think our food smells good before it's had a blood enchantment?"

Burk shrugged. "I suppose not." He reached for the casserole dish and began to serve himself.

Rosemary gasped. "Are you actually doing what I think you're doing?"

"Slowly," Marjie cautioned. "It's hot."

"You know, I think the sunlight might be changing me," Burk said.

Rosemary gulped. "That sounds concerning. I like you the way you are. I don't want you to change." She gestured to the bowl of casserole. "Are you sure this won't make you rather ill?"

"Normally, it would. I'd need the blood enchantment on it to even swallow it without being ill."

"And you don't want that?" she asked.

"Let me have a taste first," he insisted.

"All right then!" said Rosemary.

They all watched with bated breath as Burk picked up a small spoon of casserole and popped it into his mouth. He closed his eyes and groaned.

"Oh no, I knew this was a bad idea," said Rosemary, reaching for his spoon.

"Wait," said Athena, "he looks like he's doing okay."

Indeed, on closer inspection, Burk had his eyes closed in reverie, as much as when he was basking in the sunlight earlier.

"Astonishing," said Marjie. "Perhaps the sunlight is having some kind of effect on your digestive system!"

"Fascinating," Rosemary said.

"I'm not sure I should have any more right now. Could you pass the bowl over to Marjie?" Burk asked.

Marjie completed the blood enchantment quickly, and then they resumed their meal.

"So, I *can* enjoy real human food," said Burk. "I just didn't want to go overboard in case it was too much too soon."

"That's very wise," said Rosemary. "You could learn a thing or two from this man," she said to Athena.

"About not rushing into things or testing thoroughly?" Athena asked. "Point taken. So could you!"

Just then, there was a knock on the door.

"Who is it?" said Rosemary.

Athena shook her head. Marjie merely shrugged.

Rosemary went to check. On the doorstep stood a handful of

familiar terrifying and ancient beings dressed in old-fashioned clothing from various historical periods, staring at her hungrily.

"Burk, your buddies are here," she called out. She turned back to face the Vampire Council. "What is it you want?"

"We are seeking an audience with my son," said Charles, stepping forward, his blond hair perfectly suited to his pale pink polo shirt. "Good evening, Rosemary."

"Good evening," Rosemary said, greeting him with a warm smile. "Please, come in." Despite the concerning circumstances, the Vampire Council had only showed up on her doorstep a few times before, and always when there was some major problem. In the past, she'd been the one responsible for the problem, and at least this time, that wasn't the case. Still, she was concerned.

Burk appeared beside her in a flash.

"What is it? What do you want?" Rosemary asked the uninvited visitors.

"The Council is most fascinated by the recent developments that you've experienced," Charles explained.

Rosemary raised an eyebrow. "And those are?"

"We'd like you to come with us for some brief experimentation," Charles said to Burk.

"Experiments?" said Rosemary. "I'm not having you chopping him up or anything."

"Oh, no, don't worry. It won't be anything like that. We simply want to study this rather unusual turn of events. We have some questions for you too."

"Oh, you do, do you?" said Rosemary, feeling her inner-stroppiness take over.

"Is it true that you have some kind of magic that can stop werewolves from changing at the full moon?" an older looking vampire with a big beard in Victorian garb asked.

"I suppose, yes, I can admit to that," Rosemary said.

"This indeed is fascinating. We'll have more questions for you in the future, but for now, we'd appreciate it if you'd come with us, Burk," an unfamiliar vampire in a tweed vest said.

"Just like that? With no warning?" Rosemary asked.

"It'll be quicker this way," Charles promised.

"No harm will come to him," said Rosemary, stepping forward to take Burk's hand.

"I'll be fine," Burk reassured her. "I can understand the Council's interest in this situation. A vampire being able to go out in the sunlight is nearly unheard of, aside from scrawled legends from some ancient relics."

Rosemary sighed. "You can have him for three days, maximum."

Burk chuckled. "I must say, I appreciate how protective you are of me. It shows you care."

"Of course I do," Rosemary said furiously.

"It's nice of you to return the favour, Rosemary," said Burk. "You know how much I love you. And I want to reassure you. I'll be fine."

Rosemary smiled and then turned back to the council. "All right, he can go with you, but give us at least another hour or two to finish dinner and say goodbye properly."

"You want us to wait that long while you have a...meal?" the Victorian chap asked in disbelief.

"And say goodbye *properly*," said Rosemary.

Charles laughed. "We'll give you some privacy then." With that, the vampires on her doorstep all vanished, except for one – the most important one. The one who – if it were up to Rosemary – should really not be going anywhere.

"Five minutes to eat dinner," said Rosemary, "and then I want you upstairs."

"Yes, madam," Burk said with an enormous grin on his face, following Rosemary back inside. "I wouldn't want it any other way."

4
ATHENA

Athena went up to bed with an emotional rawness that made her want to curl up in the foetal position. She drew the curtains over the French doors to the balcony in her beautiful room overlooking the back garden, catching a glimpse of the surrounding forest. It stretched all the way to the village with a view out to the foggy horizon of the sea. The house had shaped this space for her so beautifully. It was even more wonderful since the winter solstice. In its re-build, Thorn Manor had given her extra space and expanded her adorable library-study with its secret bookshelf door. She pressed her hand to the wall in silent thanks, allowing a warmth to spread through her body. She really had a wonderful life...she only hoped she wasn't going to spiral again.

Deep inside, things hadn't felt so good lately.

As she pulled the last of the curtains closed she glanced out towards the dark forest and felt a shiver, a chill running down her spine. Was she being watched? It wouldn't be totally ridiculous to fathom that there might be dark forces out there, enemies of some sort or another. This was all part of life in Myrtlewood, after all. A part of her secretly longed for something terrifying – a magical calamity – an epic distraction, just so that she didn't have to face the dark emotions swirling and churning within.

She'd hoped a trip to the fae realm would lighten things, and it had, but coming back to this heavier realm where everything seemed more solid and solemn and serious...well, that only made the bad feelings so much worse.

As she prepared for bed, she noticed the aching sensation was back; she'd been grappling with it for weeks now. It was the same gnawing feeling she'd had when Elise had vanished. Only now she knew exactly where her ex-girlfriend was, and it wasn't helping.

Outwardly, Athena seemed perfectly normal. She wanted it that way. She didn't want to make anyone else miserable, after all, especially not her mother. And not tonight when they'd received the surprise news that Burk had to go away. Marjie and Athena had gone for a little walk to give them some privacy and say goodbye. By the time they'd returned, Rosemary was in the kitchen, washing up, her face slightly puffy.

She sat in her cosy armchair and held the cushion in her arms for a moment, as if it might impart some comfort. Athena wanted to be strong, for her mother and for her own sense of dignity, but inside there was that agonising ache, that dire thirst, that familiar emptiness that could never be satisfied – not by good food, good conversation, or even her beautiful room full of books and supplies for making art and magic. She picked up a book but struggled to focus on reading, which was unusual for her. Normally Athena could work through several paranormal romances in an ordinary week, but now they only made her more despairing. She couldn't face romantic tragedy novels either; she had a real one of her own.

Yes, going home to the fae realm had been a welcome release. There was something about that place that eased her pain, but now that she was back in her ordinary life, the aching had returned. Perhaps, this time Athena was prepared for it.

She opened a backpack and pulled out a bundle of fabric. It was a scarf, and carefully wrapped inside was a golden bottle in the shape of a pear, adorned with gleaming, gilded leaves.

"Take this, just one or two drops on the tongue," Queen Áine had said after Athena had confessed the deep inner pain that was apparently already obvious to her powerful grandmother. Perhaps psychic perception was one of the perks of being the ruler of the fae realm. "It will ease your worries and fill you with joy. It will help you sleep the sleep that you need, help you focus even if you're easily distracted. It will lift your spirits."

"What's the catch?" Athena had asked.

Her grandmother smiled benevolently at her.

"There is no catch."

"There's always a catch with the fae," Athena retorted.

"That's not the easiest potion to make," the Queen said slowly. "It only works on the emotional level; it won't solve any of your problems by itself. It'll just ease the pain."

Athena sighed gratefully. "That's exactly what I need." She'd reached forward for the bottle, but her grandmother hesitated slightly.

"Remember, only one or two drops. To take more could be risky."

Athena had scoffed. "That's fine, I can follow instructions. I'm not my mother, am I?" She'd reached for the bottle once more. Queen Áine pulled back just slightly.

"There is one catch for you," she said instead, eyes squinting suspiciously.

"What is that?"

"I want you to take more of a role here."

Athena shook her head. "I have to focus on my studies; it's getting serious now. Everyone's starting to worry about my future."

Queen Áine had thrown back her head in musical laughter. "You're so young, so full of life's worries. All I want is to build a relationship with my own long-lost grandchild."

"You don't need to bribe me into visiting," Athena insisted. "I'd do it of my own accord."

"Very well," said the queen, handing over the bottle with a flourish. "I look forward to seeing you again, and getting to know you better."

Athena had sensed a subtle warm glowing feeling as the cool golden bottle had slipped into her waiting hands. Now, holding the bottle in her bedroom, Athena felt that same glow. She didn't need to take the potion; perhaps she could just sleep with it nearby. Would it work if she took it inside her water bottle?

Snuggled up, she was curious to try it, to see whether what her grandmother had promised would really be the case. And so she opened the bottle and lifted it to her lips.

A single golden drop of the potion landed on her tongue. It felt sweet and divine, like lazy summer days, the bloom of exquisitely scented roses, the refreshing tang of lemonade made with real lemons.

Her shoulders loosened as her whole body relaxed and she slipped languidly into bed, falling into a glorious slumber.

5

ROSEMARY

Rosemary tied another ribbon around another bunch of early spring blossoms shivering in the frigid morning air. "Is this really necessary?" she called out.

Marjie gave her a reassuring smile from the next tree over. "We don't do ritual because it's necessary, just because it's tradition."

"Indeed," said Ferg, who had somehow materialised behind Rosemary.

She shot a glance over her shoulder. "Do you have to sneak up on me like that?"

"How else will I know if you're doing a good job?" he asked, straightening the braces holding up his brown corduroy trousers which matched perfectly with his cloak. "Which is obviously an important mayoral role for me to oversee. Those are a little skewed to the left, by the way."

Rosemary sighed. "Why did I even sign up for this?"

"Because I asked you to," said Marjie warmly, "and because you like to help the community."

"We'll see about that. I'm sure we could just write a nice thank you note to the goddess Bridget instead, since we've been in her presence a couple of times now. The preparations for Imbolc seem a little formal, after all that."

"We must respect the gods!" said Ferg.

"And besides, we're almost finished," Marjie added, and she was right.

It wasn't long before the whole row of trees leading up to the train station was decorated in bows and blossoms. Rosemary ran her hand along the bark of the nearest tree, recalling how she and Athena had first arrived in Myrtlewood about a year earlier, catching a glimpse of these blossoms through the train window as she tried to explain the unusual village to her daughter. How little did she know back then! She'd only had a fraction of an inkling about the magic of this town and what their lives here could be like.

"What are you thinking about, dear?" said Marjie as they walked away back towards the village.

"Just thinking about how so much has changed, I suppose," said Rosemary. "A year ago, I knew nothing of this entire magical world."

"Galdie made sure of that," said Marjie.

"Don't remind me," said Rosemary. "I think I've mostly forgiven her for keeping me in the dark. I know she did what she felt she had to do. She felt she did, anyway. I still don't totally agree that it was right."

"Who knows?" said Marjie. "If we had to live our lives over, we might well make different decisions, or the same decisions for different reasons. You know as well as I do that the things that don't work out teach us far more than the things that do work the first time!"

Rosemary frowned. "I'm not sure all learning experiences are worth having," she grumbled. Then she smiled at her friend. "But it does feel like a miracle of sorts that we got to meet you and become such good friends in this short time. Life is so different now, and I'd never go back. I guess at least I can appreciate the magic, having not known it so consciously before I came here. Life was so bleak back then, it does make me see things in a different light."

Marjie beamed. "Exactly. See, managing the challenges we face helps us to appreciate all the glory of what we have. You'd never know light without the shadow. If it wasn't for the night we wouldn't even know what the day was!"

"You're too wise for your own good," said Rosemary.

"Well, my extremely wise soul is telling me that we're both in sore need of a cup of tea. Why don't you come and pop into the shop with me? Tamsyn has been covering for me this morning and it's time she had a break."

Rosemary put a hand on Marjie's shoulder. "Don't *you* need a break?"

Marjie chuckled. "I have far too much crone-powered energy for that!"

Moments later, Rosemary stepped into the delicious warmth of Marjie's tea shop, blissfully inhaling the delicious scent of scones, cakes, and pasties.

Marjie was right. There was so much to appreciate, even with the struggles they'd faced. But a part of Rosemary's mind still protested. After all, it was all very well to savour the wonder of life, but every single seasonal festival in Myrtlewood seemed to be plagued with a different kind of magical mania bringing danger and chaos with it! She wondered what was in store for them next. Hopefully Athena would have some clue, being so good at researching the festivals, but she had been oddly quiet recently. The poor girl had been through a lot. She knew Athena was still missing Elise, who had chosen to stay in the Underworld, stubbornly refusing to return back to her previous life and instead becoming some kind of goddess.

"Maybe I will write to Bridget," Rosemary said as Marjie brought her and the pot of tea over to the table to sit down.

"What would you say?"

"I'm pleased to make her acquaintance and implore her to please give us one single peaceful festival. Imbolc is one of her big ones, isn't it?"

"It is," said Marjie. "But it's probably not her you have to worry about, stirring up the chaos. That's not her style."

"Maybe she could put a bubble of protection around the town," Rosemary suggested weakly, "and protect us from whatever is trying to break through."

"I wonder if that would be a good thing at all," said Marjie. "Magic can get in the way of the cycles of nature. And you know we don't want that. We need to embrace it."

"I'm all for embracing the beauty of spring," said Rosemary. "I just would like to do so in a peaceful and calm manner."

Marjie put her hand on Rosemary's shoulder. "Instead of trying to stop the tide from coming in, why don't you use your magic for good?"

"I like to think that I do!" said Rosemary, scrunching up her nose.

"I mean proactively," Marjie explained.

"How so?" Rosemary asked.

"Well, this is the time of year for planting the seeds for new things to grow in your life. What is it that you want?"

Rosemary sighed. "I suppose, aside from a bit of peace, I don't really know. I want things to go well for Athena's final year at school. Last year she missed a large chunk – I just want her to be happy."

Marjie patted her on her hand. "That's a lovely intention to set. What about for *yourself*?"

Rosemary sighed. "I don't know. For quite a while there, my goal was getting the chocolate shop up and running, and keeping it running. Papa Jack does a lot of the work for me at present, and he loves it, especially now that his family helps him out. Business is going pretty well. I still like inventing new recipes, but I sometimes don't have the drive to do anything new. I'm sort of demotivated, I suppose, when there's no magical chaos coming my way."

Marjie chuckled. "There's a deeper truth if ever I saw one, and Jack does do a brilliant job; he's freeing you up for something new. What will it be?"

Rosemary shook her head. "I just don't know. I probably need more rest, but that's hardly inspiring."

"I wouldn't say that," Marjie said. "Rest is wonderful, but is there anything that you've always dreamed of?"

"You know, when I was first training as a chef all those years ago," said Rosemary, "I did dream of having my own cookbook. I would have loved that – creating something that would last, you know? So that even in a hundred or more years' time, somebody might pick up my book and I could give them joy and deliciousness."

Marjie smiled so warmly at this that Rosemary's heart melted a little.

"What a gift to the world!" Marjie crowed. "Not that your chocolate shop isn't already doing that already…"

"But chocolate can only last for its shelf life," Rosemary added.

"Well, I think it's a perfectly marvellous idea," said Marjie. "I've thought about doing the same thing myself, only I wouldn't want to give away my secret recipes!" She giggled.

Rosemary smiled. "I wouldn't even know where to start, though. As much as I like the idea of writing – of creating recipes in a book, maybe writing about the food – I feel like I need to know more. I need to understand the herbal properties, if I'm going to include herbs and all."

"That can be learned," said Marjie. "Perhaps that's your next big adventure – becoming a magical herbalist!"

Rosemary grinned. "Yes, I suppose learning new things is fun. It's good to have a project."

"You're right," said Marjie. "Oh, can I ask you something? How is Burk getting on?"

Rosemary felt a little pang of nervousness. "I've been wondering how he's doing."

"You haven't heard from him?" Marjie asked.

"Just a few quick text messages," said Rosemary, concerned. "When he handed himself over to the Vampire Council, Charles swore they wouldn't do any harm. If it wasn't for that I'd have tried to stop him from going."

"They're trying to examine him to see what happened to make him day-walk, I take it," said Marjie.

Rosemary nodded. "I joked that they're worried all vampires will start sparkling, but yes, it's more that they're interested in his new ability to withstand sunlight. They want to understand it."

"They probably want to harness that," Marjie added, a dark look on her face. "That ability in him is connected to your magic. Don't you forget that!"

Rosemary shrugged. "So eventually they'll decide they want to capture me and milk me for all I'm worth?" She made a disgusted face.

"Not like that," said Marjie.

"Okay, I've been worrying about too many things already. The last thing I need to do is add paranoia about the Vampire Council to my list," said Rosemary.

"That's probably wise," Marjie agreed.

6

ATHENA

It was a quiet morning. Athena got up out of bed and looked out the window of her bedroom at dawn, gazing past the forest at the view that usually calmed her nerves.

It would be the first day back at school after the winter holidays, but Athena had missed so much since the autumn term. She was so behind on everything.

Her breath misted the window and an ache in her heart made her feel that she couldn't quite cope, but she pushed through anyway, getting ready and grabbing a quick piece of toast before walking the short distance to Myrtlewood Academy.

The sun warmed her skin, soothing her from the outside, but something was not right. She felt that hollowness. That absence. That pain – like shards of broken glass inside.

A part of her was still in the Underworld with Elise.

Part of her heart had broken off when Elise had chosen her own path, rather than to come back and be with her loved ones in the land of the living.

Athena didn't want to be depressed. In fact, she was rather sick of the exhaustion and pain. She had endured enough of that already, and yet she could not for the life of her figure out how to be happy... not after all that had happened. Not with that sense of longing that continued to ache within her reminding her what she had lost: the closest person in the world to her.

"Time can heal too," Marjie had told her, but Athena wasn't sure this was always the case. And on top of the pain, she had a lot of catching up to do.

She entered the school gates. Everyone stared. The students that she didn't know well stared at her the most.

They'd heard, of course – the whole town knew about what had happened at the winter solstice. They thought she was some kind of hero. Athena felt the clenching twist of guilt. Most people would never know the whole story, and she didn't want them to. She'd unwittingly participated in bringing about the turmoil and devastation. She'd gone to hell and back, creating seasonal chaos and putting the world at risk, all trying to get Elise back...

But Elise didn't want to come back at all.

Athena choked back a dry sob.

"There you are!" Sam said, wrapping their arms around Athena who leaned into the hug, taking a deep breath and relaxing in the warm comfort of her friend's embrace.

"Athena!" more voices called out from across the courtyard; Ash and Derron were headed towards her. It was good to see her friends again, good to be in the company of people who knew the full story of what had happened and not just fragments of gossip. Their smiles lit her up.

Then she caught sight of Felix. For a moment, Athena recoiled. He had blamed her for Elise, for everything that had happened, and she worried now that he no longer wanted to be her friend. But Felix's dark eyes merely crinkled into a sad smile.

"There you are," he said. He didn't blame her, then. Not this time.

Perhaps Felix understood Elise better than Athena did. Perhaps he understood *why* she had to stay.

"It's okay to be sad, you know," said Ash. "We all are."

"I wonder how Fleur's holding up," Sam said.

"Surprisingly well, by all accounts," said Felix.

Sam frowned. "That's strange. She was beside herself when Elise went missing."

"I called in to visit," said Felix. "The house seemed normal – or as normal as a rainbow sprite residence can be...and Fleur seemed okay. She was making muffins."

Athena sighed. "I'm glad she's coping. I'm not sure how I'm going to, to be honest. But at least I've got you lot of weirdos to distract me. Not to mention *schoolwork*..."

They all groaned.

"It's getting harder this term," said Ash. "They apparently really want to prepare us for whatever comes next."

"And what does come next?" said Athena. "Do you all know what you're going to be doing after finishing here?"

"My parents are set on me going to university in London," said Ash.

"Do you mean like the London School of Economics or Goldings University?" Athena asked.

Sam laughed. "No, she means a real university!"

Athena raised an eyebrow. "Oxbridge? But that's not London, right?"

"Oh no, the magical one, Herschel's," Ash clarified.

"Of course," said Athena, blushing slightly. Ash was fairly new to the magical world herself and yet she had it all worked out. Athena's heart beat faster and her thoughts cycled through confusion and distress. How didn't she know this? She'd missed so much. What hope was there of ever catching up when she was so far behind?

Sam sighed. "I don't know if I'd ever get in there. But living in

London would be cool! My uncle owns a clothing boutique there. I've been wondering if I could intern with him."

"That sounds fun," said Athena, fleeing from her anxious thoughts by focusing back on her friends. "You could learn to make fancy outfits."

Ash smiled. "That does sound like a lot of fun."

Felix laughed. "Not to me!"

"What would you rather be doing, then?" Athena prodded, grateful for the distraction.

Felix raised his fist towards the sky in a power pose. "I want to be where the action is!"

"Oh yeah? Where is that then?" Ash asked.

Felix shrugged. "I don't know yet. But it's going to be awesome."

"If you like putting out fires, there's always the magical authorities," said Ash.

Sam laughed. "Felix prefers starting fires rather than putting them out."

"Still," Athena added, "they would have a lot of action, I suppose. What about you, Derron? Do you have any plans?"

"Not sure," he replied quietly in his usual gentle-giant manner. "I'm still thinking about it."

Ash fished in her bag and pulled out some colourful brochures. "These are from Herschel's. There's an overview of the prospectus and a few different programmes in more depth." She passed them around. "If Mum and Dad are insisting I go, then I'm hoping at least one of you will come with me."

"I suppose we'll need good grades to get into these courses," said Athena, eyeing the advanced astrology programme with great interest.

"Oooh these classes actually look fun," said Derron. "Not that school isn't interesting sometimes, but it doesn't really go into great detail or teach you any practical skills."

"We could make a pact," Ash suggested tentatively. "We could all work as hard as we possibly can and try and build up our grades. And then we'll have the choice whether to go to university or not."

"This sounds like a scam," said Felix. "I'm out." He looked over towards Athena.

"Well, I'm in," she said, more decisively than she felt. "I need something to take my mind off things."

Sam shot Felix a dirty look. "The most irritating thing about you is that you get top grades without even trying. You've always done better than me at school, even when I've tried hard and you haven't tried at all."

"If that's the most irritating thing about me, you've got it easy," said Felix with a grin.

Athena shook her head. "Jesting aside, I suppose I'd better go and talk to Ms Twigg – see if there's anything I can do to get my grades up, maybe find something I can add for extra credit before the school year finishes."

"That's a great idea," said Sam. "I think being in the theatre troupe might count. You could join us – me and Ash signed up a few weeks ago, after the winter solstice."

Athena shook her head. "I don't know. I'm probably too awkward to be on stage."

"You're a Leo, aren't you?" Ash asked.

"Not all Leos like the limelight, at least not directly," said Athena. "I'd rather shine through my paintings than have to do any kind of public speaking or public performance."

"Fair enough," said Ash. "I'm sure there's something you can do. The school must surely understand why you've missed so much. You've helped the whole town out multiple times by now. Hopefully they'll be lenient."

"Ms Twigg is far from what I'd call lenient," said Athena.

"You got that right," said Felix, with a grin.

7
ATHENA

Athena approached Ms Twigg's office with trepidation.

Despite her tiny stature, the strangely reptilian librarian, mythical history teacher, and acting-Principal of Myrtlewood Academy was the most terrifying of all the teachers at the school. Even Felix quietened whenever she cast him a quelling look.

There was something about Ms Twigg, and it wasn't just the glimpse of her long forked tongue that occasionally darted out of her mouth. Or the way her eyes sometimes looked slanted like a snake, with a green, shimmery sheen. Perhaps it was her presence and the way she held herself with such stern and cutting authority.

Athena had grown to admire her because, despite being the size of an average eight-year-old, Ms Twigg wielded power without so much as lifting a finger or uttering a word, and that was something in itself to be respected. However, Athena's respect did not stop her from also fearing the teacher.

She knocked on the door at morning break.

"Come in," Ms Twigg's stern voice entreated.

Athena gulped and gingerly pushed the door open. The hinges

creaked softly, and a wave of warm, dry air washed over her. The office smelled of old parchment and something else – a faint, reptilian musk that made the hairs on the back of Athena's neck stand up.

The room seemed somehow to be both larger and more cramped than it had any right to be. Bookshelves lined the walls, crammed with ancient tomes and modern textbooks alike. A large mahogany desk dominated the centre of the room. Ms Twigg sat behind the desk, her hair in neat pigtail plaits, her demure frame nearly swallowed by a moss-green cardigan adorned with bright magenta snapdragon blooms.

"Hello, Ms Twigg," Athena said cautiously. "I...I wanted to talk to you about my prospects."

Ms Twigg raised an eyebrow. "Your prospects, Miss Thorn?"

"Err...yes," Athena said.

Ms Twigg's eyes narrowed "You mean, you're not going to go off and join the Underworld like your friend?"

Athena took a deep, shuddering breath. She really did not want to get into this. "I'm afraid not, Ms Twigg."

Ms Twigg shrugged. "I suppose that's for the best. I can't have all my students disappearing off to become minor deities, now can I?"

"I'd certainly hope not," Athena said, with a small laugh that came out rather awkwardly, especially because Ms Twigg did not look amused.

"All right then, your future prospects?" Ms Twigg said.

"Ah, yes," said Athena. "I...I know there's a university for magical beings in London, and I know I've missed a lot of school, but I'm wondering if it's too late to make up."

Ms Twigg turned brusquely and began searching through a drawer of files, muttering to herself, until she reached Athena's name. Athena's eyes darted around the office, taking in the rows of ancient-looking books lining the walls, their spines adorned with strange symbols that seemed to shimmer and move when she wasn't looking directly at them.

"Athena Thorn, here you are." Ms Twigg sighed heavily as she opened the manila folder, which seemed rather thick, especially considering it only covered a single year.

"I take it most of that isn't because of my schoolwork," Athena said, gesturing at the pile of papers.

Ms Twigg's eyes lit up in amusement and a cold smile stretched across her face. "We keep records on all the students here as the magical authorities require us to. Any strange occurrences, any unusual abilities...I think you'll find your file is rather full of those kinds of details."

Athena shrugged. "Fair enough." She waited awkwardly as Ms Twigg flipped through the folder, and then with a resigned sigh, she closed it again.

"You do have quite a lot of work to make up," said Ms Twigg.

Athena's shoulders slumped. "I know, and I promise I will study hard. I won't be distracted again like last term."

Ms Twigg's eyes gleamed slightly. "I'm glad to hear it. Have you considered doing additional activities for extra credit?"

"I wanted to ask you about that too," said Athena. "Ash and Sam say they joined the local theatre troupe, but I'm not sure that's quite my thing."

"Well, you never know," said Ms Twigg. "Acting can be a good way to express the emotions that one might be suppressing." She gave Athena a look which only increased the tightness in her chest.

"What else could I do?" Athena asked. "For extra credit, I mean."

"The Imbolc ritual is coming up," Ms Twigg replied. "You could volunteer. That would count."

"Help to organise the ritual? Really?" said Athena, feeling a sudden burst of fear and excitement – a refreshing change from dread and grief. "I suppose I could do that."

"Have you ever done anything like that before?"

"No, but Mum has," said Athena. "So how hard could it be?"

Ms Twigg smirked. "Indeed...Well, you'd be taking on a leadership role, as no one has volunteered to lead this season's ritual. The mayor cannot understand why there are so few people stepping up." Her eyes crinkled in amusement. "He has very little self-awareness at times. However, if you can tolerate his majestic, orotund, toplofty officiousness telling you what to do at every turn..."

"Oh, I think I know Ferg well enough to handle him," Athena said with a level of confidence that made Ms Twigg's smile tighten. She almost looked impressed.

"Very well," she continued. "If you step up to the challenge – and you see it through – we could add some additional credit to your record," said Ms Twigg. "Besides, there's creativity involved in organising a ritual and learning about the seasons and the history of the traditions, of course."

"Of course," Athena agreed readily. "I love history, especially magical history the way you teach it."

"Do not try to butter me up, Ms Thorn. I am immune to the flattery of students, as your chum Felix well knows."

Athena laughed. "I wasn't just saying that. I really do love history and research. I'm not sure how I'll go with the leadership part."

"Perhaps it'll be a little test for you," said Ms Twigg with a chilling iciness to her tone.

"I will do my best," said Athena eagerly. "I'm not afraid of hard work."

"Good to hear it," said Ms Twigg, "because aside from any additional credit you might earn, you have several key assignments due in the next few months and you'll also need to pass your final exams. You've done well in astrology, and of course your automancy comes naturally, as it runs in your family. However, you'll need to really pick up the slack in potions. I can see you're behind in herbalism too. Perhaps you could ask Ms Flarguan for help."

Athena shuddered. "I don't know if Beryl would ever want to help me."

Ms Twigg narrowed her eyes. "Don't tell me you're still fighting with her."

"Not so much anymore," Athena assured her. "That doesn't mean we're exactly friends."

"Believe me when I say that you could use the extra help," said Ms Twigg sternly. "Herschel's University has a high bar for entry. Only a small number of students are accepted in every year."

"How does that even work?" Athena asked. "I mean, I know Myrtlewood is a small town. Surely most places don't have that many magical people. Where do the other students come from?"

"I'll excuse your ignorance as you're still relatively new to our world. You'll find most magical communities have their own ways of schooling children, either in groups or at home, around the country. And there are other schools besides us that feed into Herschel's. It is a globally recognised establishment. People come from all across Europe, the Americas of course, even Australia and New Zealand. In fact, they boast students from every continent, even Antarctica."

Athena's mouth fell open. "Antarctica? Who lives there?" Athena blurted out, not meaning to sound rude. "I'm sorry, but I thought it was populated by penguins."

"Indeed, it is," said Ms Twigg.

Athena laughed. "Oh, you weren't joking," she said a moment later. "I didn't realise penguins...were magical."

"Have you not watched them as they swim majestically through the water?" Ms Twigg sighed in wonder.

"You're saying penguins attend the university?" Athena narrowed her eyes. "Really?"

"Only a few," said Ms Twigg. "They'll be in human form, just like most of the seals tend to be on land."

Athena beamed. "Seals? Well, I've heard of selkies."

"Thank the goddess Brigid for small mercies," said Ms Twigg. "I'm afraid you're going to need her grace, and a lot of hard work and dedication, to meet the entry requirements."

Athena sighed. "I'll see what I can do..."

"What is it? Why do you still look so defeated?" Ms Twigg asked.

"I suppose I'm not really sure what I want to do."

Athena noticed Ms Twigg's gaze drifting to the windows overlooking the forest. "Is everything alright, Ms Twigg?"

The teacher startled slightly. "Oh, yes, quite. It's just...have you noticed the forest seems quieter these days? Probably nothing to worry about."

Athena looked out the window towards the thicket of woodland. "I haven't really," said Athena. "But I was looking out at the forest last night and something about it...never mind. Erm, Ms Twigg, I know I've missed a lot of school and I keep feeling like I really don't know what I'm doing. I need your help."

Ms Twigg focused back on Athena, looking her so sternly in the eyes that she squirmed. "You really think you're up for the challenge of going to university?"

"Well, yes," said Athena, feeling less sure than ever but not wanting to back down now. "I suppose so."

"Any idea what you want to study?" Ms Twigg asked sharply.

"Astrology, maybe some other things, I suppose. I might as well lean into my automancy, since it is a family gift and all."

"That would be wise," said Ms Twigg with a small nod of approval. "I advise you not only to focus on your strengths, but also on your weaknesses."

"You want me to study things I'm not good at?" Athena asked.

"We often learn far more with things that are hard. When I was at school, I always struggled with history." Ms Twigg's words came out like a small confession, complete with a mischievous grin. "In fact, history and folklore was my most challenging subject."

"And why do you teach it now?"

Ms Twigg's smile spread more openly across her face this time. "Because I know what it's like to struggle to learn it. If I only taught things I was good at, what kind of teacher would I be? If things come too easily to you, how would you know how to teach somebody who struggles with them?"

Athena nodded slowly. "I suppose that makes sense. But I don't want to be a teacher—"

Ms Twigg's gaze narrowed. "What's wrong with being a teacher?"

"I don't know," said Athena. "You have to put up with all us pesky students, I suppose."

At that moment, Ms Twigg leaned back in her chair and a hearty laugh escaped her lungs. Athena watched wide-eyed because she'd never seen Ms Twigg laugh, not properly anyway. As her mouth gaped so wide open, it revealed row upon row of extra sharp teeth. Athena tried to suppress a small gasp, but it escaped her lips nonetheless.

Ms Twigg's teeth snapped back into their regular position and her eyes narrowed into slits. "Is there anything else, Miss Thorn? Can you leave me in peace now to enjoy what's left of my morning tea?"

Athena smiled, tight-lipped. "Thank you, Ms Twigg, you've been very helpful," she mumbled.

She scurried out of the room. The teacher's laughter followed her all the way down the hallway like a stray dog.

8

ROSEMARY

"Penny for your thoughts?" Papa Jack asked warmly.

Rosemary had been gazing out the front window of Myrtlewood Chocolates. She was supposed to be planning the new Imbolc-themed storefront display and had started several times.

"Nothing seems to be quite working for me," said Rosemary in frustration. "I keep getting distracted. I just feel like I'm going in circles. There are lots of things I could be doing for the sake of the shop, but none of it seems important now after last night..."

"What happened?" Papa Jack asked with caring concern.

"The Vampire Council came and escorted Burk away," said Rosemary. "They're going to do some tests on him."

"That sounds concerning indeed," Papa Jack replied. "Against his will?"

"Well, not exactly," Rosemary admitted. "But against *my* will, I suppose. I let him go, of course. He's a grown up, after all. He seemed very relaxed about it. His dad, Charles, was there – he's a member of the Council as you might recall."

"So surely it's not all that terrible..." said Papa Jack.

Rosemary shrugged slightly. "I'm just worried about him."

"Is this because of the sparkly sunlight situation?" Papa Jack asked. Rosemary nodded.

"I'm not surprised they're taking an interest in that," said Papa Jack. "Not that I know a lot about vampires."

"You know a lot about everyone," said Rosemary. "Everyone confides their life stories in you, because you're so warm and understanding."

He grinned at her. "Right. So confide your worries in me. See if that helps."

"Change is scary," said Rosemary. "And if I'm going to be completely honest, I was worried before this…"

Papa Jack put a hand on her shoulder and looked her in the eye. "It makes sense. You were worried that the man you love was going to be different after what happened at the winter solstice."

"Silly, I know," said Rosemary, looking away.

"It's not silly at all," he assured her. "Change is scary, not just to you. It's normal to be afraid…or excited. You know, fear and excitement are two sides of the same coin."

"You sound like Marjie," said Rosemary. "Always so full of wisdom."

"That's the thing," said Papa Jack, with a wink. "Maybe Marjie's wisdom has rubbed off on me."

Rosemary grinned. "You two do seem cosy lately. Can I be happy for you?"

"We'll see," said Papa Jack, blushing slightly. "My point is that when change happens you can either be fearful and resistant or you can look for the thrill of it all."

Rosemary scrunched up her nose at that. "It's not exactly thrilling having your boyfriend carted away by scary blood-sucking creatures, even when he is one of them himself."

"That's not the thrilling part." Papa Jack chuckled.

"So tell me what is," Rosemary insisted.

"Well, if it was me, I would think about what was interesting in the situation. Aren't you curious about what's going on? Just a little bit in a state of wonder about how it is that your magic not only saved Burk, but gave him this new ability to sparkle in the sunshine?"

Rosemary giggled. "A little. It is rather fascinating. You know I have fearful, worrying tendencies that get in the way of me appreciating just how weird and interesting and wonderful everything is too. It's just...there's so much going on in the chaos of life and it's easy to look for the threats."

"That's what our survival brains do, or so I've read," said Papa Jack. "The psychologists say that our minds stick like glue to all the potentially dangerous or worrying things and bounce off the happy things looking for more problems to solve."

Rosemary narrowed her eyes. "I'm pretty sure they don't say it like that, but your way is better." She smiled and then sighed. "And perhaps the council have really good intentions here. They say they'll protect us at any rate. Apparently there's a risk that rogue vamps might come after us seeking daywalking powers...the Council are keen to minimise that kind of mess if at all possible and I appreciate that."

"Exactly, that's the spirit," said Papa Jack. "And who knows, there might be some silver lining to the situation. Perhaps they're going to develop some new kind of medicine that can help vampires to have a different kind of life."

Rosemary shrugged. "I'm not sure if that would be a good thing? I mean, like you say, they are powerful blood-sucking, terrifying creatures. What are we going to do if they walk around in the daytime too? I mean, surely it's a good thing that they have some weaknesses!"

"Perhaps they won't even need blood anymore," Papa Jack mused.

"Oh, that's funny," said Rosemary. "Last night, before Burk left with the council, he ate human food! He thinks the sun was doing something to his metabolism. He's not sure."

"So – wonder of wonders!" said Papa Jack. "Perhaps it's even a good thing the council are taking this seriously. They might understand the situation better. They could be your allies. They don't have to be your enemies."

Rosemary shrugged. "You have a wonderful, if slightly delusional, way of looking on the bright side. And I love you for it."

Papa Jack smiled warmly. "And I love you too, Rosemary. You are like a daughter to me."

"Perhaps I'm more like a spoiled niece," Rosemary suggested.

"Perhaps," said Papa Jack with a grin. "Now let me make you a hot chocolate and then let's get back to work."

"If only I could focus," said Rosemary. "I just really don't care about this display."

"How about I do the display this time," Papa Jack offered. "It will give me a new kind of challenge and you can focus on inventing some new recipes in honour of the season."

"That's not a bad idea," said Rosemary. "And it kind of makes sense to do something different. After all, winter is the dormant period. The seeds lie in the soil. And then as we move into spring, they start to sprout and new things blossom. Change is always happening whether we embrace it or not."

"Now who's the wise one?" said Papa Jack, nudging her with his elbow. "I'm going to put on a new batch of orange blossom hot chocolate for us to sip while we work. It'll refresh our minds."

"Sounds perfect," said Rosemary, beaming at him.

For a few hours her worries subsided as she poured herself into the creative process of experimenting with new flavour combinations. It was only later that afternoon that her worries returned, bringing with them a salty tangy sensation and tightness in her chest. This time she wasn't worried about Burk, but something else was tugging at her mind and she couldn't help but think of Athena.

9

ROSEMARY

Rosemary stirred a large pot of chicken soup. She was hoping the nourishing meal would help to ease Athena's concerns after her first day back at school. She'd seen the slightly stricken expression on her daughter's face upon arriving home and the tension in her shoulders, mirroring Rosemary's own stress. Athena was upstairs now, studying. Rosemary could think of no better support at a time like this than homemade soup.

As Rosemary stirred the pot, the smell of thyme wafting through the air, Papa Jack's reassuring words came back to her, and Rosemary's stress eased a little, only to return at the sound of the doorbell.

"Not again!" Rosemary grumbled.

"Do you think it's the Vampire Council?" Marjie asked.

"I wish," said Rosemary. "I'd like to give them a piece of my mind."

"Oh, another one of *them*," said Marjie, bustling into the kitchen. "Shall I get it?"

"I might as well," Rosemary said. "Will you keep an eye on the soup?"

"Of course, love," said Marjie, taking the wooden spoon from her.

Rosemary wiped her hands on the tea towel and then opened the door to find an unfamiliar woman standing on the doorstep, just as she'd expected.

"Is this the house of the great witch Rosemary Thorn?" the woman asked, holding up the bundle in her arms. It was a baby.

Rosemary's heart sank. In recent weeks, she'd had more and more of this kind of visit – people who'd heard of the Thorn family magic, especially after the winter solstice, had come to seek her out with all kinds of problems.

The baby in the woman's arms looked pale and young – far too tiny to be out in the cold despite being wrapped in a warm blanket.

"I'm not sure I'd be able to help you," Rosemary said, wanting to carefully manage the woman's expectations.

"You haven't even heard what it is..."

Rosemary probably could have guessed, but instead, she shepherded the uninvited visitors inside out of the cold and allowed the woman to explain.

"My baby...something's wrong with her. She's not eating properly. She always wakes in the middle of the night, crying out. At first, I thought it was just colic. But it's always the same time. I think she's been haunted...or cursed."

"Well...I'm not an expert in that," said Rosemary.

"Perhaps you have some herbs that can soothe her," the woman asked.

Rosemary reached into her pocket for a card. She'd keeping a stock of them for this kind of situation. "Take her down to the apothecary," Rosemary said, handing over the business card with its simple and soothing design. "The details are on here. If there's something affecting her health, then they might be able to help you with that. And if not, if it is a curse, then maybe they'll know a bit more about what to do. It's really not my field, you understand?"

The woman smiled. "Thank you. I'll do that!"

Rosemary closed the door as the woman hurried away, to find Marjie hovering nearby.

"You heard that, then?"

Marjie nodded. "Another one, just like you thought."

Rosemary shook her head. "I'm not the town's most powerful witch like Granny was. You've told me about how everyone would come from far and wide to seek out the magical advice of Galdy Thorn. I'm not an expert on anything except maybe magical chocolate."

"Which cures a lot of problems," Marjie added.

"Not all of them, though," said Rosemary. "I can ease some emotion, but I can't find a missing child or undo ancient curses or even heal a broken heart. I'm starting to think I should put together some sort of directory of experts who can help people with various problems. Because I really don't know much at all."

"I'm sure you would be able to help most of them, in one way or another," said Marjie. "But you're right. There are other people who are probably better placed to do it. And you've got enough on your plate. A magical directory sounds like a great idea. Perhaps we can put it together over dinner."

As she turned back towards the kitchen, the doorbell chimed again.

Rosemary sighed deeply.

"I'll check on the soup," Marjie promised and headed to the kitchen.

On the doorstep was a man, this time, looking dishevelled and panting slightly.

"What is it?" Rosemary asked, mildly concerned about the man considering the wild gleam in his eye.

"I was just on a walk through the forest," he said, "and I...I saw something from a distance. Something terrifying."

"Could you be a little more specific?" Rosemary inquired. *Some-*

thing terrifying was hard to picture without any details, but she didn't want to come across as rude unless it was for a very good reason.

"Some kind of creature, I think. I didn't get close enough to see what it was," the man said. "But everyone knows you're a powerful witch. I thought you might want to know."

"Which forest?" Rosemary asked, her concern growing.

He gestured towards the woods near the house. "There."

"Just what we need." Rosemary eyed the forest with some suspicion. "Some sort of monster, do you think? Or humanoid creature?"

"Both, I'd wager," he replied. "There was something unnatural about it. Not just regular supernatural – but wrong. Very, very wrong."

Rosemary shrugged. "I'm not really sure what I can do about that, right now. I'm trying to make soup. And I'd better get back to it."

The man held up his hands. "I don't know," he said. "I'm going to stay away from those woods. I just thought I'd better warn you. I had to do something!"

"Consider reporting it to the police, then?" Rosemary suggested.

"Oh, I never thought of that," he admitted.

"They're in the middle of the village," said Rosemary. "The police station is easy enough to find."

"I know where they are," he grumbled.

"Alright then. See what they say. I'm not exactly a magical authority," Rosemary added.

"At least you know what you're doing," the man said with a sigh.

Rosemary shook her head. "I suppose you've had dealings with Constable Perkins in the past."

"I certainly have," said the man.

"What's your name?" she asked him, feeling slightly more sympathetic. After all, dealing with Perkins was dreadfully frustrating and unpleasant even at the best of times.

"Trevor," the man replied.

"All right, Trevor." Rosemary reached into her pocket and found another card. "You go and find Detective Neve. Give her a call at this number. She's highly competent. Don't waste your time with Perkins."

The man smiled at her. "All right, then. I'll do that and then consider my civic duty done. I'm staying away from the forest."

"Fair enough," said Rosemary. She closed the door after bidding him farewell and headed back to the kitchen.

"Now, about this directory idea," she said to Marjie, who was lifting a teaspoon to her mouth, tasting the soup. "Where do we start?"

10

ATHENA

Athena finished the school day utterly exhausted. The classes had been overwhelming, the level of difficulty seeming to have escalated well beyond what her brain could keep up with, even in the subjects she was normally used to doing well in. Dr Corvus had gone on and on about astrological progressions when Athena had no idea what that meant. She'd made a note to look them up when she got home, but at this point of tiredness she felt she couldn't face any new information.

"Cheer up," said Ash, approaching Athena as she picked up her bag. "We were gonna hang out after school. Do you want to join us?"

Athena shrugged. Part of her just wanted to go home to bed, but she didn't crave being alone with her feelings at this point either. Perhaps some light socialising would help to ease the tensions in her mind. "I suppose I won't get any more behind than I already am."

"Oh, come on," said Ash. "Don't stress about school. It all seems too hard at the moment, but it won't stay that way for long. You'll be fine."

Athena sighed deeply. "I hope you're right. I thought Mum was being hard on me last term, but now I think she was being far too lenient. I shouldn't have gotten away with missing so much and now I'm paying the piper."

"That nefarious pied piper always creeped me out in the story," said Sam, joining them. "Why are you talking about him anyway?"

"We're not," said Ash. "Athena is just feeling behind on schooling and is beating herself up on what should or should not have happened in the past, which my grandmother says is never a good idea, you know. The past is only useful if you are taking those lessons forward, not using them to make yourself feel worse."

"Ash's gran sounds very wise," said Sam, smiling sympathetically at Athena. "Don't be hard on yourself. Besides, I'm sure if you'd been here at school with everything going on it would have only made things harder. Your mind wouldn't have really been here at all."

Athena sighed dramatically and flung her hands up in mock desperation. "So I'm a lost cause, regardless!"

"Don't be ridiculous," said Ash, giggling.

"Or maybe do be ridiculous, if it makes you feel better," said Felix. "A dramatic absurd Athena is better than a sad desperate Athena."

Athena shot him a glaring look. "If you weren't being hilarious right now I might seek revenge, you know…"

"I love a good threat," said Felix, crossing his arms. "But I do always find it pays not to take ourselves too seriously. It lightens the mood."

"It doesn't help my grades though, does it," said Athena as they walked towards the school gates.

Sam put their hand on Athena's arm. "You're one of the best students here. Really, when you set your mind to it."

"It doesn't feel that way," said Athena. "Thanks for trying to cheer me up though."

"So, you're coming to hang out with us?" Sam asked.

"Of course," said Athena. "What do you have in mind?"

"It's a sunny day. Why don't we go for a walk?" Ash suggested.

"Perfect," said Sam. "Derron is going to meet us by the front gates."

"Sounds great," said Athena. Things seemed strange still between her and Felix. Emotions had been high when it came to Elise, and Athena didn't know where she stood. He'd been his usual friendly cantankerous self lately, but she wondered whether his cockiness and jokes were masking other more complicated emotions around Elise. Afterall, they had been so close.

Athena followed her friends up towards the school gate where they waited for Derron while Felix threw pebbles from a nearby garden towards the road, absentmindedly.

"Whoever takes care of the school gardens isn't going to be happy if you keep depriving them of pebbles," Athena said lightly.

"Is that so?" said Felix, turning towards her. "Caught red-handed by Athena Thorn, powerful witch of Myrtlewood. What are you going to do to punish me?"

"Feeling guilty is punishment enough," Athena replied primly.

"Where are we going?" Derron asked as he bounded up enthusiastically. His bear-like manner evident in his expression and movements even in human form. Athena appreciated his gentle-giant nature. It made her feel safe, whereas Felix's foxy shifter vibe was sly and challenging. As they walked, she momentarily pondered how the animals within shifters might affect their personality, but she had too few examples to make any proper comparisons. She thought about asking her friends but then wondered whether it was invasive to pry, or whether they, like werewolves, had stigmas and stereotypes that were painful to talk about.

At this point they were walking towards town. Athena pulled herself out of her own rabbit hole of thoughts in order to join the discussion of where they'd go.

"We could go for a beach walk since it'll be windy, as you pointed out," said Ash.

"What about the forest?" Felix asked.

Athena had a creeping sense of unease. Her mother had mentioned something about the forest over dinner, hadn't she? Had a stranger come to the door raving about some new problem again? Or was it something Ms Twigg had said? It was hard to keep track, but something about the forest had set her on edge lately.

"I heard there was some kind of monster in there," Athena said, though she wasn't sure if that were true. Everything inside her head felt strangely blurry, weighed down by exhaustion, or was that grief?

"A monster?" said Ash, sounding fascinated. "Really? What kind?"

"Sounds great. Let's go!" Felix crowed. "Monster time!"

Athena folded her arms and raised her eyebrows. "Are you serious?"

Felix tutted. "Come on, a powerful witch like you shouldn't be afraid of a little monster."

"What if it's a big monster?" Sam asked.

"I'm not afraid," said Felix. He held up his hand, allowing it to momentarily transform into a clawed paw, his teeth taking on their fox form.

"I see," Athena said as he growled at them all.

Felix's growl turned into raucous laughter, but he persisted with the idea of heading into the forest and a part of Athena was curious. What was it about threats that was so compelling? Why do people tell ghost stories and watch scary movies if not for the sheer thrill of the shadowy danger? Perhaps she needed that level of exhilaration now to cut through the emotional swamp that threatened to pull her under like quicksand, creating a gulf between her and everyone she cared about. She took a deep breath, determined to be as present as possible – to stay connected with her friends even though the pain made her want to isolate. Everyone else was in agreement about the forest and they all looked to her to make sure she was onboard. She took a deep breath and smiled as warmly as possible. "All right then, let's go."

"Excellent," said Sam. "If we stop at my house on the way, I'll grab some food. We can have a picnic."

It didn't take long for them to swing by the modest cottage where Sam's family lived. It was only just large enough, Athena realised, to house a family of this size. Sam had a lot of siblings, but the house was cosy and not too chaotic.

Sam's mother, Miriam, greeted them warmly. Athena recalled seeing her working at the local grocery shop and always making people smile. Miriam was delighted to properly meet Sam's friends, sending them off with a basket of sandwiches and a flask of lemon myrtle tea. "Don't get into too much trouble," she called out as they left.

"Athena's always trouble," Felix jibed.

Athena rolled her eyes. "Look who's talking, the greatest trouble-maker in all of Myrtlewood Academy."

"Now there's a title I can be proud of," said Felix.

They wandered towards the forest. Being among the trees almost always made Athena feel relaxed, and today was no different. Though the forest was wintry and many of the trees bare, it was calming to be in nature. Some of her worries melted away.

They made their way towards the stream. There they found a clearing where Sam spread a picnic blanket and they lounged around, still wearing their coats, sipping from Sam's thermos as they ate the sandwiches.

"It's all going to be fine, Athena," said Ash. "No one has a perfect school record. No one expects you to."

Athena raised an eyebrow. "Says the girl with the perfect school record."

"Surely some of the things you've done to help save the town should qualify for extra credit," said Ash.

"It's not exactly school-sanctioned," Athena replied. "Although, apparently, I can help to organise the Imbolc ritual."

Felix scoffed. "That's bound to go well! Set the whole thing on fire and create a magical explosion." He sounded excited about the prospect.

Just then, there was an odd shuffling sound and even Felix looked worried. Athena stood up and looked around. "Probably just an animal. Maybe a squirrel."

"Speaking of squirrels, how's Nugget going?" said Ash. "I miss having him at school."

"Same as always," said Athena. Her familiar was among the many reasons her school record was far from perfect. Especially the incident involving him attacking Beryl, who happened to be closest thing to a prefect that Myrtlewood Academy had.

"He was defending us," said Sam. "I don't see why he's banned from the school."

Athena shrugged. "I suppose he did step out of line."

"You're lucky you have a familiar," said Sam. "Nobody in my family does. Our magic isn't strong enough."

Ash shrugged. "Don't be so sure. I was reading the other day about a theory about magical lineage that posed an interesting idea."

"What was that?" Sam asked.

"Well, it basically said there's far less predictability in magical genetics," said Ash.

"I've always thought that," said Derron. "Like, my grandfather Gerald doesn't have a magical bone in his body."

"And apparently research shows that non-magical people can develop incredibly powerful magic," said Ash. "If they do the work to connect to it and practice a lot."

"You mean by signing my soul away to the Bloodstone Society?" said Felix. "I'll give it a whirl."

Athena punched him playfully. "No, by connecting deeply to their intuition."

Sam chuckled. "Maybe. There are lots of people with seemingly no magic at all, like Detective Neve."

"She has a magical baby now," said Derron. "She doesn't even need powers of her own."

Athena laughed. It was interesting to think about the magical potential within everyone. If only they could access it. "I didn't realise I was magical at all until a year ago. In fact, if we'd never come to Myrtlewood, I would still be living an entirely mundane life. Aside from all the paranormal books I read..."

There was another sound from the forest, a twig breaking.

"Do you think...?" Ash asked, looking around, concerned.

"I don't know," said Athena. "Maybe. Maybe we should go."

They packed up the picnic and began to make their way back along the forest path.

"Look there," said Derron. "Something's coming."

Athena stared into the gloom at the shadow on the path in front of them. It looked like an old man, ambling towards them.

"So...hungry," his dry raspy voice carried ahead. "Have any food? Spare any food?"

"Of course," said Sam, reaching into a bag with the remnants of their sandwiches. "Mum always makes way too much."

They held out the package of leftover sandwiches towards the man. Athena caught sight of his face, his eyes sunken. There was something not quite right about him, something that sent a chill through her, but she didn't want to be rude and stare.

"Thank you," the man said, trembling as he stuffed the sandwiches into his mouth. "So hungry, so starving."

"You're welcome, Mister," said Sam as they continued on.

When they were well out of earshot, Felix asked, "That wasn't the monster people have been talking about, do you think? Everyone's getting worked up about an old hobo? Disappointing."

"There was something weird about him," said Athena with a shrug.

"He gave me the creeps," Ash admitted. "I didn't want to be rude."

"That makes one of us," said Felix.

Athena rolled her eyes at Felix but smiled at him. "I'm ashamed to say that I missed you."

"Finally, she speaks sense," said Felix.

They cleared the forest and found themselves on a quiet suburban street not too far from Thorn Manor. Athena felt her nervousness dissipate. There was something strange about the forest, she had to admit, and she was glad to be away from the trees. She would feel even better when she was home, despite the fact that this very same forest bordered on the periphery of Thorn Manor.

11

THE DEVOURER

The hunger gnawed at him, a relentless, all-consuming ache that hollowed out his insides. He stumbled through the darkening forest, leaves crunching beneath his feet, each step more agonising than the last. The scent of damp earth and decaying foliage filled his nostrils, but it did nothing to satiate the void within.

His magical senses, once a source of pride and power, now betrayed him. They reached out, grasping at the very essence of the forest around him. He felt the life force of every tree, every creature, pulsing just beyond his reach. It was maddening.

A rat scampered across his path. Without thinking, he lunged, his fingers closing around its small, warm body. As he absorbed its life force, a momentary relief washed over him. But it wasn't enough. It would never be enough.

The spirit that had taken root inside him whispered like a hungry ghost, promises of unimaginable power. It spoke of an endless feast, of consuming entire worlds. He knew he should resist, but the hunger was too strong, the temptation too great.

His body began to change. Oil-slicked growths erupted from his skin, rough and unyielding. His fingers elongated into gnarled talons. The transformation was excruciating, every cell in his body screaming in protest.

But with the pain came power. He could feel the forest bending to his will, the very earth trembling beneath his feet. The hunger grew stronger, more insistent. He needed more. Always more.

His consciousness began to fragment, memories slipping away like water through cupped hands. Who he had been, what he had loved – it all seemed so insignificant now. There was only the hunger, the insatiable desire to consume everything in his path.

As the last vestiges of his humanity slipped away, he threw back his head and roared. The sound echoed through the forest, a promise of the destruction to come. He was no longer a man. He was the Devourer, and the world would tremble before him.

12

ATHENA

Athena teetered precariously out of the school library with an enormous pile of books owed in no small part to Ms Twigg, who had loaded her up with almost every book in the vast library of particular relevance to Imbolc. As she walked along the hallway towards the classroom, Athena wondered if there was a spell with which she could shrink the books down in order to carry them home.

Something unusual caught her eye – a face she didn't recognise. Someone new wandered down the hall and into her classroom. Myrtlewood Academy had small classes, and Athena felt sure that she knew everyone in potions class by now. The young-looking girl, with a pale round cherubic face and long dark hair, had something otherworldly about her. A shiver ran down Athena's spine – was this girl infiltrating the school?

Athena was trying to decide whether she should drop the books and try to get to the room as soon as possible, but Ash and Sam stepped up to her, each taking a section of her pile, making the rest of the short journey much easier.

"Thank you," Athena said.

"No problem," said Sam.

"Err...did you see that girl going into our potions biology class?"

"I think so," Ash said. "Why?"

"She looked too young to be in our class," said Athena, not wanting to voice her more paranoid thoughts.

They pushed the door open to find the unfamiliar girl sitting at a table.

"Are you in the wrong room?" Athena asked, keeping her tone gentle but unsure how else to proceed with her discomfort.

"I don't think so," the girl responded, a charming lilt to her voice. "Isn't this level five potions?"

"It is, but you're not usually here," Athena said, wondering about the accent. It was an unusual one.

"I'm new," the girl said, raising her hands in a slightly defensive way. "My name is Liliana. It's nice to meet you."

Ash and Sam both smiled and Athena followed suit, but something seemed strange. "We're almost about to finish the school year," Athena pointed out. "It's only a few more months to go and then it's all over."

"My family just moved from Ireland," Liliana explained, and indeed, now that she mentioned it, the lilt sounded Irish, though not in a way Athena was used to. Perhaps it was some rare regional variety of accent.

"She seems nice," Sam whispered to Athena as they took their seats.

Athena shook her head. "She seems suspicious to me," she whispered back. "Why would her family move this late in the year? Why wouldn't they wait a few months?"

"Maybe they didn't have a choice," Sam said. "You could always ask her if you're worried. During class, you know, casually. Just don't be rude about it."

"I'm not going to be rude!" Athena whispered. "I'm just, you know... usually right."

Sam smirked and nudged Athena. "Don't get too full of yourself."

Athena smiled and shook her head. After carefully arranging her pile of books, she turned her attention back to Liliana. "So, Liliana, you just moved from Ireland, right? That's what I heard you say."

"That's right," said Liliana with a half-smile.

"I was just wondering, why would you move at this time of the year? Wouldn't it have made sense to wait for a few more months until you finished whatever school you were at?"

Liliana sighed. "We've moved around a lot. My mum was just finishing up a position in Bermuda and we had to leave there because her role was ending. I was top of my class and now I have to start all over again. But at least the curriculum won't be too different."

"Top of your class?" said a cold voice on the other side of the table. It was Beryl of course, sizing up the competition.

"I didn't mean to sound snobbish," Liliana said quickly. "It's just been a challenging time. I asked Mum if we could stay in Bermuda and she insisted that we come here. She said it would be good for me to finish off the year in a different place."

"What was your mum doing in Bermuda?" Athena asked. "I mean, I don't mean to pry, but I have been there myself."

"Oh, have you?" said Liliana, sounding genuinely interested. "What for?"

"It was for diplomatic reasons, I can't really go into the details. You understand," Athena said.

Although her friends all knew the details quite thoroughly by now, Athena wasn't about to tell this complete stranger, who she was still suspicious of.

"Cool," said Liliana. "Mum's a specialist on Irish magic, and particularly when it comes to our magical creatures. It seems there's been a problem occasionally, in other parts of the world, where some very specific Irish creatures, known and mostly only remembered in our folklore, somehow find themselves wandering where they're not really supposed to be at all. So I suppose the Arch Magistrate wanted her to consult for six months with the subcommittees in Bermuda. But before that we were in France for several years where Mum took up a teaching position at *Académie des Arts Occultes de Lysmont*."

Ash sighed. "That sounds like a glamorous life."

"Yeah, I wish that I could grow up to be an academic, take up teaching positions in all sorts of interesting countries around the world," Athena mused.

"There's no reason why not," Liliana said.

"You've got to have the best grades for it, surely," said Athena with an edge to her voice.

"It's more complicated than that, I must say," said Liliana. "Academics these days are always so stressed. I'm not sure that I would want that kind of high pressure, competitive work. But don't beat yourself up so easily," she added, turning to Athena. "I have total faith in you."

Athena felt flushed and anxious. "Why? We've only just met."

"Well, I've been reading some magical blogs about you," Liliana admitted. "You've got a bit of a fan club."

Athena felt a cold sensation in the pit of her stomach. "People talk about me on the internet?"

"You look disgusted," Ash noted with a tone of deep amusement.

"It's nothing to worry about," Sam said quickly. "Mostly people just speculating about what other abilities you might have."

"How do you know all that?" Athena demanded.

Sam shifted uncomfortably in their seat. "I kind of...search up all my friends periodically. Especially you, because you're the one that gets the most attention on magical websites."

Athena shook her head. "I didn't even know there were magical communities online, but I suppose it makes sense."

"That kind of thing is mostly used by people in isolated places,"

Sam explained. "Most magic users prefer face-to-face community but not everyone has that opportunity."

Athena frowned. "I thought magic was mostly hidden though…"

"Hidden in plain sight," said Sam. "Mundane folk would assume it was all role play or make believe."

"Actually, the witching authorities worked with tech mages to help establish the internet," said Liliana. "It needed a particular type of mysterious connection magic to get everything going."

Athena shook her head. "Wonders never cease…It does creep me out that people are talking about me though." She shot Liliana a questioning look but didn't know what else to say. "Thanks for the warning, I guess. It's a bit weird though. Just because I seem strange to people on the internet doesn't give them the right to speculate about my life."

"Just pretend they're writing fanfiction about you," Ash suggested.

Athena laughed. "I'm not sure that's any better!"

Liliana hesitated, then smiled at them. "This is all a bit overwhelming. But I'm keen to meet other students, because it's not easy to make friends."

Athena wondered whether her judgements had been too hasty. She and her friends looked at each other. Maybe this new girl could hang out with them. Athena couldn't very well put her foot down at this point, especially not when her suspicions told her she needed to know more about the situation. If this new girl was just innocently invading the school for no more nefarious purpose than to finish her education, that was fine, but perhaps there was something else going on.

It was normal to regard new people with suspicion, wasn't it? At least until they proved that they were trustworthy. Athena hated to think that she was turning into her overly paranoid mother.

She gave Liliana a small smile. "You can hang out with us some time," she said with a shrug, trying to be as casual as possible, before returning her attention to her enormous pile of books.

"I have something for you, actually," Liliana said, reaching into her satchel. "It's a reusable shopping bag." She extracted a flimsy fabric drawstring bag. "It's charmed," she explained, handing it to Athena. "So you can fit a lot of things here, even though it looks deceptive. It will hold all those books with very little weight."

"Wow," said Athena. "That's exactly what I need! When Ms Twigg gave me these books I'd wondered if I could do something like this myself."

Liliana shrugged. "That kind of magic is complicated. Usually it takes professionals. There was a market in Paris where they do it for twenty Euros, though. And a tiny donation of magic."

"That sounds dodgy," said Ash. "You really gave away some of your magic for this?"

Liliana shrugged again. "I don't need all of it."

"But isn't it weird?" Athena asked. "Kind of like giving blood. There's a part of you out there that somebody else has. Couldn't they use it to control you?"

Liliana shrugged. "There are protections that you can use. You're right, though, it will carry my magical signature. It could be a risk but there are laws in place prohibiting that."

Athena shook her head. "You could be framed for a crime if you're not careful."

"That seems a bit far-fetched to me," Liliana said.

"Not as far-fetched as you would think. It happened to my mother. In fact, she almost felt the full wrath of not only the Witching Parliament but several other magical authorities around the world. Somebody was framing her deliberately."

"Perhaps she shouldn't have given it away so easily," Liliana suggested. It wasn't framed as an insult. She seemed sweet and naive.

Athena smiled gently. "Hopefully there's nothing to worry about. Are you sure I'm not going to lose all these library books in your magic bag and then have to face the wrath of Ms Twigg?"

"Athena, you make her sound so scary!" Ash laughed.

"How can she be so terrifying when she's so tiny?" Liliana asked.

"Just you wait until you have History and Folklore with her," said Felix, sidling closer to the conversation.

"Who's this?" Liliana asked.

"My name is Felix," he said, extending his hand. Liliana went to shake it, but Felix raised her wrist to his lips and planted a small kiss there.

Athena and Sam looked at each other, eyebrows raised. Felix had never been quite so gentlemanly or affectionate before.

Liliana didn't seem to mind.

"You have to watch out for this one," Ash said, gesturing to Felix.

Athena took one more look at the new girl. She seemed innocent enough, with her long dark hair and pale complexion, but something told her to keep her guard up, at least a little.

The tingle of magic rising on her forearms told her something nefarious was afoot.

13

ROSEMARY

Rosemary yawned as she entered the kitchen to find Athena huddled amidst enormous piles of books.

"What on earth is going on?" she asked sleepily.

Athena took a deep breath. "I'm studying. Just doing some research for the Imbolc festival, remember? I told you."

Rosemary yawned. "How long have you been up?"

Athena looked around guiltily.

Rosemary's gut tightened. "Don't tell me you didn't sleep."

"I didn't really feel like sleeping. It's fine," Athena insisted.

"I really don't think that's fine. Everyone needs sleep. How are you going to function at school today without it?"

"I'll be okay. I'm...just using a wake-up charm."

"Don't rely on magic like that, love. You know how things can go badly if you're not in a good mental state. Sleep's important for getting your brain to rest, you know, processing and stuff."

"I know, Mum," Athena sighed. "It's just...there's a lot to do. I don't know how I'm going to pack all my study in on top of this ritual."

"Perhaps you're taking on too much," said Rosemary. She wanted to go into a more in-depth conversation on the importance of looking after oneself using her own history of bad examples as evidence, but she was interrupted by a knock at the door.

Rosemary yawned again as she put the kettle on. "I wonder who would be visiting at this time? And more importantly, what do you want for breakfast?"

Athena shrugged. "Marjie already made me an omelette before she left." She gestured at her half-full plate. "I can get the door if you like."

"Sit," said Rosemary. "Eat your omelette. I might have some toast in a minute."

Rosemary shot one more concerned glance towards her daughter before going to the door. Standing there was her good friend, Detective Constantine, known to her friends as Neve.

"Good morning, Detective," said Rosemary with a smile.

"That's awfully formal," said Neve.

"Well, you're wearing your blazer, so I assume that you're on duty," said Rosemary. "Please tell me it's not something awful."

Neve frowned. "It's not exactly good news."

"You'd better come in," said Rosemary. "Something tells me we're going to need a little extra something in our tea this morning. I'm sure Marjie will have something for us."

She followed Neve into the house; the detective sat down comfortably amid Athena's piles of books at the kitchen table.

"So what do we need to be worried about?" Rosemary asked as she began making tea. "Is there anything I need to sit down for?"

"I'd hope not," said Neve. "We've definitely dealt with worse situations but..." She hesitated.

"What's going on?" Athena asked, taking another bite of her omelette.

Neve took a good look at her and squinted. "You look like you need a nap," she said, patting Athena on the shoulder. "Did you not sleep well?"

Athena shot her mother a warning glance. "No, I did not," she said quietly. "I'll be back in a minute."

"What's going on with her?" Neve asked.

"I wish I knew," said Rosemary. She carried the tea tray over. By the time she'd finished pouring Neve's cup of Earl Grey, Athena had re-emerged, looking bright-eyed and bushy-tailed, as though she had just woken from a blissful slumber.

Rosemary eyed her with more scepticism. "What did you do?"

"Nothing! Just a little charm, like I said."

"Fine, but don't rely on it, love. You can't fix everything with magic. Try to get a good night's sleep tonight."

"Maybe I'll need a nap in the afternoon," Athena muttered. "Stop fussing, Mum. Neve's here to tell us something and I bet you haven't let her get a word in edgewise."

"That's not fair," said Rosemary with a cheeky smile. She turned back to their guest. "Neve's the one who's stalling. Tell us what's going on."

Neve sighed. "Well, now that we're all sitting down, I suppose I've run out of excuses."

"Sounds serious," said Athena, frowning.

Neve held up her hands. "Well, a body tends to be serious."

Rosemary gulped. "I thought you said it wasn't that serious!"

"I'm being deliberately optimistic. This might have been natural causes."

"You're going have to fill us in on the details a little more," said Athena. "What dead bodies? Whose dead bodies? Where are the dead bodies?" She suppressed a laugh. "That really shouldn't be funny. What kind of hellscape are we living in?"

"Okay, it's probably nothing too serious. It could just be a total coincidence, but the body of a man was found nearby."

"In the forest?" Athena said with a tone of fear that set Rosemary on edge.

Neve nodded. "How did you know that?"

"Just a guess..." said Athena. "I mean, Ms Twigg said something strange to me about the forest. Besides, I was hoping it wasn't right on our lawn."

"Okay, fair," said Rosemary.

"Of course, I'm not accusing you two of anything," said Neve. "I'm hoping you can help out in some way, though."

"What do you know about the man?" Athena asked.

"He looks like an old straggler, probably homeless. Unkempt, scraggly hair. Extremely weathered and dehydrated. So I'm guessing it was natural causes, only...there's something odd about it. His face was so sunken in, his body wasted away, as if he hadn't eaten for days."

"I suppose that could happen in the forest," said Rosemary. "Somebody who was already a bit malnourished and then perhaps they get lost and don't know how to get out or eat wild food."

"Perhaps," said Neve. "Obviously, I have to ask everyone who lives around here if they've seen anything suspicious, and if you did, we might need to file a report."

"Great," said Athena, pressing both palms into her face.

"What is it, love?" Rosemary asked.

Athena sighed deeply. "Well, this is probably not going to be all that useful and will just create more paperwork for you. But I did see an old man in the forest the other day."

"You didn't tell me that!" said Rosemary reproachfully.

"I was with my friends," said Athena. "We were having a picnic after school and a man came towards us on the path on our way back. He looked starving, so we gave him some leftover sandwiches from Sam's mum. He seemed ravenous. He ate all that food and he was still wasting away. Perhaps it wasn't enough...or perhaps it was too late."

"Anyway, you've done nothing wrong. There's no need to hide that you were just doing him a good turn, giving him the extra food you had," said Rosemary.

"I still don't like the sound of it," said Neve. "Please do come down to the station." She handed Athena a form from her briefcase. "And tell your friends to come in and do the same. The more we know, the better position we'll be in."

"But what for?" Rosemary asked. "He's already dead, isn't he? Or do you think there's magic involved?"

"I certainly hope not," said Neve. "But you know in Myrtlewood, you can never be too careful."

"I suppose you're right," said Rosemary. "And I'm glad we've got our best detective on the case."

"Our only detective," said Neve.

"Well, better you than Constable Perkins, that's for sure," said Rosemary.

Athena giggled. "Don't let him hear you say that or he will lock you up for insulting a police officer!"

Neve shook her head. "I suppose I better get going."

"Wait, before you go – how's Nesta and the baby?" Athena asked.

"Yeah, I want to know too," said Rosemary. "How are they doing?"

"Brilliantly," said Neve. "Charming and happy. I've never seen Nesta so lit up."

"Literally," said Athena. "When you have a glowing baby—"

"The glow has subsided somewhat since you last saw her," said Neve.

"That's probably for the best," said Rosemary. "Glowing babies are bound to attract undue attention, especially when they grow up. Can you imagine the glowing superpower of toddlers?"

Neve gritted her teeth. "I'm not looking forward to that stage. There's a reason they call it the terrible twos."

"That's funny," said Rosemary. "I read that they don't have a term for that in Spain."

"I've heard that too," said Athena. "...that people are more respectful of the children and let them explore naturally with healthy boundaries, and enjoy their curiosity. And so instead of telling them not to do things and telling them off all the time, it's just a fun and sometimes intense life stage that children go through."

"I'll bear that in mind," said Neve, smiling at Athena. "I also hope you're volunteering to help out at times. Something tells me we're going to need all the trusted babysitters we can get."

"I'm sure Athena will promise to visit soon. Nesta would love that, and so would I," said Neve, and with a warm hug for both of them, she left.

As she began to leave, Rosemary said, "You know, it's funny. Despite your rather unsettling news, I was pleased to see you at the door and not some random stranger. We've had a lot of callers lately."

Neve gave Rosemary a wry look as she walked her to the door. "I'm not surprised."

Rosemary sighed. "Yeah, it seems like everyone near and far has heard about some powerful witch who lives at this house and wants me to solve all their ills. I was thinking about setting up some kind of directory because I don't know anything about...well, most things!"

"That's not a bad idea," said Neve. "Let me know if it gets out of hand. We'll see if there's some kind of support we can provide you."

"Well, there's been nothing like that yet," said Rosemary. "But I suppose sometimes people do get a bit demanding. There's only so much I can do myself."

"We're going to need to put on a parade for you, Rosemary Thorn," said Neve. "The woman who keeps saving the town, even if she sometimes endangers it almost as often."

Rosemary laughed. "Now off with you!"

14

ROSEMARY

*L*ater that afternoon, Marjie popped into the chocolate shop, jolting Rosemary from her worried thoughts about the body in the forest near Thorn Manor.

"I come bearing lunch," said Marjie, brandishing a paper bag, "and it's delicious."

"I'm sure it is," said Rosemary. "Papa Jack's not in today, unfortunately."

"Oh, I know," said Marjie with a beaming grin. "He told me Zoya had a cold and he was going to stay home with her. Such a thoughtful and caring man."

Rosemary smiled at her friend. "Indeed he is. You two are getting closer lately."

Marjie smiled mischievously. "Perhaps we are. But I won't say anything further than that on the subject. Not right now, anyway."

"Fair enough. I won't pry. What did you bring me?"

"Your new favourite – I promise! Basil and goat's cheese scones that I've made with little chunks of quince paste and cream cheese embedded in the dough."

"That does sound amazing," said Rosemary. "So when's your recipe book coming out?"

"Oh no," said Marjie with a dismissive wave and a chuckle. "I'll never, ever share my secret recipes. I enjoy them far too much for that."

Rosemary laughed. "Fair enough."

"What about you?" said Marjie. "Are you going to create that book you mentioned?"

Rosemary took a deep breath, inhaling the scent of chocolate and spice in the air as she poured one of Marjie's favourite hot chocolate drinks. "You know, I have thought about it. I feel like I do need a new project. Athena's so busy with school and it won't be long until she's flown the coop altogether." She shivered at the thought. "I'm going to need some kind of focus, something to take my mind off things, and to keep me grounded when things turn to custard and chaos, as they inevitably do around here."

"Do you think Athena will move to London, go to university?" Marjie asked.

"I don't know," said Rosemary. "Gosh, I would love to keep her wrapped up nice and warm and safe with me. But another part of me really hopes that she does, that she has opportunities to live her dreams in a way that I never really got to do when I was younger. I only made it through the beginnings of chef school and that was so many years ago. Athena's got so many options that we never even knew existed, even if she doesn't know it yet."

"She's a smart girl," said Marjie. "And I'm sure she'll figure it out."

"I must admit, I'm worried about her," said Rosemary. "I don't think she slept at all last night. In fact, she said as much to me. I found her amid a pile of books this morning."

"I noticed," said Marjie. "We live in the same house, remember?"

"That's right," said Rosemary. "Sometimes I forget that because you're busy doing your Crone thing. It sometimes feels as though I hardly see you for days at a time."

Marjie smiled at her. "Glad to know I'm not overstaying my welcome."

"Never," said Rosemary. "I'm going to need you even more when Athena inevitably does leave. She's welcome to stay at home as long as she likes, of course, but children need to spread their wings eventually, don't they? Not sure how she'll cope. She's self-sufficient in some areas, but having a self-cleaning house doesn't exactly teach you how to look after yourself in a normal residence."

"She'll have flatmates, I suppose. Eventually."

Rosemary sighed at the impending future. "Yes, I suppose. So perhaps I do need a project. Like a book. Although I'm terrible with recipes, so a chocolate recipe book sounds challenging..."

"Recipe books aren't hard," Marjie said, shaking her head. "You're overthinking this. How is it that Jack knows how to make your truffles?"

"Because he follows the instructions," said Rosemary. "He watches me make things and takes notes from all my rambling and makes his own magic with them."

"Exactly," said Marjie. "It's the very same thing. You already have a whole lot of recipes. Just because you're not good at writing them out – or following instructions on your own – doesn't mean that you don't already have a whole lot of recipes under your belt."

"I don't know," said Rosemary. "A recipe can't just be a set of instructions, can it? I mean, that sounds a little boring. Besides, how do I explain how to do the magic?"

"Well, that's going to take some skilful writing," said Marjie.

"And it somewhat narrows my readership, doesn't it?" said Rosemary. "I mean, how many people out there even live in the magical world?"

Marjie shrugged. "My guess is that it's at least a couple of million in the world. Probably more."

Rosemary took a bite of the scone, savouring the exquisite flavour. "And how many of those people want a magical cookbook or even speak English?"

"Well, you could always get a translator," Marjie said.

"So that a few more people can read it in Brazil?"

"I don't know," said Marjie. "Perhaps it doesn't matter how many people read it. I mean, if you wanted lots and lots of people to read your book, you could write something totally different, aimed at a mass market. Make the magic so subtle that people would really have to look to find that part of the instructions."

"Now there's an idea," said Rosemary. "Do you think it's possible to mass produce a book with hidden magical instructions?"

"It's out of my area of expertise, but I suppose," said Marjie. "Perhaps it's not even a recipe book that you want to write, but something else."

Rosemary shrugged. "I haven't considered myself to be much of a writer."

"Maybe that's because you haven't tried it yet," said Marjie. "Not properly. Give yourself some credit. It might be a book you want to create, or it might be something totally different. But there's no harm in dabbling, starting a new project and seeing where it goes. It doesn't have to be the best thing you've ever created, or the most amazing thing in the world. It's just an outlet for your creativity, and a project to keep you occupied."

"It would actually be good to have something to occupy me right now," Rosemary sighed. "With Burk away."

"Has he called?"

"Briefly," said Rosemary. "Last night we had a quick chat. The Council tests aren't too arduous, fortunately. He seemed very relaxed about it all, which put me at ease a little, but he's afraid it might be another couple of weeks before he's back."

"Are you worried?" Marjie asked.

"I'm a little bit worried about the Council. And there's something else too," Rosemary admitted.

"What?" Marjie prompted.

"I'm worried he's changing, I suppose," said Rosemary. "I mean, what is a vampire who can go out in the sun and eat human food? Is he becoming somebody different? And will that different person even like me?"

Marjie chuckled. "I'm sure he will. There's so much to like when it comes to you, my love. Don't let your insecurities get in your own way."

"Sage advice, as always," said Rosemary.

"Oh, sage!" Marjie exclaimed under her breath. "That's what this scone could really use. A little sage butter." She grinned at Rosemary.

15

ROSEMARY

Rosemary had just put the kettle on when Athena arrived home from school the next day, an hour later than usual, looking exhausted.

"You alright, love?" Rosemary asked, seeing her daughter's slumped shoulders as she sighed. Her hair looked tangled and like it could do with a good wash. Rosemary knew better than to say anything when Athena clearly wasn't in a good mood.

"Tea?" she offered.

"Yes, please," Athena replied. "And can we have chicken soup for dinner? I feel like I need some comfort food."

"Of course we can," said Rosemary. "What did you do after school?" she asked casually.

"I was being a good citizen," said Athena. "I went to the police station with my friends, you know, to give a statement about what we saw in the forest."

"How was that?" Rosemary asked. "You didn't happen to bump into Constable Perkins, did you?"

"No, thank goodness," Athena replied. "It was just Neve. But I don't know…it was exhausting, having to try and think…There wasn't really much that we saw, but making a formal statement was a bit of a process. We didn't want to be misleading, but really, there's not much to say. I wish I could have been more helpful."

"Is that all that's bothering you?" Rosemary asked. "You seem a bit low."

Athena shrugged. "I do feel a bit stressed, you know, with school and everything. I just feel like I don't have any time. And I'm running out of…" Her voice trailed off.

"Running out of what?" Rosemary asked patiently.

"I'm running out of patience."

Rosemary's spidey senses were tingling. There was something else going on with her daughter, but whatever it was, Athena wasn't ready to tell her. And it wasn't the first time Athena had behaved strangely. Yes, there had been some disasters in the past, like the rather terrifying painting incident where she'd found Athena floating in the middle of her room surrounded by artwork.

Not to mention Athena sneaking off to the fae realm when she was only sixteen and accidentally unleashing chaos on Myrtlewood, though technically that might have been their cousin Elamina's fault for secretly summoning the fire sprites.

But Athena seemed much less of a child now; day by day, she was becoming more and more adult, and Rosemary had the feeling she needed to give her daughter space. Rosemary had to come to grips with her overprotective urges, after all. She was determined not to try and overwhelm her daughter with questions, because she knew it would backfire. At least she knew all this in her mind. Actually living up to that knowledge was a different matter entirely.

She hoped Athena would tell her what was going on and trust her not to totally overreact again. Rosemary held up the tea tray. "Shall we sit on the window seats and relax for a bit?"

Athena was nibbling at a biscuit from the tin Marjie always kept well-stocked in the pantry. "I don't know. I probably should get the books out again, figure out what I'm going to do for this Imbolc ritual."

"I'm a bit worried that you're taking on too much," said Rosemary.

"I'm not, Mum," Athena said defensively.

"I'm just expressing my natural concern for your wellbeing. I'm not going to tell you what to do," said Rosemary, restraining herself from telling Athena what to do. "Maybe I can help you," she suggested instead. "With the Imbolc ritual."

"Sure," said Athena. "But it's not really me organising the ritual if you do it for me."

"I didn't say I'd do it *for* you," said Rosemary. "I merely said that I'm here to help. What do you need – research? I can read. I can make notes."

Athena smiled, though it seemed a little strained. Rosemary wondered how much of her daughter's mood was still being affected by a certain ex-girlfriend who was apparently quite happily living in the underworld, becoming a goddess, thank you very much.

"Where do we start?" Rosemary asked, carrying the tray to the kitchen table where Athena's books were still piled high.

"I want to do something fairly traditional. A lot of Imbolc has to do with Brigid, you know."

"Oh yes," Rosemary replied, "I remember her from Beltane." She pictured the enormous, towering goddess who'd appeared to save them in the nick of time. It was strange to ponder that an old god apocalypse had been looming at the time, which again was Elamina's doing. Goodness, if the Witching Parliament ever found out about her sinister manoeuvrings, Elamina's political career would be all but over. Rosemary had been sworn to secrecy at the time. Somehow she didn't feel like it would be the right thing to do to dob Elamina in now.

"We saw Brigid in the underworld, too. Remember?" said Athena.

"The winter solstice..." Her voice took on a tender note and Rosemary gently patted her arm but didn't broach the topic of Elise.

"Oh that's right," said Rosemary. "There were rather a lot of gods down there. You know what. I think I saw Brigid not long after we first moved here. Not properly, just a vision of her in the sky around the time of last Imbolc, you know, when the Bloodstone Society was attacking us?"

"Well, Brigid is important to Myrtlewood. And her energy is strongest at Imbolc," Athena said knowingly. "She's coming back, coming to power after the winter dormancy, taking some of the power back from the Cailleach. It's the only thing that makes sense."

"What else do we know about Imbolc?" Rosemary asked.

Athena gestured at the books spread out around the table. "There seems to be a lot of traditional bread baking, and weaving special shapes to honour Brigid. Most modern traditions have included those sorts of things. I've been looking at records from past years' celebrations. It seems like people just take the elements of the season they enjoy and adapt the ritual to suit whatever they're most interested in."

"That sounds fine," said Rosemary, "but I hardly remember any of the Imbolc ritual last year. I think we wore flower crowns. How did we end up getting roped into that?"

"Probably Ferg," said Athena, shrugging.

"Probably. He is usually to blame for that kind of thing."

"But I don't want to do something random," Athena said with a serious tone. "I want to do a more traditional ritual. I feel like it'll help me more with the extra credit – it'll show that I've done research. And it'll be more meaningful. Maybe it'll even help me with my exams – who knows when a history of magic question might arise relating to Imbolc."

"These are all excellent points," said Rosemary with a gentle smile.

Athena blew out a breath. "I'm just hoping that the extra research I do now on magical customs will help me, at least in some small way, compensate for not growing up knowing any of this stuff at all."

Rosemary put a hand on Athena's shoulder. "Don't stress too much about that, love."

"How can I not?" said Athena. "My whole future is at stake."

"Well, yes and no. I did terribly in high school and my life's turned out okay."

Athena shook her head. "Sure, it is now. But it wouldn't it have been so different if you'd excelled? And if you'd never met dad…"

"No point dwelling on the past," Rosemary said, feeling a tightness form in her gut. It was a thought she'd had many times. "Besides, if I'd never met Dain I wouldn't have you, and I'd not change a thing about that."

Athena pressed her lips into a smile that didn't reach her eyes.

"Everyone's got their own path," Rosemary continued. "You know, love, a lot of people don't figure out what they want to do for a career until they're in their thirties or forties or even later on. You don't need to put pressure on yourself as if it's the end of the world. So many examples of people who failed at school and then went on to make huge contributions. What about Albert Einstein – wasn't he like that?"

Athena smiled. "Actually, I heard Einstein was a magic user. They called him the time-wielder mage."

"He seemed a bit mystical, by all accounts," said Rosemary. "What does that make Newton – the gravity mage?"

Athena shrugged and took a sip of her tea.

Rosemary pointed at the book – an impressively thick volume titled *Seasonal Festivals and Their Celebration in Britain* by none other than Agatha Twigg. "Oh, look – you could ask Agatha for more details."

Athena laughed. "While it is amazing to have a world-class historian living locally in our village, I'm not sure I can tolerate Agatha's grumpiness. Getting good information out of her is like getting blood from a stone."

"I suppose it is," said Rosemary. "We could buy her a bottle of sherry, see if that helps."

Athena laughed, passing the heavy tome over to Rosemary. "Just read the book, Mum. You tell me if there's anything interesting that Agatha has to contribute."

16

ROSEMARY

Rosemary was just putting some finishing touches on her latest batch of experimental truffles when her stomach growled. "I think it's lunchtime," she called down to Papa Jack.

"Bring me back something tasty, won't you?" he replied.

"It's your turn to do the lunch run!" Rosemary said with a cheeky smile. "But I can go if you like."

It had become a running joke between them. Papa Jack *always* did the lunch run given half the chance because he enjoyed it, but he liked to pretend otherwise.

"Ah...I suppose it is my turn," Papa Jack conceded.

"Any excuse to see Marjie!" Rosemary winked.

"Actually, I'm preparing a little surprise for her later," he admitted. "Perhaps it would be better if you go this time. It will give me an air of mystery if she misses me just a little bit."

Rosemary grinned at him. "Don't worry, I won't spoil the surprise."

She took off her lavender-and-sage striped apron and headed in the direction of Marjie's tea shop.

Of course, Marjie never charged her for food, but Rosemary liked to find sneaky ways of paying, such as slipping money under her plate or leaving it on the counter when Marjie wasn't looking.

She entered the tea shop to find it bustling, as it often was around the middle of the day, and was promptly waved over to a table by Una and Ashwyn, who were thoroughly enjoying Marjie's roasted aubergine and feta sandwiches.

"It's good to see you, Rosemary!" said Una, hugging her warmly. "It's been a little while since we've properly had a chat, isn't it?" Una's long dark hair was tied back into a plait, while Ashwyn's wavy blonde locks flowed loosely around her shoulders. Rosemary smiled as she greeted them, admiring how the two sisters always looked so impeccable and effortlessly elegant. Rosemary normally identified with being a frazzled mess, often even when she was dressed up, but she didn't mind that too much these days. She smiled to herself and gave herself permission to be as much of a mess as she needed to be as she sat down with them at the table. "I can't stay for too long though – I've got to bring Papa Jack his lunch."

"Feel free to sit with us as long as you like," said Una, before taking another large bite of her sandwich and sighing.

Something stirred in the back of Rosemary's mind.

"What is it?" Ashwyn asked.

Rosemary realised she must be frowning as dark images flicked through her mind. "I just remembered – I had the strangest dream last night. And then I forgot it. Now I've remembered it again." She rubbed her temples.

"My mother always told us never to disregard dreams, especially vivid ones," Ashwyn noted. "Whatever it was, it must have been powerful if it's giving you a right headache now."

Rosemary was indeed feeling the beginnings of a tension headache creep in. "Do you happen to have a remedy for dream headaches on you?"

"I could whip something up especially for you and drop it by your shop after lunch," said Una. "The Apothecary has been quiet today, and headache remedies tend to work best when they are attuned to the person's immediate situation."

"And your dream..." Ashwyn added. "What was it about?"

"Here you are, dear," said Marjie. Without taking her order, Marjie brought over exactly what Rosemary felt like – a pasty with a nice fresh side salad and a pot of Lady Grey tea. Marjie took a moment to sit down with a look of concern in her eye. "Yes, dear, tell us about your dream. I always find them important to ponder."

Rosemary took a deep breath as the dark and slightly terrifying images flashed through her mind again. "Well, I woke up in the night and there was a thunderstorm. The house was dark. The light switches didn't work. I went downstairs and the Morrigan was in my living room. And she screamed at me." Rosemary shivered. "It gives me shivers just to say it."

"That sounds like more of a nightmare," said Una, with compassion in her tone.

"It almost was," said Rosemary. "It was scary at first, except I woke with more of a sense of guilt than fear."

Marjie patted Rosemary's hand. "The Morrigan is formidable even when she's being friendly."

Rosemary sighed. "Do you think she's sending me a message?"

"What kind of message would that be?" Ashwyn asked.

"Okay, this might well sound absurd," said Rosemary. "But at Samhain, the Morrigan told me she wanted an invite to cocktails."

Una snorted into her tea. "You're joking!"

"I'm afraid not," said Marjie, patting Rosemary on the shoulder. "And it's not the only time she's made the request either. Is it, dear?"

Rosemary gritted her teeth for a moment and grimaced. "Marjie's right. When I was in the underworld, I saw the Morrigan again and she brought up the invitation. It wasn't a joke."

"So you've got one of the most terrifying dark goddesses in the northern hemisphere trying to invite herself over for drinks?" said Ashwyn with a wry smile. "Quite the predicament."

Rosemary burst into laughter. "When you put it like that, it's hard to be terrified, because it sounds so ridiculous. But yes, I'm afraid so."

"What do you think..." Ashwyn asked. "I mean, what does she want from these cocktails?"

Rosemary shook her head slowly. "I've got no idea what a goddess would even like to drink."

Una's eyes gleamed as she half-smiled. "With the Morrigan, perhaps something extremely strong and sour and spicy all at the same time."

"Well, at the very least we can whip something up," said Marjie.

Rosemary blew out a breath. "It seems highly impractical."

Marjie shook her head. "Sometimes a little impractical magic is necessary, or a little more openness to the somewhat ridiculous situations that arise in our lives..."

"Do I really *have* to?" Rosemary asked.

"I'm afraid you do, my dear," said Marjie. "She's not giving up on this, and you do *not* want to get on her bad side, no matter what."

"I suppose I actually have to do it then. How does one even host a cocktail party for a deity? And who would come along?"

"Well, I wouldn't want to miss it," said Ashwyn.

"Neither would I," said Una. "I'm expecting my invite promptly." She laughed.

"So go ahead and joke about it," said Marjie seriously, patting Rosemary on the shoulder, "but this is no joke. Strange and absurd as it might be, I think we're going to have to take this seriously. But don't worry, love, you have all the support in the world and the most wonderful friends," she added, smiling at Una and Ashwyn.

"Thank you," said Rosemary. "It seems like life is always throwing things at me – things that test my worst fears, and I just have to go along for the ride."

"That's exactly what life is like...probably for all of us," said Ashwyn sagely.

Marjie nodded. "Indeed it is. But you know what? It's wonderful too...and it's all magic in its own way. Even when things are horrendous and horrible, there's something to learn. And having good friends and people who care about you in your life, having wonderful conversations and good food and tea – well, that makes all the chaos and fear worthwhile. That's what I reckon," said Marjie.

Rosemary smiled at her. "I don't even know where to begin in inviting the Morrigan for cocktails, but I'll see what I can do. And if I get too scared, at least I have some friends to help me. Just don't be surprised if I hide behind you!"

17

ATHENA

The next morning, Athena lay in bed feeling tired. Her whole body ached. She'd barely slept in days. She wasn't going to tell her mother that – the last thing she needed now was Rosemary cracking down on her. She already had too many things to worry about.

She glanced across to her bedside table. There was only a small amount of potion left.

*I need to make more...*a voice inside her insisted.

Another more sensible voice insisted that she needed to have a break from it – she was becoming too dependent on the good feelings and the energy the potion provided. Yet, that was exactly what she needed to get through all her schoolwork, because underneath the magic wearing off, the creeping sensation of the deepest well of pain she'd ever known threatened to overwhelm her. Carrying so much despair was exhausting and she simply could not function.

Athena cringed at the woozy sensation of feeling out of control of her own life. She didn't want to have to beg for the potion from her grandmother over and over. She couldn't bear the thought.

*Perhaps I can get that recipe...*Somehow, she doubted the queen would give it to her, not easily. Perhaps she wouldn't be able to make it at all in the earth realm.

Sighing, Athena took the tiniest sip of the remaining potion and prepared her mind for school and the day ahead.

In the back of her mind she was speculating...perhaps Queen Áine would come to a gateway Athena could make...and bring her more potion. Was that wishful thinking? Right now, everything positive seemed like wishful thinking. The last dregs of the potion clearly weren't enough.

Athena washed her face and dragged herself downstairs to where Rosemary was already setting out tea and toast for breakfast.

"You look tired," said Rosemary as Athena slumped down at the table.

"I suppose I am. Just need a little rest," Athena replied. "What's up with you?" she asked her mother who looked rather pale.

"Oh...apparently, I have to invite the Morrigan over...I mean, the Morrigan!"

"Seriously?" said Athena.

"I am serious! I forgot to tell you yesterday that I had a horrible dream the night before last where the Morrigan appeared to me. It was terrifying."

Athena shook her head. "You do get yourself into the strangest situations, Mum. I don't even know how to rationalise any of it."

"It was shocking for me, too," said Rosemary. "But Marjie and Ashwyn and Una all say that I need to invite her. So I'm going to have to be brave. I'm going to do it. Perhaps we can just hand her some margaritas on the night of the dark moon, and it'll be all over."

Athena rolled her eyes. "Yeah, that sounds very likely."

"Your sarcasm is inspiring," said Rosemary dryly.

"That was sarcasm too, if you didn't realise," said Athena. "So how are you going to invite her? It's not like you can just call her up on the phone."

"I wonder if I could maybe find a spell for that..." said Rosemary.

"Telephone to the divine realm?" Athena shook her head.

"Actually, I found this," said Rosemary, holding up a small black leather-bound book. "The house helped me find it, I suppose. It appeared on my bedside table this morning."

Athena didn't want to touch the book but looked at it with some fascination. Etched in silvery letters on the front cover were two ominous words.

The Morrigan.

"What does it say?" Athena asked.

"Apparently people can communicate with her by going into a river or lake, especially with the blood of your enemies, or something like that..."

"Dark stuff," said Athena, taking a sip of tea.

"...or you can go into a cave," Rosemary continued. "Which sounds a lot less cold than being in the water at this time of year."

Athena laughed. "So you're going to go into a cave and call Morrigan on your phone?"

Rosemary sighed and smiled lovingly. "Don't be silly, Athena. It's too early in the day for that kind of carry on."

"It's never too early for absurdity, mother," said Athena. "Alright, are going to go by yourself?"

"It sounds like I have to," said Rosemary, sounding nervous. "...According to the book. It will be fine though...I mean, it's just a conversation."

"Good, because I'm too busy to come with you," said Athena. "I need to get some studying in before school."

Rosemary narrowed her eyes. "Something strange is going on with you and you're not telling me what it is."

"Maybe," said Athena with an evasive smirk, "but I'm not telling you what it is, am I?"

"I suppose I'll see you after school then," said Rosemary.

Athena gave her Mum a quick hug, scarfed down the last of her toast, grabbed her backpack, and then, checking to see that nobody was looking, she slipped away into the garden. Reaching up into the air at the outskirts of the forest, she closed a door, feeling that familiar gentle flowing sensation of being *home*.

The fae realm feeling had shifted for her.

It used to be that feeling was forbidden, a source of delight and allure. Now, she was used to the fae realm. It was a secondary home. Now...she had cravings of a slightly more specific variety.

It's not an addiction, she assured herself. *It's just something I need right now to get me through.*

But Athena was smart enough to know in the back of her mind that wasn't entirely the case. She was using the potion as a crutch.

Sometimes a crutch is helpful...

And she was in so much pain, after all. While part of her felt resistance, the rest of her mind was quite happy carrying on in this way indefinitely. As long as she had proper access to the potion, everything would be fine...or at least she'd have a higher chance of feeling fine, given the circumstances.

"Queen Áine!" she called out. There was no response at first, but moments later, the purple leaves in the forest seemed to glow and a bright golden light swam towards her. The delicate features of the queen emerged from amidst the glow.

"Athena, my dear gracious granddaughter. It's good to see you," said the fae queen's musical voice.

"Err...it's the thing you gave me. I mean...I seem to have trouble when I don't have any left. I mean, my life—" Athena began, but the Queen cut her off.

"What in all the realms does this mean?"

"You know what it means," said Athena. "The potion, Grandmother. I was wondering if I could have some more of it."

Queen Áine looked at her sceptically, as though seeing into her mind, which perhaps she could... "Of course you can, my dear. But only take a tiny amount at a time. And make sure you sleep. You still need sleep."

"I was afraid you'd say that," said Athena. "But I don't have any time to sleep. I have so much to do."

"What are you doing that sleep is no priority?" asked the Queen, looking confused.

"I missed so much school last year. And on top of everything else, everything with Elise...I haven't been feeling good. The potion helps me feel better. It gives me energy, like you said."

The Queen looked at her gravely. She raised her left hand and a tiny portal appeared above her upturned palm, shimmering in golden light. With her right hand, she reached in, and a moment later, withdrew another bottle. "This should tide you over."

The bottle glittered and seemed to shrink as she handed it to Athena. It was tiny.

"I will give you the potion, but Athena, I'm concerned. This could be dangerous."

"I'll be careful," said Athena, though she had the sudden urge to cross her fingers. Was she really being careful? Careful wasn't a priority, was it?

"Promise to use it sparingly," Queen Áine advised. "Put it somewhere safe and only use it when you really need to. Don't make me regret this, Athena." Her voice hardened.

"Okay," said Athena. "I will. I'll see you at the equinox and we'll have a wonderful time."

The fae queen vanished before her eyes, leaving Athena alone. She closed the gateway, holding the tiny bottle in her hands.

I need to work out how to make more...

18

ROSEMARY

The wintry forest was just beginning to stir with the green of early spring as Rosemary made her way out towards the cave. This particular forest, which she had driven to the outskirts of town to reach, seemed so much lighter and more serene than the woods surrounding Myrtlewood recently, and Rosemary hoped that the ominous vibe was just an effect of the body that had been discovered. She also hoped it had been natural causes and not nefarious magic at play, though part of her seriously doubted it, and her worried mind continued to find dangerous possibilities to speculate about whenever she looked out the window lately.

She wished she knew what was going on, but leaving the area was a welcome respite and besides, what she was doing now was almost certainly going to be dangerous enough!

The cave she was seeking was one of the many rumoured to have a historical association with the Morrigan.

Rosemary meandered along the well-worn forest path, carrying a wicker basket like a fairy-tale character, enjoying the peace of birdsong and dappled light as she walked.

Eventually she caught sight of the cavernous entrance and the ominous feeling returned.

She wanted to run away, but a deeper current pulled her forward and words swam through her mind, perhaps calling to her from the ocean of intuition within.

Sometimes we have to seek out darkness to find more light...

She slowly crept inside, her steps echoing in the air.

"Hello?" she called out nervously, unsure whether she was checking for other humans or signalling to any Morrigan related supernatural elements that she was encroaching on their territory.

The cave was still and quiet aside from the occasional dripping sound from further ahead. The air smelled of minerals and moss. The ground below her feet was solid, studded with rough rocks and smooth pebbles.

Rosemary unpacked the basket she'd brought, carefully placing a black mirror on the ground in front of her as the book had instructed.

She set up a single black candle.

She had considered bringing a cocktail as an offering, reasoning that the goddess might not take too kindly to any delays in supporting the actual invitation. But the book hadn't mentioned cocktails and Rosemary suspected it might come across as offensive – as if she was offering the dark goddess a single drink instead of the full hospitality she'd demanded.

Rosemary had dithered in her preparations. In the end she'd simply brought a piece of black obsidian shaped like a raven as a kind of token.

She found the right page in the book: 'Invocation to the Morrigan'.

A thrill of fear rushed through her.

Rosemary took several deep breaths.

When she was ready, she lit the candle and began to read the invocation, her voice echoing through the damp cavern.

A moment of deep silence followed.

A cold gust of wind swirled around Rosemary, prompting the candle flame and shadows to dance. She stared into the mirror but could see only darkness, not even her own reflection. She squinted, trying to make out any kind of shape. Then she heard the sound of a throat clearing behind her.

Rosemary jolted, turning to see the figure she was looking for standing right behind her. "You scared me!"

"That's my job," the Morrigan replied with a wry smile. "Nice to see you finally have the guts to call on me properly. You'd better not tell me that you want something else. I'm not here as your servant, Rosemary Thorn."

"Errr..." Rosemary started nervously. "I'm here to give you an invitation." Then she narrowed her eyes in suspicion. "Actually, I have a question to ask you first."

"More than just the one?" said the Morrigan, her sly smile creeping into a more mischievous expression.

"Have you been messing with my dreams?" Rosemary asked.

The Morrigan threw back her head and cackled. "Is that the question you want to ask me?"

"No," Rosemary conceded. "I'm finally inviting you to have cocktails with us. I just wanted to know if that was you...in my dream."

"If it's me, it's me," said the Morrigan with dramatic flair. "I can see you've finally come to your senses and plucked up the courage to summon me with my demanded tribute. Good for you. It would have gotten rather dangerous for you, had you delayed much longer, you know..."

Rosemary took a small step back. The way the powerful goddess's words resonated, they almost sounded like a warning of the inevitable, rather than a threat, though perhaps they were both. She decided to take it as a compliment rather than running terrified from the cave because something inside her told her that this was the safest and wisest course.

Rosemary stood her ground and simply nodded.

"So when is this cocktail party?" the Morrigan asked.

"Err..." Rosemary hesitated. "That depends. How many people would you like me to invite?" She didn't want to endanger any quests, but she also needed to know the goddess's expectations if she had any hope of meeting them.

The Morrigan looked her dead in the eye. "The more the merrier, I say."

Rosemary gritted her teeth. "I'm still planning it," she said. "But we're getting fairly close to Imbolc now...so I was thinking..."

Rosemary needed to keep this powerful goddess on side, but her hopeful rational brain had struck upon another idea.

Sometimes a little impractical magic is necessary...

Marjie had said something like this, and it had sparked an idea. What if she could take a pragmatic approach to this absurdly impractical situation. Gods and goddesses had shown up in Myrtlewood before and used their enormous power to resolve utterly hopeless and dangerous situations. Wasn't that what mere mortals prayed to deities for?

She'd started to wonder whether it might pay to have the Morrigan around during the inevitable chaos of the upcoming seasonal festival, especially given the ominous situation that seemed to be unfolding on which they had no useful information with which to prepare.

"Imbolc?" said the Morrigan, raising an eyebrow. "Well, that is a pickle, isn't it?"

"How so?" Rosemary asked, taken aback.

The Morrigan turned her palms over in the air. "It's not really my thing, Imbolc."

Rosemary gulped. "Would you prefer we wait until Samhain?" she asked hopefully.

The Morrigan drew her neck back. "I do not wait. I am always Samhain. No. I will come to your Imbolc cocktail party, but…"

Rosemary waited as the Morrigan considered something. Eventually the goddess spoke.

"It would be rude not to invite Brigid."

"Brigid?" said Rosemary.

"It's her time of year, Imbolc." The Morrigan wiggled her hands slightly, patronisingly. "So it's sort of like her birthday. It would be discourteous to have a party in my honour, especially in a town so close to Brigid's heart…"

"I suppose I could invite her too," said Rosemary, trying not to be too enthusiastic about the possibility of having another Goddess around to keep this wicked wild deity in check.

"Oh, why not invite all of us?" the Morrigan continued.

"All. Of. You?"

"Yes, you remember…" said the Morrigan. "You've met us now…our little sisterhood. *I* could still be the guest of honour because I'm the most fabulous, but we could pretend it's to honour Brigid's big day." She rolled her eyes at her own words.

"Sure…if that's how it works," said Rosemary. Then she narrowed her eyes again. "Wait a minute. Would you promise to be on your best behavior and not destroy the town?"

"Of course!" said the Morrigan with a pout. "Destroying the town – that's no fun if it's destroyed, is it? And we wouldn't want all the gods to come. Only the nice ones, the ones that have fun at parties. I mean, Brigid's okay. Get a bit of fae wine in her and she can actually be a lot of fun. Obviously Cailleach and Cerridwen are a right pack of larks. You're right to be intimidated but we really are a merry crew, if a little roguish."

Rosemary couldn't help but smile subtly at this.

"And besides, it's getting on in the seasons," the Morrigan continued. "It'll be like a last hurrah for them for the year before it gets all warm and sweaty." She scrunched up her face in disgust at the very thought. "Oh, that sounds brilliant. What a great idea, Rosemary Thorn."

"That...wasn't my idea," said Rosemary. "It was yours. Remember? I just had to invite you here first."

"And my dark divine brilliance emanated through us both," the Morrigan said with a proud stormy expression.

"Err, okay," said Rosemary. She couldn't help but mutter under her breath. "Now it seems like we might have a whole lot of deities on our hands…"

"Don't worry," said the Morrigan, catching her with a sharp glance. "Worrying is for the weak and ill-informed. It is beneath a powerful witch. The event will be brilliant. I can provide the decorations."

"I think...err...My friend Marjie has already offered to do the decorations," said Rosemary, unsure of what she was trying to get across, but sure she didn't want the goddess to go to too much trouble.

"Oh, I suppose she can assist," said the Morrigan. "I can do them better. They will be dark and terrifying."

"For Imbolc?" Rosemary asked.

The Morrigan put a hand on her hip and frowned. "You're right. Imbolc needs something a little more sunny, even if that's dreadfully boring," she grumbled.

"Alright…" said Rosemary, "you can all come. And maybe you can do some decorations if you want to. I'll take care of the cocktails. And your job is—" She suddenly started to feel fear under the goddess's glowering glare.

"My job is what, exactly?"

"To have a lot of fun, of course!" said Rosemary, in as jolly a tone as she could muster. "And to invite the other goddesses…as long as nobody causes too much mayhem."

"But there's all sorts of fun mayhem," said the Morrigan, sounding slightly disappointed. "I'm longing for a good dollop of debauchery! Perhaps a little dramatic death on the side?"

"Jovial debauchery, perhaps," said Rosemary, trying not to grit her teeth. "But I'd prefer not to have deaths, if at all possible. That's a hard boundary for me."

"Suit yourself," said the Morrigan. With a dismissive wave, she vanished into a gust of wind and raven feathers.

The candle went out, leaving only cackling laughter echoing in her wake.

"Well," said Rosemary to herself. "I suppose that could have gone a lot worse. So I'm going to count my blessings..."

19

ROSEMARY

Rosemary was curled up on the sofa with Fuzzball and Nugget, occasionally stroking the familiars as they napped. It was a very comfortable situation.

Athena had been studying in the next room. Rosemary heard her footsteps as she approached.

"What's for dinner?" Athena asked.

"What do you feel like?" Rosemary replied. "Soup?"

"No, I think I've had enough soup recently. What other ideas do you have?"

"Let's check the pantry."

"Oh, wouldn't it be good if we could have some lamb ragù?" said Athena.

Rosemary smiled at her daughter. It was a game they liked to play. "Is that what you most feel like?"

"I feel like rich lamb ragù made with Pinot Noir and capsicum, served with pumpkin gnocchi and Parmesan."

"Well, I can tell you now, we have about three of the required ingredients, and none of the main ones!"

"And now how many do we have...now?" said Athena, striding towards the fridge. She opened it. "Oh, what a surprise!" she said, pulling the newly appeared ingredients out in their paper bags. "Pumpkin, capsicum, lamb...I'll check the pantry for the wine, but you know what, the house provided again. Everything we need is right here."

"It's the best," said Rosemary as Athena closed the fridge again. "Sometimes life is so magical here in Thorn Manor that I wonder if it's like that fable about the porridge pot."

Athena quirked an eyebrow. "The porridge pot?"

"The one where you just have to say the magic word, and it produces porridge. But then nobody knows what to say to make the porridge stop, so it just keeps going and the whole house gets overrun with porridge."

"Never heard of it," said Athena. "Is it like an old story or something?"

"Yes," said Rosemary. "You don't know it? It was in a book that I read to you as a child."

Athena shrugged. "I don't recall. If you've never noticed, I've never been that into porridge. I mean, it's okay, but it's not my favourite."

"Blasphemy," Rosemary teased. "You didn't get enough good Scottish oats as a child."

"What's the fable supposed to be a warning about anyway?" said Athena. "Not making porridge?"

"No, it's a little bit like 'be careful what you wish for' because the porridge is very delicious. And the people know how to use the magic words to get it, to produce more porridge, but then in overusing that, they don't know how to stop it and it sort of takes over everything."

"It sounds a bit like a magical omen," said Athena. "One of those ones, like in *The Sorcerer's Apprentice*. Or that story about the king who turned everything into gold, and then he got very miserable and hungry."

"I wonder what gold tastes like..." Before Rosemary could think any more on the topic, there was a knock at the door. "You know," she said, "it's been a few days. I thought random people might have stopped coming to ask me for magical help. I suppose I was being too optimistic."

"I can tell them to go away, if you like," said Athena.

"No, it's fine," said Rosemary, giving Fuzzball one final scratch behind the ears. He skittered away, disappearing to wherever he went when there was company. Nugget sat there, pretending to sleep and also pretending to be unperturbed, though his little ears twitched.

Rosemary reluctantly got up and went to see who was at the door.

She was surprised to find a familiar face. "Zade! It's been a long time."

Athena crept up behind her, putting her hand on her mother's shoulder. "Hello!"

Zade was perhaps not quite a friend. But he'd been an ally, though he'd had the misfortune of being married to that sleazeball scheming trickster Don June who Rosemary and Athena had been involved in getting locked up after he tried to steal the election. They hadn't seen Zade since.

"It's been a long time," Zade acknowledged. Something in his eyes seemed rather sad. "I'm sorry. I just had to get away after everything that happened...I needed a break from Myrtlewood."

Rosemary looked at him more closely. Zade was usually the picture of composure, yet his shirt wasn't quite right, his face showing all the tell-tale signs of sleeplessness. There was something about him that was uncharacteristically harried and slightly unkempt.

"What's going on?" Rosemary asked. "It's not that I'm not happy to see you. I'm just wondering..."

"Why I'm here?" Zade sighed deeply.

Athena, of course, caught on immediately, stepping in front of her mother and gesturing for Zade to come in. "Something's wrong," she whispered as they slowly followed him in. "And we're going to find out what it is."

They led him into the kitchen and offered him tea. Zade sat down heavily at the table.

"Right. So what's the problem? Is it Don June?" Athena asked. "What's he done now?"

"I wish I knew," Zade admitted. "Obviously, well...things have been challenging and we're not really together anymore. Although we're still technically married. But I haven't forgiven him for what he did."

"That's understandable," said Rosemary. "He put a lot of people in danger just for his own ego gratification."

"I feel so guilty about the whole thing," said Zade. "I should have done more to stop it. But by the time I found out it was already too late."

"But he was sent away to jail, right?" said Athena.

"He was sentenced, but it was a short sentence. I'm not sure why," said Zade. "Anyway, he's been released. I was expecting him to come and find me, but he never did. So I came back to our house here in Myrtlewood. And the place is a mess. I mean, Don always was a bit messy. I was always having to use my magic to tidy up after him. But it doesn't seem like a normal level of mess. It's chaotic. And I figured out he must be staying there."

"That sounds a bit off," said Rosemary. "Maybe he was too ashamed to get in touch with you."

"That's what I thought, at first," said Zade. "So I waited. I cleaned up. Eventually, he came back. This was a week ago. He was looking strange; wild-eyed and rambling. And then he disappeared again. I reported it to Neve at the time because I was worried about him. And I checked the local hospitals, but nobody fitting his description turned up."

"What happened to him?" Athena asked.

"I just don't know," said Zade. "I spent a few more days getting the house back in order because it was a shame to see it in such a state. And that's when I found it..."

"Found what?" Rosemary asked.

Zade pulled some crumpled pieces of paper from his pocket and laid them carefully on the table. "It doesn't quite make sense until you look at it closely. It looks like scribbles that don't add up..."

"What do you make of it?" asked Athena curiously.

"Well, there are fragments here and there," Zade said, brandishing the crumpled paper. "And when I pieced them together, it suggested… as far as I can tell, that he's on a quest for revenge. Your names both appeared."

A heavy weight settled in Rosemary's gut. The last thing she needed was a crazed former politician armed with magical powers coming after her. Not now.

"Well, it wouldn't just be us, surely," said Athena. "What about Ferg, his arch-nemesis and rival in the mayoral race?"

"Yes, his name was there too," said Zade. "And I'll report all this, I assure you. I just thought I'd better check in with you. I wondered if you'd heard from Don. I'd really like to get him the help he needs."

"That's very compassionate of you," said Athena. "If somebody was going to ransack my house, even if they were the part-owner, I'd be looking to give them something other than just help!"

Zade released a mirthless chuckle. "I don't have hope that Don and I will ever be together again. If I'm honest, it wasn't working for us. He was just always so obsessed with power, you know?"

"Oh, yes, we had some inkling of that," said Rosemary. "Though at least we didn't have to live with him."

Zade chuckled. "But there's a part of me that still cares for him. It wouldn't be right to let him harm anyone else or himself. And I fear right now he's a danger to both. I just wish I knew where he was."

The conversation was promptly interrupted by another knock at the door.

Athena shrugged and rose and a moment later returned with none other than Ferg.

"Speak of the devil," said Athena.

"Who's the devil?" said Ferg, stepping into the room with his characteristic serious expression. "We don't do devils in Myrtlewood, unless you count appeasing the darkness of Samhain."

His eyes fell on Zade and filled with anxiety or perhaps suspicion. "Mr June. What have you been up to? I keep track of the goings on in Myrtlewood and I wasn't informed of your return."

"I've been out of town," Zade explained. "I actually came here because I'm worried about Don. He might be seeking revenge."

"Suspicious," said Ferg. Then he turned to Rosemary. "And what are you here for?"

"I live here, Ferg," said Rosemary. "What are you here for?"

"I'm here to meet with Athena," said Ferg.

"Uhh, that's news to me," said Athena.

"What's this about?" Rosemary inquired.

"Well," said Ferg, preening. "Your very intelligent daughter has taken it upon herself to help organise the next Imbolc ritual. And I wanted to check in on how it's going."

"Sure…" said Athena, blushing slightly. "I can show you my plans if you like." Her face lit up with something akin to pride. Rosemary was pleased to see it. Athena had been working so hard on the ritual and she deserved some recognition. "I've been going over all the traditional rituals. I have some ideas."

"Brilliant," said Ferg. "This is music to my ears. I so admire your dedication to tradition. It is something sorely lacking in this town. What we need is a return to simpler times where people listened more and valued the wisdom of their elders.

"I'm not going to argue with you, Ferg," said Rosemary. "But perhaps this isn't the best time. Didn't you hear that Zade is worried that his ex is going on a revenge rampage and we might be in danger?"

Ferg looked at Zade. "I'm going to take you in for questioning, young man."

Though Zade must surely have been within Ferg's own age bracket, he simply said, "Sure, I have nothing to hide."

Rosemary shook her head, wondering if taking people in for questioning was even in the Mayoral job description, but she supposed it must be. Ferg was a stickler for the rules. "Is that really necessary?" she asked.

"Indeed it is," said Ferg. "Because this could be some nefarious scheme that you corrupt Junes are cooking up and I need to ensure that I have all the details."

"That's fine, I'll come with you. Like I said, I have nothing to hide," said Zade.

"Very well," said Ferg. He turned back to Athena. "But first, show me your plans."

Approximately thirty-three minutes later, Athena was glowing with pride at Ferg's praise for her deep research and the two visitors were out the door, to begin what promised to be an awkward interrogation process.

"One problem solved for now," said Rosemary as the front door closed, leaving them in peace.

"What problem?" Athena asked.

"The problem about having uninvited guests, at least for the moment." Rosemary smiled at Athena. "Now, let's make that ragù."

20

ROSEMARY

Rosemary bolted awake at the loud atmospheric cello music piercing her dreams. She reached for the phone on the bedside table, feeling bleary and confused as she answered. "Hello...What is this?"

"Miss Rosemary Thorn," said a reedy voice.

"Excuse me?" said Rosemary, reaching for words when her brain still wasn't quite ready to form them. "Who is this? What's wrong?"

"Why do you assume that something's wrong?" the voice replied.

"Well, only because it's..." She looked at her screen. "Well past midnight."

The voice chortled. "That's right. I forget you mortals need your static rest."

"What is this all about, then?" Rosemary asked, feeling a particular fear down her spine.

"Nothing of great concern or consequence to me," said the voice. "We merely would like to meet with you."

"Who is this?" Rosemary asked. "Why would you like to meet with me? What's going on?"

"My apologies for the miscommunication," said the voice. "It took me a long time to figure out how to use this device. They keep changing and I haven't been keeping up with the technology."

Rosemary was slowly coming to her senses after the rude awakening. "You're some kind of vampire, I presume."

"She's not entirely stupid," the voice muttered quietly. "This is good news."

"And let me guess..." Rosemary added as rage flared through her. She wasn't sure if this creature of the night was being deliberately rude or just didn't realise the modern technology could pick up on their quieter voice. "You're something to do with the council, aren't you?"

"Sharper and sharper, Miss Thorn. And you're correct, we are indeed calling about matters involving Perseus Burk."

"Good news, I hope," Rosemary said, bracing herself in case of otherwise.

"Not so much," came the reply, tightening Rosemary's gut. "We have determined very little from all of our studies. However, we understand that you are the witch who imbued young Mr Burk with this rather unusual gift."

"I wasn't trying to," Rosemary insisted as she wondered how old this creature must be to call a thousand-year-old 'young'.

"Be that as it may..."

"Who am I even talking to?" Rosemary asked.

"My name is Elvadora Sharp."

"Elvadora?!" said Rosemary. "Elvadora...doesn't that sound like some kind of fake name?"

"Bite your tongue," said the voice, sounding terribly offended.

"What is it that you want, Elvadora?" Rosemary asked.

"We're wondering if you will acquiesce to our request in allowing us to study your magic."

Rosemary coughed in an attempt to stop herself from swearing. "You call me in the middle of the night to ask me to be your lab rat?"

"I suppose I could apologise for the timing," the voice said stonily. "This really is important, you see. If we do not fully understand what's happening with the case of Perseus Burk and communicate effectively on this matter, other vampires might get it in their heads that they must kidnap him or even you in order to try to imbibe the magic themselves. Day walking is something that vampires crave more than anything else, for the most part."

"Why? Because you want a suntan?" said Rosemary, rolling her eyes.

"No, simply because we have very few limitations," the vampire said, not even bothering to laugh at Rosemary's joke, "and we're not used to not getting our way. When a vampire becomes obsessed with a limitation, like day walking, the situation can become rather dangerous, putting you and those you care about in grave danger."

"Yes, yes, so I've heard. If I don't come and be your guinea pig, some other mad, bloodthirsty fiends are going to come after me and everyone I care about?"

"That's about the size of it, yes."

"Oh, whatever," said Rosemary. "If I spend a couple of days with you – wait, how long would this testing take? Burk's been gone for days, almost a week already."

"I do believe that if you're active and willing, we'll only need two or three days of your time," said Elvadora.

"And where exactly would I have to go?" Rosemary asked, mulling over her options.

"Our main base is north of Edinburgh."

"You want me to go to Scotland so you can run tests on me and my magic?" said Rosemary. "Getting to Scotland could take me days."

"Days? What are you riding in? A carriage? Why not simply take your private jet?"

"Oh yes, my private jet." Rosemary rolled her eyes even more dramatically. "I suppose I could catch a plane, but that's a whole lot of admin in booking tickets. You're quite out of touch with most people, aren't you?"

"Well, I don't get out much. The catacombs need tending to, after all."

"Having a normal one then," said Rosemary. "Well, I'm not going to go anywhere without talking to Burk about it. Maybe his family too. "

"Very well. We will schedule for him to call you. I take it you'd prefer a daylight phone call?"

"At this point," said Rosemary, "it doesn't seem to matter, does it? Is he there? Can you put him on the line?" She was feeling wide awake and a rather odd mixture of frustration and terror at the thought of what lay ahead.

The phone call abruptly ended. Rosemary frowned at her phone and then saw that it was ringing again. Burk's voice came through.

"Rosemary?"

"Burk, what's going on?" Rosemary asked.

"I apologise. Vampires keep odd schedules."

"I realised that," said Rosemary, "and whoever Elvadora is, they just told me that they want me in Scotland to be a lab rat...like you."

"I understand that this isn't great news," said Burk.

"It's not your fault," said Rosemary, resting her head in her hand. "What should I do?"

"Go back to bed and rest, my love," said Burk gently.

"Well, that I can do. If I can actually get any sleep now after all this."

"Rosemary," Burk said, his voice low and soft. "If you're willing to come, I can arrange everything. I hate to drag you into vampire politics like this. I'd love to make it up to you...perhaps we could go to Portugal for a few days – there's a special place I'd love to show you."

Rosemary's heart warmed at the thought. "When?"

"Whenever you'd like. We could go from here if Athena could spare you."

"I don't know," said Rosemary. "I'm a little worried about her. But I suppose things are rather quiet at the moment, and we are in between the seasonal festivals. Better now than at Imbolc...but Burk, are you really sure about this? Do you want me to come to Scotland?"

"Believe me, I've weighed up the options and this is the best possible route...for now."

Rosemary gulped. She was no longer tired. The thought of diving into the strongholds of vampire power was not exactly appealing, but perhaps it was the best idea to have ancient bloodsuckers as strong allies rather than enemies.

"Will they promise that it's only a few days?" Rosemary asked.

"Let's get them to sign a contract," said Burk. "Vampires are strict on rules."

"Well, I'm glad you're a lawyer. Sort that out for me, will you?" said Rosemary, becoming more resigned to her fate. "Is there really a risk that crazed vampires will come after me or Athena for my magic?"

"I'm afraid so," said Burk. "Fortunately, the word hasn't spread far. Yet. But trying to stop rumours is like trying to stop the tides from changing, as you probably know."

"I suppose so," said Rosemary. "Well, at least I'll see you soon...in Scotland. How do you think I should get there?"

"Don't worry, my love. I'll arrange everything. Just rest now."

Rosemary went back to sleep, though it took her a long time. And when she finally did, her slumber was restless and filled with dreams of Athena shouting, and vampires chasing her.

21

ATHENA

Athena had been tossing and turning all night. She couldn't get the potion out of her mind. Without it, the pain came back – the heaviness, the tiredness that made everything impossible. She needed a recipe. She needed to be able to figure out how to make it herself so that she wasn't relying on her grandmother's good grace. If she could just have a regular supply, everything would be fine.

She crept out of bed and up to the attic room, the tower room that held the large cauldron and old spell books. There was something special about this room with its gold-rose ceiling reaching the outside. The circular shape of the room had a special kind of magic to it. Perhaps that was why Granny Thorn had liked it here so much.

Now, if only there is a way of replicating this potion...

She remembered a spell that might be useful which she'd come across a while back. It took several minutes of paging through the old books before she found it again: A revealing spell.

It was quite simple, really. The spell called for fresh spring water, rosewater, sea salt, and several large, polished pieces of black onyx. All ingredients she had to hand.

"No time like the present," Athena muttered to herself as she gathered the ingredients and began to combine them in the large cauldron, stirring the water counterclockwise eight times. When it stilled, the surface appeared silvery, mirror-like. She took a small vial of potion from her pocket. There was barely any left in it, but she could spare a drop.

One golden droplet fell into the mirror-like surface. She held a blank page of parchment over the cauldron and was delighted to find words scrawling themselves across the page in silver lettering.

Athena's heart sank as she took in the words.

The potion was a complex one and called for ingredients that could be hard to find if one didn't know where to look.

She pored over it, trying to figure out what they all were.

The purple mushrooms she could get easily enough from the fae realm. They were a common kind that grew readily there. But the recipe also called for specially enchanted colloidal gold, which she didn't have to hand.

She looked around at the house.

"I don't suppose you could provide me with some of these?" The tower room trembled just a little.

Rosemary...

Athena was worried she might wake her mother. "Never mind," she said. "You're a good house and you're doing a good job." She patted the wall, which seemed to purr beneath her touch.

"Fae potions might be different from witching potions," Athena muttered to herself. "But if I can get all the ingredients, I'm sure I can get this to work."

22

ROSEMARY

Rosemary stumbled downstairs the next morning, exhausted and bleary, to find Athena bright-eyed and bushy-tailed, making pancakes in the kitchen.

"What's gotten into you?" said Rosemary, grinning at her daughter. "You're in a good mood."

"I think things are finally turning around," said Athena.

"Well, that sounds promising," Rosemary replied. "I'm afraid I have some bad news."

"What is that?" Athena asked.

"You know how Burk's gone to be a lab rat for the vampires?"

"Yes," said Athena, concerned. "Is he okay?"

"He's fine," said Rosemary dismissively. "But apparently, they can't figure out what's going on with him. And they've decided the only way to get to the bottom of it is to get their hands on my magic too."

"What does that mean?"

"Well, apparently I need to pop over to Scotland for a couple of days," Rosemary explained.

"Scotland?" said Athena. "As opposed to where vampires usually like –Transylvania?"

Rosemary shrugged. "I suppose Scotland is quite dreary. Not a lot of sunshine."

"And are you going to do it?" Athena asked.

"Well, by the sounds of it, I have to," said Rosemary. "The council is worried that obsessive vampires will come after us to try to get the secret."

"And how will being a lab rat help with that?" said Athena.

"Well, the very rude person with the elvish-sounding name, who I talked to in the middle of the night – because vampires have no sense of decency apparently – told me that if they can figure out what's really going on, they'll be able to manage the situation far better. I don't know, maybe they'll put out a press release or something to stop any rumours. They seem to think they'll provide security for us, at least. So I suppose it's a good idea to keep them on our side."

"You're going to have vampire bodyguards?" said Athena, laughing.

"This is not a funny situation," said Rosemary. "I'm doing my best to contain my extreme anxiety right now."

"You're doing a great job, actually," said Athena.

"Thank you, daughter. Somebody's gone and replaced you with a polite fae creature while I was asleep."

"I am a polite fae creature, thank you very much, Mother," said Athena.

Rosemary sighed and laughed at the same time. Then she eyed Athena with caution. "Will you be all right if I'm away for a few days?"

"Of course. There'll be nobody to stop me from studying."

"Get yourself under control, young lady," said Rosemary. "You're obsessed."

"Everything is under control," Athena insisted. "And I will be perfectly fine. Besides, Marjie's here. She'll make sure that I'm eating and mollycoddle me. I don't need you to do that as well."

She batted Rosemary away with the spatula so that she could flip the pancake.

"And how are you getting there?" Athena asked a minute later as she added more batter to the pan.

"Burk's going to arrange everything," said Rosemary. "And he's going to sort out a contract to make sure that the council keeps to their word."

"I do like having a lawyer in the family," said Athena.

Rosemary smiled. "It's quite convenient, I must say. And hopefully they'll let me bring him back to Myrtlewood afterwards."

"Bring him back? You mean he can't just come back of his own accord?"

Rosemary shrugged. "You know what I mean."

"Well, perhaps you two could have an extended getaway. You know, you've never had a proper holiday together or anything."

"That is a nice idea," said Rosemary. "And the weather is awfully cold at the moment. But I can't just leave you and swan off to the Caribbean or something."

"Mum, I'm practically an adult," Athena answered. "I'll be fine for a few days. Take a whole week if you want to."

"Well, I will see how I feel after being a lab rat. I might just want to come home, hang out with you."

"You might," said Athena, "or you might decide that a holiday is just what you need."

Rosemary shrugged. "At least I can rest easy knowing that Marjie's around."

"Are you saying that I can't take care of myself?" Athena asked, bringing a plate of pancakes generously drizzled with lemon juice and sugar over to her mother.

Rosemary scoffed down a pancake and then licked her fingers. "Actually, if you make pancakes this good, I think you're doing just fine."

"Who's doing just fine?" said Marjie, coming into the kitchen.

"Did you sleep in?" Rosemary asked.

A slight blush touched Marjie's cheeks. "Well, I was out a little late last night, I must admit. Jack took me to a wonderful restaurant by the ocean where they serve the food that you most crave in the world without even having to ask you what it is."

Rosemary smiled. "I love that place. I need to go back there again. It was delicious."

"Yes, and after all the talking and the wining and dining, I didn't get home until after midnight. There was a light on upstairs."

"I got a late night phone call from the council," said Rosemary, before filling Marjie in on the details.

"I don't like the sound of all that," said Marjie. "It's bad enough that they've taken Burk. They have to take you as well?"

Rosemary shrugged. "Apparently it'll only be temporary. So that's, I suppose, one saving grace. Besides, I've never really been to Scotland, except for a school trip when I was twelve."

"Well, I suppose you could think of it as just another adventure," said Marjie.

"There you go, looking on the bright side again," Rosemary replied. "I knew I could count on you for that. I'm glad you had a lovely time last night."

"It was delightful," said Marjie, before taking a bite of delicious pancake with lemon and sugar. "And this is just what I needed. A brilliant breakfast. You've done a great job, love."

"Why, thank you," said Athena, smiling proudly.

"It really hit the spot," said Marjie. "And I hope it's okay that you'll be away for a few days."

Rosemary shrugged. "I could take Athena with me…"

"No, Mum. I don't want to go to Scotland just at the moment. It's too cold. And besides, I've got far too much to do."

"And it's probably best to keep you away from the vampires

anyway," Rosemary conceded. "I mean, Burk and his immediate family seem to be fine about not trying to drink your delicious fae-witch blood. But I'm not sure the rest of that lot will be so restrained."

"Stop talking about my blood like it's some kind of irresistible cocktail," said Athena with a mock frown.

"Can I count on you to make sure everything is fine here?" Rosemary said to Marjie.

"I wouldn't have it any other way," said Marjie.

"Well, I suppose that settles it then," said Rosemary. "I'm off to be a lab rat. You two sit around eating pancakes and having a jolly time."

Marjie and Athena shared a cheeky look.

"Help me convince Mum that she should take an extended holiday with Burk," Athena whispered conspiratorially.

"That sounds like a fun idea," said Marjie. "Why don't you do it, my dear? I'm sure you're overdue a break."

Rosemary sighed. "You know, maybe that would be a nice way to make the most of this very strange situation."

"Now you're talking sense," said Athena.

"What is this world coming to?" Rosemary made a funny face and then returned her attention to her delicious plate of pancakes once more.

23

ROSEMARY

Rosemary was ready at seven in the evening, just as Burk had asked. She was just finishing up her packing when Athena knocked on the half open door and walked into the room.

"I don't see enough bikinis there, Mum," Athena teased.

Rosemary shook her head. "I really hope it's not a bikini-requiring occasion. All my swimwear covers much more of me – deliberately. As hard as it is to find swimmers larger than luggage tags these days!" she said, rolling her eyes.

Athena laughed. "I'm just glad you're taking my advice."

Rosemary looked at her daughter with just a hint of scepticism. Athena's deep coppery hair looked a little unkempt, and there were hints of dark circles under her eyes, but other than that, she did seem happy.

"Are you sure this is okay?" Rosemary asked.

"Yes!" Athena insisted. "It's only a few days."

You're not just trying to get rid of me, are you?" Rosemary squinted at her daughter slightly.

"When you interrogate me like this, it hardly makes me want to keep you around for much longer, doesn't it?" Athena retorted.

"Excuse me?"

"I'm just being silly, Mum. I'm fine. Marjie will look after me. Besides, we've got so many friends here in Myrtlewood. If anything goes wrong, the whole community will come out to help. You know they will."

"If anything goes wrong, or looks even slightly concerning, you tell me straight away – before you call the whole village in, okay?"

"Alright, alright," said Athena. "But we know that nothing is going to go wrong. We're still miles away from the Imbolc festival, for starters."

"Three weeks is not miles away," said Rosemary.

"Point taken. But you've really got to go for a quick holiday now or you'll miss your chance. I want to study, and you need to build up your strength. Besides, you've got to be on your best behavior for that goddess cocktail party. The situations we find ourselves in!"

"Indeed," said Rosemary, sighing.

The doorbell rang, and Rosemary clomped downstairs to find that Marjie had already opened the front door.

There stood Azalea, Burk's stunning vampire mother, in a black, shimmery dress with drapey sleeves and a plunging neckline.

"You can relax, my dear. Just be yourself," said Azalea, kissing Rosemary on both cheeks. "Perseus cares for you so much. Let me do that. It'll be quicker this way, trust me." She picked up Rosemary's bags as if they were nothing more than feather-light. Azalea smiled, slightly maniacally, as she looked from Marjie to Athena. "Don't worry, she'll be in good hands, and we'll return her to you in no time."

"You'll make sure of that!" said Marjie. "We need our Rosemary, and I want her back in one piece when this is all over."

"I will personally ensure she returns safely."

"Does that mean you're coming on holiday with us?" Rosemary asked, hoping the answer was no.

"Not this time, I'm afraid," said Azalea. "I have some important business to attend to. But I'll be there in a flash if I'm summoned. I doubt I'll be needed."

"Thank you for helping with this," said Rosemary. "I don't feel comfortable navigating vampire politics by myself. It's all kinds of terrifying."

"And that's what makes it so delightful," said Azalea with a flourish. "Now, do you need to be carried, or will you follow?"

"I can walk on my own, thanks," said Rosemary. She hugged Marjie and Athena, and after several more goodbyes, followed Azalea out to the car.

It was a sleek sports car, and as soon as Rosemary was settled in the front seat, Azalea accelerated with astonishing speed that made Rosemary wonder if her fear of vampire politics was misplaced; this driving situation was obviously far more dangerous!

Moments later, she found herself in front of the family castle. "What are we doing here?" she asked. "How are we getting to Scotland?"

Azalea grinned. "I figured we'd drive to the airport and fly from there."

"Of course you did."

Azalea whistled, and a trapdoor opened up. A platform rose, bearing with it a gold-coloured private plane. "Here it is," said Azalea.

Rosemary tried to smile. "Can you fly planes as well as submarines?"

"No, planes are terribly boring. But I have Charles for that." That was when Rosemary noticed him, already seated in the cockpit, wearing a 1950s style pilot's cap, his angelic blond hair peeking out from underneath. He saluted her; Rosemary waved back.

"I'm just gonna go with it," she muttered to herself.

It wasn't the first time she had travelled in style with the Burk family, even if last time she'd had some moral support. She wished Burk was here now. She supposed she would see him soon enough.

Rosemary got onto the plane with slightly shaky legs. What was she really getting herself into? She trusted Burk with her life. And she was starting to realise that, aside from the unnerving driving and all the bizarre eccentricities, she trusted his parents too. She certainly did not trust the other powers of vampire politics, however.

"Will you stay with me when we get there?" Rosemary asked.

"I'd be happy to," said Azalea. "We wouldn't want it any other way."

Charles fired up the plane. "Alright, fasten your seat belts, keep your tray tables folded away, and let's get this party started."

The plane took off, and Rosemary looked out the window to see all of Myrtlewood and the surrounding countryside recede into miniature.

She glanced at her hands, hoping that she wasn't flying into some kind of terrible trap, and that she could handle this situation with grace.

She looked across at Azalea, who had pulled out a gold basket. "Do you mind if I craft?" she asked.

Rosemary smiled, raising her eyebrows. "You craft?"

Azalea shrugged. "Every hundred years or so, I swear off all crafts because it's a nightmare with all the clutter. And then I remind myself that I actually rather enjoy nightmares." She winked. "I can't help myself. I get back into crafting again." She pulled out a travel-loom and began weaving what appeared to be a rather intricate tapestry.

"Are you making a family portrait?" asked Rosemary.

"Indeed! It's going to be marvellous. And you know what? I think I'll include you in it."

Rosemary couldn't help smiling. "Why, that's perfectly sweet of you."

"Sweet?" Azalea wrinkled her nose. "I suppose a little sweetness is okay, so long as it's paired with another flavours. Sweet and sour, perhaps. Or bittersweet...or sweet with a heavy dose of spice."

Rosemary chuckled. "I should have known better."

24

ATHENA

Athena opened the door to a very frazzled-looking Detective Neve. "What is it?" she asked. "Has something terrible happened?"

Neve stumbled into the entryway. "No, no," she said. "I just haven't had enough sleep and…I need to talk to you about something."

"Well, come in then," said Marjie, coming out from the kitchen. "I'll put the kettle on."

"Where's your mother?" Neve asked Athena.

"Off to Scotland."

Neve's jaw dropped. "Why? What's that about?"

"It's a long story," said Athena, "involving the vampire council."

Neve sighed as she followed Athena to the kitchen and took a seat at the table. "I'm not sure I've got time for long stories. But I suppose it wouldn't hurt to get advice from you two."

Athena raised her eyebrows. "You really came to see Mum for advice?"

"Your mother is actually quite wise, you know," said Neve with a scolding note.

"Several weeks out of the year, on a good day," Athena retorted. "The rest of the time, she's a bit of a mess."

"All the best people are," Marjie assured her. "Now, what is it?"

"Nothing even close to good, I'm afraid," said Neve. "You remember when you saw that man in the forest, Athena?"

Athena felt a sudden tremor of fear. "Yes? What is it? Have there been other bodies?"

Neve slumped forward in her chair. "Bodies is probably not the right word for them. It was bones."

"Bones?" Athena gasped.

Neve nodded slowly. "A pile of bones was discovered near one of the pathways through the forest."

"Human bones?" Athena asked.

"I'm afraid so," said Neve, tension rising in her voice. "We suspect that it could have been the remains of a small group of tourists visiting town. They went missing after being spotted going into the forest."

"What do you think happened to them? Something that...ate them?" Athena asked.

"Magical forensics said it looked like teeth marks on the bones," said Neve.

"What kind of creature would do that?" Athena asked, mortified. "Eat whole carcasses and just leave the bones?"

"It's very rare," said Neve. "I haven't actually heard of it happening before. Not like this. I'll request for a magical barrier to be put up. That should be in place in the next few days and give us some time to figure out what's going on. It won't hold forever but it should protect innocent people from wandering in and whatever is in there from leaking out."

"It's understandable that you're so worked up," said Marjie. "I've been feeling strange about the forest for days. I tried to scry for it, but even with my enhanced powers, all I'm getting is darkness and a deep craving for scones!"

"That's not surprising," Neve added. "When I went in to investigate, there was definitely a dark presence. An ominous feeling, so foreboding that I had to run away. I'm not easily spooked. Hence why it wasn't too hard for me to become a police officer, even in a strange place like Myrtlewood. I've seen a lot of things in my time, horrendous things. But something about that feeling, something about that presence, it chilled me right to the bone. And I don't know how to explain it."

"You've done a great job of explaining," Marjie assured her. "Some things just can't be completely described or understood. Life is mysterious, magic doubly so!"

"And you wanted Mum's help with this?" said Athena. "Let me try and think like her…I'm not sure what she would do. Maybe make some chocolates to tempt whatever's in there away from eating people?"

"That could be worth a try, actually," said Neve. "I mean, everyone loves your mother's chocolates. And besides, they are bound to have magical properties."

"Or perhaps it would just give whatever is in there a sugar rush?" Athena pointed out. "I suspect whatever ate those people has a taste for flesh, and human flesh in particular, which is a horrifying thought. It makes me doubt truffles are going to cut it…unless there's a new raw meat variety."

"I don't know what I was thinking," said Neve, shaking her head.

"You know, I'm doing a bunch of research anyway," said Athena. "I could compile a list of creatures that might relate to this time of year and send you notes. It will be useful for my essay on the history of Imbolc and I love doing things when they serve a double purpose."

"That would be fabulous," said Neve. "Especially as Agatha hasn't forgiven me for running out of sherry at our wedding, and we've already caused a lot of trouble for the witching authorities getting this barrier set up. I doubt they'll have much patience for us."

"Well, we'll help," said Marjie.

"You are suspiciously powerful these days," Neve said, looking Marjie in the eye. "Are you going to tell me what's going on with you and Agatha and that new witch in town, Delia. Getting up to all kinds of mischief?"

"Indeed we are," said Marjie, hands on hips. "Like you said, I'm a rather powerful crone."

"I do believe you," said Neve, "but that still doesn't answer my question."

"I don't know where to start with all that," Marjie said. "It's a long story, but back to the matter at hand. You've got some of the sharpest minds and most powerful beings in Myrtlewood on your side. So don't you worry about that."

"Perhaps we could have a town meeting," Athena suggested, and then she shook her head. "That sounds like a nightmare considering all the personalities who could show up. Maybe we could just talk to the people we actually like, who aren't terribly annoying."

"That's an idea," said Neve. "Let's make a list of names." She turned to Marjie. "You wouldn't happen to have any of those pasties handy, would you? I believe you that you're a powerful crone, but I'm also starving and in need of your more kitchen-witchy powers."

"I'll whip you up a batch," said Marjie with a smile.

Later that evening, Athena's room was a maze of open books and scattered notes, the air thick with the musty scent of old paper. Her eyes, tired from research, darted between texts as she pieced together the puzzle of the forest's corruption.

"Imbolc," she murmured. "Why does it have to be both a time of renewal, but also of desperate hunger?"

She pored over a passage about Brigid, the goddess associated with Imbolc. Brigid's crosses were said to protect homes from evil and fire. "But what if something's twisting that protective power?" Athena wondered, scribbling notes.

Her attention shifted to the Fomorians, monstrous beings, ancient enemies of the Tuatha Dé Danann. They were associated with chaos and destruction. "Could their influence be seeping through?"

Next, she read about the Cailleach, who she'd met personally not so long ago. The winter crone goddess, said to drink from lakes and rivers, freezing them with her staff. "Water to ice, life to death," Athena noted, but there was no ice here...

She delved into lesser-known entities: the Sluagh, restless spirits that traveled in flocks, stealing souls; the Questing Beast associated with cursed kings; the Each Uisce, a water horse that devoured its victims.

Athena's pen flew across the page as she documented the Baobhan Sith, vampire-like faeries that drained their victims' blood; the Nuckelavee, a skinless sea creature that caused crops to wither; and the Kelpies, shape-shifting water spirits known for drowning their prey; the fear gorta: emaciated, ever-hungry spirits that roamed during times of famine. Their presence outside Ireland was rare but not unheard of.

Something struck a chord. The new girl at school had given Athena chills. She was Irish, yes, and her mother was an expert on folklore...surely a good person to ask, unless they were somehow involved.

Athena shook her head, afraid of becoming paranoid like her mother tended to be. There was no evidence that the problem in the forest was definitely a fear gorta, even if some of the pieces fit. Still, Athena made a mental note to keep a closer eye on Liliana. After all, her sudden arrival at Myrtlewood Academy just as strange things started happening in the forest seemed like too much of a coincidence.

As the night wore on, Athena found herself reading about Crom Cruach, a deity associated with sacrifice and fertility. The juxtaposition of life and death, abundance and hunger, struck a chord.

Exhausted but exhilarated, Athena read over her notes like pieces of a puzzle that didn't quite fit. The common threads of hunger, darkness, transformation, and the delicate balance between life and death wove through them all.

Athena's hand brushed against the golden potion bottle. For a moment, she felt a flicker of kinship with these entities of insatiable need. Shaking off the thought, she picked up her pen again.

*Just keep going...*she told herself.

25

ATHENA

Athena took a deep breath as the bell rang for lunch. The classroom around her bustled with the other students packing up after an alchemy lesson from Mr Venturi. She looked across the room at Beryl who was sliding her perfectly curated folders into her immaculate satchel.

Ms Twigg had suggested it would be in Athena's best interests to talk the student who'd been her arch nemesis into helping her out with potions...

"No time like the present," Athena mumbled under her breath.

She made her way across the room. "Beryl...do you have a minute? I'd like to talk to you."

Beryl looked up at Athena. "Well, well, well. Athena Thorn. To what do I owe the pleasure? Are you here to grace me with your presence or is this some kind of childish prank?"

Athena took a deep breath. "Look, Beryl, I know we haven't always been friends."

Beryl turned up her nose and looked away. "We haven't ever been friends, Athena."

"True. But we might not always have to be enemies..." Athena struggled to find the right worlds. "Oh, look, Beryl, regardless of how you want to frame it, I have a favour to ask you."

"Oh, yes?" Beryl quirked an eyebrow. "Is it rare and dodgy potion ingredients you're after? Perhaps some kind of spell that you need to get yourself out of the trouble that you've already gotten yourself into?"

"I suppose I deserve that," said Athena. She hesitated. Beryl was getting too close to the truth for comfort. "It's more that...I thought we could perhaps study together."

Beryl rolled her eyes. "Why would I want to study with *you*?"

"I don't know," said Athena. "And maybe you don't. But Ms Twigg suggested that I ask you if you'd help me with potions."

A sly smile crept across Beryl's face. "It's nice to feel appreciated...I suppose."

Of course, the truth was that Athena would dearly like to ask Beryl for rare potion ingredients. But a request like that was hardly going to go down well. Athena didn't know if Beryl would want to study with her either. In fact, she doubted it. But it seemed like there might be more of a possibility. Beryl loved being the cleverest person in the room, and when it came to potions, she almost always was.

"It would be a great opportunity for me to learn," said Athena. "I could learn from the best. When it comes to potions, you are amazing, Beryl."

Beryl practically glowed at the praise, making Athena's heart a little sad. Had the poor girl really had so little praise in her life? Coming from such a snobby and bigoted family, that did seem likely.

Beryl considered Athena carefully, and then tentatively asked, "And what would I get out of this arrangement of helping you study?"

"I could help you with Automancy," Athena suggested, her body tensing slightly. There was a chance that the suggestion would backfire. After all, Beryl did not like being second best in any subject. She seemed to take it as a personal affront.

Beryl's expression right now reflected that. She looked as though she'd just bitten into a lemon.

She was definitely going to refuse, Athena thought, bracing for rejection.

"If we helped each other with the subjects we're best at, then there'd be no magical university in the world who would want to turn either of us down," said Athena, allowing herself to be a little desperate in that moment.

Beryl's eyes narrowed and then her shoulders slumped. "I don't know if you can help me. It's hard for me to ask for help from anyone…really."

"I understand that," said Athena. "If you don't want to hang out with me, I mean, I haven't always been kind to you. We haven't exactly been friends."

A moment of awkward silence passed between them.

"I suppose I can see the good in your suggestion," Beryl finally conceded. "Alright. How about we ask if we can stay after school and use the potions laboratory?"

Athena's eyes widened, eyebrows raised. "Really?"

"Don't sound so surprised, Athena," said Beryl. "We may not get along, and I may despise you, especially when you beat me in certain subjects. But there's one thing I despise more than losing to you: losing in exams!"

Athena smiled. "I'm looking forward to learning a lot from you."

∽

AFTER LUNCH, Athena sat with her friends in the courtyard.

"We saw you talking to Little Miss Nose-in-the-Air," said Felix. "Does that mean you're going to hang out with Beryl now?"

Athena laughed and explained the situation.

"She's just going to insult you the whole time," Sam warned.

"I can handle a little bit of constructive criticism," said Athena.

"It won't be so constructive, I'm afraid," said Felix.

"Well, I can live with it," said Athena. "It's a way for us to help each other study for exams."

"Are you sure everything's okay with you?" Ash asked. "Something's not quite right. It's good to have goals and everything, but you're not planning to go off into the Underworld again, are you? Because if you do, you should take us with you."

Athena shook her head. "Don't be silly. It was reckless and dangerous. But I felt like I had to do it at the time."

She glanced around at her friends wondering if they had the capacity to understand the emptiness, the sadness, the feeling of separation...and at least some of the reasons why. Of course they did. It was written all over their faces. They all missed Elise dearly, yet it was painful to talk about her.

"Seriously though," said Felix. "What's going on, Athena? You know we've got to stick together, right? We can all help each other study."

"It's a good idea," said Ash. "I've been meaning to ask about that. Let's have a study session. I was thinking of inviting the new girl, Liliana."

Athena looked across the courtyard to where Liliana was sitting peacefully under a tree, reading an old book. There was something about her that seemed off, though she couldn't quite put her finger on what. Liliana's long, dark hair had an otherworldly sheen to it, catching the light in ways that didn't seem entirely natural. Her eyes, too, were peculiar – they seemed to shift colour subtly, from deep brown to an almost violet hue depending on how the light hit them. Around her neck, Athena noticed a pendant in the shape of a raven, which Liliana often absently touched as she spoke.

"I'm not sure about the new girl," Athena admitted.

"Just us then," said Sam. "What about after school?"

"Well, after school today, I might be having a potions lesson with Beryl," said Athena.

"Beryl!" Felix cackled. "That's a good one."

"I'm serious," said Athena.

"Sure, sure...Later then?" Felix asked. "We could all go to Thorn Manor for dinner. I'd love to see what your house cooks up!"

"Thorn Manor doesn't cook," said Athena, smiling. "At least not usually, though I'm sure it's possible..."

"That'd be great," Sam said, smiling at Athena. "We'd love to visit your magical palace – we always do!"

"Agreed," said Ash with a grin.

"Very well, perhaps you could come over sometime soon," said Athena. "There is something else that happened though. It's just—" She sighed. "I'm afraid..." Athena filled them in on what Neve had told her, about the strange feeling she got in the forest. "I think it's worth steering clear for now, at least until we find out what's really going on."

"Wouldn't the best way to find out be to go into the forest though?" Felix suggested.

Athena rolled her eyes. "Seriously, Felix, how've you lived as long as you have?"

∼

The day wore on, and Athena was exhausted by the time the final bell rang. She found Beryl in the potions classroom.

"You're late," Beryl said, not bothering to raise her head from the old tome she was reading. "I was wondering if you'd show up or not."

"I'm only a few minutes late," Athena said, trying not to sound defensive. "Thank you for doing this. I really appreciate it. I'm sorry for—"

"Shut up," said Beryl, but her tone was warm. "I know you've been through a lot. And I have too, of course."

Athena nodded. Beryl's parents had been locked up, partly due to Athena and Rosemary's role in unmasking their dodgy plan to sabotage the treaty with the fae. Not to mention the fact that, from what Athena had seen, Beryl's parents seemed awful to begin with. It reminded Athena that growing up with a family like that, who cared so much for pretences and was so emotionally cold, distant, and controlling, could hardly have been a pleasant childhood. Now was hardly the time to acknowledge that.

"So what is it you need help with when it comes to potions?" Beryl asked.

Athena sighed. "I really don't know where to start. I mean, I follow the instructions. It usually works. So what's the problem?"

"The problem is," said Beryl, "you're just so new to potion making. And while sometimes following the instructions is enough, other times it backfires. Potions are not just a combination of magical ingredients. They are complex. We have to take into account the chemistry, the various energetic factors, and the careful balancing of other forces..."

Athena nodded. "And I don't completely understand the basics. I mean, I've only been at this school for a year, and before that, before the age of sixteen, I had an entirely mundane existence."

Beryl scrunched up her nose. "That's why it pains me to see you beating me in other subjects. And I don't want to give you the advantage in potions either, really. But I suppose it won't really matter after this year. We'll be over and done, and I can go to the Avalon Academy for Advanced Magic and finally start my life."

"It sounds like you've got some good plans," said Athena, having no idea what fancy school Beryl referred to.

"I suppose, to be honest, one of the main reasons I agreed to help you was because I am really struggling with Automancy."

"You don't need it," said Athena. "It's hardly going to be the entry requirement to do that kind of advanced magic."

"That depends on what kind of course you're trying to get into, doesn't it?" said Beryl. "To get into the top programmes, I'll need to pass the extended tests and not just be good. I need to be the best, Athena. That means I need a much better grasp of Automancy."

"Alright," said Athena. "Let's make a deal, you teach me the basics of potions, including all the things that I might have missed from not growing up in a magical family, and I'll see what I can do to help you with Automancy. I really do mean it. I'll try my best."

"Very well," said Beryl. "Let's start with measurements."

"Thank goodness," said Athena. "I never really know why they can't use teaspoons or tablespoons. Why is it always a pinch of this and a splash of that?"

Beryl laughed. "I've often wondered that myself."

Athena pulled out the potion-making textbook. "Maybe we could practice on one of these spells?"

"Sure. Which one?"

"Here, how about this one? Is there a potion for getting a good night's sleep?" Athena suggested.

"If only it was that easy," said Beryl. "Oh look, here's one for prophetic dreams."

"Alright, that sounds fun. Let's try it." Athena scanned the ingredients. "Mugwort, passionflower...I think we've got all these things in store. Do we need to ask a teacher about that?"

"It just so happens that I know where the spare key is," Beryl said with a glint in her eye. "I'm sure they wouldn't mind Myrtlewood Academy's most advanced students, who are just studying for their exams, popping in to get a few common ingredients."

Athena grinned. "Wow, I didn't know you were such a rule-breaker."

"There's a lot you don't know about me," said Beryl.

"I suppose you're right," Athena admitted. "I like to think I'm a good judge of character, but maybe I've judged you very poorly."

"Right. Let's go." Beryl fished around in the desk and extracted a large bronze key. "It's through this way."

She led Athena to the back of the room and opened the door to the enormous supply cabinets. From the outside, it looked like an ordinary pantry door. On the inside, the storeroom went on for what seemed like miles.

Athena eyed the shelves greedily. There were several ingredients here for the potion she and Beryl were about to make, but also for the other one – the one she really wanted to make.

While Beryl was carefully selecting stems of dried mugwort and muttering her advice on the type of stems and leaves to look for, Athena scanned the shelves for the colloidal gold she needed.

It was up high, inside another cupboard with a glass front. A sign on the cabinet said "Restricted Ingredients".

Athena tried the door anyway, finding to her surprise that it wasn't locked.

"What are you looking for?" Beryl asked.

"I'm just being nosy," said Athena. She waited for Beryl to turn back to the mugwort before reaching into the cabinet and pocketing one of the small bottles of colloidal gold.

It fit so nicely in her pocket.

26

ROSEMARY

Rosemary sighed in awe as the helicopter drew near the ancient stone castle. The plane had landed on a private runway near Edinburgh, where Rosemary, Azalea, and Charles transferred themselves and their belongings to the helicopter, which apparently Azalea was better at driving than Charles.

Rosemary supposed that over the many centuries they'd been alive, they'd picked up many bizarre quirks and skills, though it was impressive they still adapted to new technology so well after all this time when Rosemary struggled to learn how to use every single new phone she'd ever owned.

She shook her head now, looking out over the spires, tracing the old stonework and masonry of the ancient castle with her eyes. All other thoughts flew out of Rosemary's mind, along with the worries that she'd had, as the helicopter swooped nearer, across the mountain range and towards the castle. The fleeting beauty of the moment took Rosemary's breath away, but the distraction was short-lived.

A minute later, as Azalea brought the helicopter down onto a landing pad atop one of the castle wings, all of Rosemary's doubts and fears flooded back. In a place like this, it would be impossible to escape, especially with a horde of vampires on her tail.

Even in the daylight, she could only get so far in these mountains.

"I hope that contract Perseus drafted is watertight," said Rosemary. It was always strange to call Burk by his first name, but it made more sense when around other Burks.

"Don't worry, my dear," said Azalea. "We will take good care of you. Besides, Charles is still on the council for Britannia."

"Britannia?" said Rosemary.

Azalea's smile flashed across her face. "The vampires use a somewhat different map than most humans, based on our own ancient kingdoms. And Britannia is what – England, Ireland, Scotland?"

Charles laughed. "You must be joking if you think Ireland would want to be part of this. Scotland's not keen either, actually. The Scottish vampires' enthusiasm for independence goes back centuries, but they've stayed connected to the rest of Britannia because they get a lot of power out of keeping this stronghold here. They are notorious for not following ordinances, but that's Scotland for you."

He seemed rather too chuffed about this.

Rosemary found it strangely amusing but also disconcerting. "They can hold the rest of Britannia to account for their regular foolishness?"

Azalea cackled. "Yes, I'd say much of the historic agitation for Scottish independence involved several feisty activist vampires," she crooned. "We've long been arguing over blood-enchanted scones and the order in which the ingredients and magic go in together."

Rosemary raised an eyebrow. "Vampire politics is more complex than I thought. Are scones important?"

"Don't be ridiculous," said Charles. "Blood-enchanted scones are dusty and tasteless. They're hardly a priority. It's more about the principle than anything else."

Rosemary smiled wryly. "Well, I won't pretend to understand how all the different vampire councils work or fit together. But perhaps I should know something more before I go in..."

She gestured out towards the castle.

"The various global councils maintain some independence," said Charles. "However, on the important things, we work together for consistency."

"And being in Scotland means we're not under the jurisdiction of the same sub-branch of the council that you're part of?" Rosemary asked wearily.

Azalea nodded.

"That makes me uncomfortable," said Rosemary.

"It's not exactly how it works," said Charles. "There are overarching systems and structures, larger conglomerates of regions. I won't bore you with the details. But rest assured, the vampires of Scotland would not do anything to violate our trust, as long as we don't try to manipulate them or get them to do anything that they don't want to do."

"And why would we do that?" said Rosemary.

"Exactly," said Azalea, her smile deepening. "There's nothing to worry about."

"Really?" Rosemary took a long slow breath as the engines of the helicopter wound down.

"Really," Azalea assured her.

"Alright," said Rosemary. "I'll just need a moment. An extensive history lesson on vampire politics isn't exactly what I need right now. I feel like I'm walking into a lion's den, totally unprepared."

"Ancient territories are probably not top on the list of priorities in terms of what you need to know about right now," said Azalea. "What would be the most useful?"

"Tell me, very quickly, what do I need to know?" said Rosemary, wishing she'd thought to ask much earlier in the journey, or perhaps to read up on vampire politics in her spare time.

"Our system of governance is ancient," Charles began. "We have councils and tribunals, but also circles of elders that wield significant influence. The old lore that preceded our current laws still holds sway in many circles."

"How does that work, then?" Rosemary asked, frowning.

Azalea chimed in, "It's a constant struggle between tradition and progress. Some edicts from millennia ago are still hotly debated. For instance, the interpretation of 'blood tithe' varies wildly depending on who you ask."

Charles nodded. "Indeed. And when it comes to modernising our rituals, well, that's where things get truly contentious. Some push for change, while others cling to tradition as if their immortal lives depended on it."

"It sounds...complicated," Rosemary ventured.

"Oh, it is," Charles agreed. "Power dynamics shift based on arcane knowledge as much as political manoeuvring. And don't get me started on the things we all know are outdated but can't agree on how to change."

"Vampires are not particularly sensitive," said Azalea, assuring her. "They've been around long enough to have pretty thick skin."

Rosemary couldn't quite believe that, after several encounters with easily offended vampiric creatures. However, she couldn't stay put forever.

Moments later, as they approached the castle's entrance, Azalea added, "Just remember, not all vampires are fans of modernity. Some here have seen empires rise and fall. They're not easily swayed by contemporary notions."

The massive oak doors swung open, revealing a vast hall that was a jarring mixture of ancient and cutting-edge. Gothic arches soared overhead, while sleek computer terminals hummed below. Vampires in lab coats hurried about, carrying both ancient tomes and holographic tablets.

"Welcome," came a crisp voice with a hint of a Scottish brogue, "to the Britannia Hematological Research Institute."

Rosemary turned to see a tall, imperious woman striding towards them. Her silver hair was pulled back in a severe bun, and she carried a clipboard that seemed almost comically mundane in this environment.

"Elvadora," Charles greeted her with a respectful nod. "May I present Rosemary, our...guest research subject."

Elvadora's piercing violet eyes fixed on Rosemary with an intensity that made her want to step back. "Ah, yes. The human who's caused quite a stir." She tapped her clipboard. "I have your intake forms here. I trust everything is in order?"

Rosemary gulped at the stack of paperwork, but nodded and followed along as Elvadora led them deeper into the facility, Rosemary couldn't shake the feeling that she was crossing a threshold from which there was no return.

"In a moment, I'll introduce you to Dr Drake, who is heading up the research on your...fascinating adaptation. Please sign here."

She brandished the clipboard.

Rosemary swallowed hard, suddenly very aware of the ancient power dynamics at play in this modern facility. "I...I'd like to speak with Perseus Burk first, if that's alright."

A flicker of something – amusement? annoyance? – crossed Elvadora's face. "Very well. But do remember, dear, that even he must abide by our protocols. We may be ancient, but we're not without structure."

27

ATHENA

Athena stashed the small, golden vial under her desk in her room, next to several other items she'd collected so far. She just needed to go to the fae realm and get a few extra things. She didn't want to leave it until night, because to access the door through to the fae realm, she knew she needed to be in the forest.

She had tried it from her bedroom before. Something about the house, perhaps, was blocking her. Either that, or it was the other way around – something about being near the forest made it easier to connect with the home realm of her father's people.

Checking to make sure that Marjie's car was nowhere in sight along the driveway, Athena slipped downstairs and out the back door near the edge of the lawn. She stood in the spot marked by a stone, the place where she and Elise had buried the powers of the misguided minstrel who'd tried to steal her heart.

It had been a strange moment in her relationship with Elise, and Athena still had a lot of regrets about the past she had not figured out how to process. Neither of them had felt ready to continue as girlfriends at that point, and so they had agreed to be friends. Even that had been better than the current situation, with Elise in the Underworld.

At least then, there was somebody close. At least a friend was better than no Elise around at all.

She hadn't heard from Fleur, Elise's mother, for a while. She wondered how the poor woman was doing. She should call in and visit, or at least send her a letter and some flowers. Maybe Fleur could advise her on the proper etiquette in the magical world for comforting each other in times of grief. There might even be particular fae realm customs that she should be observing, but she was still too new to all of this...and the thought of seeing Fleur made Athena's heart clench painfully in her chest, just as thoughts of Elise only brought back that sad, hopeless, aching, heavy feeling she'd been doing her best to avoid.

The potion would help.

The potion would ease that pain, would enable her to focus, to study, to move on with her life. Wouldn't it? Perhaps it was just masking her pain. Perhaps it was just a crutch. But wasn't that okay if it helped her get through the day...at least for now?

Athena raised her hand, about to open the doorway, when she heard a sound.

"Hey, Athena!"

Athena turned to see Felix striding across the lawn towards her. "What are you doing here?" she asked.

"Checking on you," he replied. "Something's been off with you lately. I wanted to make sure you're okay."

"I'm fine...busy actually. Umm, maybe I can meet up with you later."

Felix stood his ground. "Look, I know something is going on with you and it's not good. Losing Elise was bad enough. I don't need to lose another friend."

"Don't be silly," said Athena. "You're not losing me."

"Then what are you about to do? And don't lie to me, because I already know it's something..."

"I'm just hopping over to the fae realm. It's not a crime, you know," she said, shrugging.

"Don't you remember what happened last time? When you just hopped off to the fae realm without telling anyone about it? We all had to come looking for you," Felix reminded her.

"That was a long time ago, Felix, and I'm not going very far. It's not a risk. I just need to gather some potion ingredients."

"Something tells me that you're telling the truth," said Felix, "but it's not the entire story."

"Sherlock Holmes, you are," said Athena, nudging him with her elbow. "So what, are you going to try and stop me?"

"Why would I do that?" said Felix, striking a pose with his head cocked to the side. "I'm not going to stop you. I'm going to come with you."

Athena rolled her eyes. "No, you're not. It's not safe. The fae realm energy affects people strangely."

"I've been there before. And you know, in my shifter form, I'm totally fine."

"Alright then, you can come with me. If you remain a fox," said Athena with a sigh. She could see no other way forward.

Felix threw back his head in laughter. "You're saying you like me better when you can't hear me talk?"

"Well..." Athena blinked at him, innocently. "I've always thought foxes were rather sweet animals."

"Sweet is not the look I'm going for," said Felix, but a moment later he transformed into a large fox, dashing about in circles around Athena's feet.

"We're not going to be there for long," said Athena. "Stay near me. I just need to collect a few things."

Felix sat down to heel near Athena's feet as she raised her hand

and cut the door to the fae realm. The familiar feeling of homecoming swept over her. She breathed it in.

"Alright, remember we're not going to be gone too long. Stay close. And remember, don't eat anything. If I recall correctly, last time you got yourself in trouble and quite sick by eating the wrong thing."

Felix yipped and leapt through ahead of her.

Athena wandered around the purple forests, searching for the familiar mushrooms. The book on fae realm botany she'd borrowed while staying at the fae palace would have come in handy with identifying the right ones. She wished she'd brought it back with her. However, she was sure the violet ones, with the slightly flat tops and the long, dainty stems, were the right mushrooms.

Athena went to work, deciding she might as well get enough for several batches of the potion. Because if all went well, she wouldn't have to come back in a hurry.

There was something eerie about coming here alone, even though she wasn't entirely alone with the fox Felix sniffing around the bushes and chasing the occasional pixie or sprite. Perhaps it wasn't quite as eerie as the forest around Thorn Manor had seemed today, especially after Neve's stories.

Felix dashed out ahead, then returned, nudging Athena's legs with his snout, encouraging her.

"I haven't petted you enough?" said Athena, scratching him behind the ears. It was a little bit odd, considering he was one of her school friends, but it seemed harmless enough.

"Alright, you've got enough. It's time to go, boy," she patted him on the head. Felix whimpered.

"Look, if you're going to behave like a dog, I'm going to treat you like one," Athena growled, and Felix yipped in laughter. "Come on, I think this is roughly the same place where we cut the door." At least, so she thought.

Felix barked uncertainly as she raised her hand and began the process of going back through to the Earth realm. But it was darkness that greeted her on the other side.

Athena gasped.

Something was dreadfully wrong.

"Felix, stay close. I don't think this is quite right."

They were far too deep in the forest. She knew she needed to close the gate again. But she couldn't help but stare in horror at the darkness, the trees stripped bare of life, the barren emptiness. She wasn't sure how far into the forest she was. This wasn't right, not at all. There was a hollow feeling, as if some mythic nothingness had been swallowing the very life force of this place that was usually so vibrant, peaceful, and full of life.

"I don't like this at all," said Athena, sealing up the door. She tried again to retrace her steps, closer to home this time.

"Okay, here goes," Athena said. She took a deep breath and began cutting again, creating another door. This time, as the layers fell away, Thorn Manor was visible. She was at the edge of the forest on the road.

She leapt through, Felix close behind, and sealed up the door again. But it wasn't what was on the other side, in the fae realm, that terrified her. It was what she'd faced so nearby, so close to home. It made her heart tighten, as if it had shrunk up into her chest in fear.

Felix shook himself and then transformed back into his usual state, his clothing magically reclaiming him as well. "So what was that about?" he asked.

"Something bad is going on in that forest," Athena said. "I saw...Do you think it's the Morrigan?"

"I wish it was that simple," said Felix. "Do you remember the haunted house from Samhain?"

"It was nothing like that," said Athena. "Well, a little like that. But maybe it was just the creepy feeling that was similar. Something very different is going on."

"Is that what you're making the potion for? Is it some kind of defensive spell that you need to protect the town?"

Athena nodded, just slightly. It wasn't really a lie. She did need to make a potion to protect the town, after all, and how could she protect anyone when she wasn't functional? "Something like that," she muttered.

She rubbed at the tightness in her jaw.

Was this who she was now? Somebody who stole ingredients and potions components from school? Somebody who lied to her friends?

It's for the greater good, she told herself. But even in that moment, she couldn't be totally sure that she wasn't also lying to herself.

28

ATHENA

"Are you alright, dear?" Marjie asked Athena.

Athena blinked and looked around, finding herself surrounded by books as she sat by the fire in the living room of Thorn Manor. "I must have nodded off," she said.

"Well, I'm glad you're getting some sleep," said Marjie with a wink.

Athena felt her shoulders stiffen. Had Marjie noticed something? She was getting far too intuitive, especially these days. Had she discovered Athena's secret?

"I stayed up late studying and preparing for the ritual," Athena explained.

"I think you're pushing yourself too hard," Marjie said gently.

Athena shook her head. "I'm fine, really. I've just got a few assignments to do. I can combine both my prep for school and for Imbolc."

"How does that work?" Marjie asked.

"Well, I have a History of Magic essay to do, and I decided to choose the season to focus on so that all my research would have a dual purpose."

"How clever you are," Marjie said. "Are you ready for dinner? I've made a chicken and thyme pie."

Athena inhaled deeply, trying to catch the scent from the kitchen. "I can smell it," she said. "It smells delicious."

"Will you be joining me in the kitchen? Or would you like to eat in here surrounded by books?"

Athena smiled. "We could both eat in here, and you could keep me company."

"I'd love to bring a tray in," said Marjie. "It is awfully cosy by the fire, isn't it?"

"Exactly," said Athena.

Moments later, they were tucking into Marjie's delicious pie paired with fresh Granny Smith apple juice.

"Is this seasonal?" Athena asked, picking up her glass.

"Well, apples tend to be stored throughout the winter so that they're available for more than just one season, you know."

"Thank you for this. It really hit the spot," Athena said. She took another big bite of the pie, chewing the pastry for a moment before swallowing it down and reaching for another mouthful ravenously.

"But tell me, you didn't skip lunch again, did you?" Marjie asked.

"No..." In truth she couldn't remember. "I'm just feeling hungry. You know, it might be from reading about the season of Imbolc. People got so hungry over the winter. In the history books, that's why the seasonal festival was so important. Coming out of the winter and hoping for a good harvest that would carry them through for the next year. Most of the supplies run low by that point. The spring is just beginning at Imbolc...and doesn't bring much in the way of food, not for a while anyway."

"That's right," said Marjie. "Sounds like you've got a pretty good grip on the season. It's good to see you so focused and devoted to schoolwork."

Athena smiled. "I suppose I'm compensating for all the months that I spent moping around."

Marjie reached over and patted Athena on the shoulder. "Moping around is necessary sometimes, you know. There's a season for everything."

"I suppose," Athena replied. "I just needed to find that feeling sorry for myself didn't exactly get me very far."

"No, probably not," Marjie agreed. "Though it can be good to indulge yourself from time to time, as long as it's not too much."

Athena sighed. "If I'd been more focused, I wouldn't have so much to catch up on. Some of these assignments I could have done last year. The school has been pretty lenient letting me catch up like this."

"It's not just schoolwork that's scaring you," Marjie said. "It's because of what comes after, isn't it?"

Athena nodded. "Who knows what will become of me?"

"To be wise beyond your years is a good thing in the long term, my dear," said Marjie. "And you are a wise one, even if it hurts sometimes."

"Being a teenager sucks," Athena said, sounding more petulant and immature than she intended. "What happens afterwards? I'm just scared I'll miss my whole life."

"Nonsense," said Marjie. "Most interesting people I've known in my life had no idea what they were doing when they were younger, even at the tender age of forty like your mother. Some people know what they're doing from a young age and stay focused on it. But those are the rare minority."

"Mum keeps saying that."

"Because your mother is actually wiser than you'd like to give her credit for," said Marjie. "A lot of us take our time to figure it all out. But we get lots of chances to start again, to learn more, to do different things. It's what makes life so interesting, and it's just as well too. Otherwise, I'd be stuck with one of my old businesses."

"Like the recycled toilet paper?" Athena asked with a smile.

Marjie laughed. "That never quite worked out right. I couldn't figure out where to transmute the soiled particles, you understand."

Athena was glad she'd finished eating. "If it had worked, perhaps it would have been a raging success."

"I'd like to think so," said Marjie. "But then again, if it had worked and I'd become a magical toilet paper magnate, I wouldn't have my wonderful tea shop. And who knows? Maybe I wouldn't be living here with you."

"New wonderful mistakes await the world," Athena said.

"Don't worry about it," Marjie replied. "You'll be fine."

"Are you sure?" Athena asked.

"I think you need to figure this out on your own," said Marjie. "I always feel that it's everyone's right to make their own mistakes in life."

"Thanks for the vote of confidence," said Athena, pretending to be offended.

"I do have the utmost confidence in you," Marjie assured her. "And I'm sure whatever is troubling you, you'll figure it out."

"I wonder how my mother's getting on," Athena mused.

"She sent me a message earlier," Marjie said. "She said she's in some kind of grand castle and that vampires are really weird."

"That does sound exactly like what she'd say," Athena replied. "In fact, she sent me something similar. I hope it all works out."

"Can't hurt to have the vampire authorities on your side," Marjie said.

"Powerful allies indeed," Athena agreed.

29

ROSEMARY

Rosemary's head was spinning as she followed Dr Drake through the winding corridors of the vampire research facility. The castle's stone walls were adorned with an eclectic mix of ancient tapestries and modern holographic displays, creating a jarring juxtaposition of old and new. The air hummed with an energy that made her skin tingle, as if the very atmosphere was infused with centuries of magical experiments.

"Watch your step here," Dr Drake cautioned, his pale hand gesturing towards a sudden dip in the floor. "This part of the castle is over a thousand years old. We've had to get creative with our renovations."

Rosemary nodded, carefully navigating the uneven stone. "I'm surprised you don't just level it out," she commented.

Dr Drake chuckled, the sound echoing off the walls. "Oh, we could. But where's the fun in that? Besides, it's a good reminder of our history. Speaking of which..." He paused, turning to face her with an excited gleam in his dark eyes. "Have you ever heard of the Sanguine Scrolls?"

Rosemary shook her head, and Dr Drake's grin widened. "They're ancient prophecies, said to be written in the blood of the first vampires. Most of us thought they were just myths, but recently..." He trailed off, glancing around as if checking for eavesdroppers. "Well, let's just say recent events have made us take a second look."

Before Rosemary could press for more information, they rounded a corner and entered a vast circular room. The ceiling soared impossibly high, adorned with intricate frescoes depicting scenes from vampire lore. Rosemary craned her neck, trying to take it all in.

"Welcome to the Grand Atrium," Dr Drake announced proudly. "This is where we conduct our most important experiments."

The room was a hive of activity. Vampires in lab coats bustled about, their movements a blur to Rosemary's human eyes. Strange machines whirred and hummed, emitting occasional puffs of colourful smoke. In one corner, a group of researchers arguing in hushed tones huddled around a large device which appeared to be a conglomeration of whirring cogs.

Rosemary was curious but it seemed the researcher vampire had other priorities.

"Now then," Dr Drake said, clapping his hands together. "Shall we begin?"

The next few hours passed in a whirlwind of tests and examinations. Rosemary cast spells while connected to whirring machines, provided samples of her magical essence (which briefly turned the lab into a disco ball of sparkling lights), and even participated in a peculiar obstacle course designed to test how her magic interacted with vampire abilities.

Throughout it all, Rosemary couldn't help but notice the vampires' enthusiasm. She'd almost describe it as a 'zest for life' if perhaps she wasn't acutely conscious that she was among the undead.

They approached each task with boundless curiosity and enthusiasm, savouring every moment. During a brief break, she watched in amusement as a group of vampire researchers debated the merits of different tea blends with the passion of sommeliers discussing fine wines.

"You all seem to enjoy...well, everything," Rosemary commented to Dr Drake as he handed her a steaming cup of Earl Grey.

He grinned, revealing perfect teeth. "Immortality teaches you to appreciate the little things. Every sensation, every experience is a gift. If not, it gets awfully gruelling after a few hundred years."

Rosemary pondered this, sipping her tea thoughtfully.

As the day wore on, Rosemary found herself in a room lined with ancient texts. The scent of old parchment and leather bindings filled the air, reminding her of Myrtlewood's library. An elderly vampire with spectacles perched on her nose pored over the results of their tests.

"Fascinating," she muttered. "Simply fascinating. Ms Thorn, your magic is unlike anything we've seen before."

"What does that mean?" Rosemary asked, trying to peek at the parchments spread across the desk.

"It seems, your magic—"

A commotion erupted in the hallway. Dr Drake excused himself to investigate, returning moments later with a harried expression.

"I'm terribly sorry, but we'll have to cut this short," he said. "There's been an...incident in the Eternal Archives."

"The what now?" Rosemary asked, raising an eyebrow.

Dr Drake sighed. "It's where we keep all our records. Millennia of vampire history, all meticulously catalogued and cross-referenced. Or at least, it was." He ran a hand through his hair, looking genuinely distressed. "Apparently, someone tried to modernise the filing system without consulting the Archival Committee. Now we've got centuries of documents out of order, and the nightwalker's union is threatening to strike if we don't sort it out by moonrise."

Rosemary blinked, trying to process this information. "I'm sorry, the nightwalker's union?"

"Oh yes," the elderly vampire chimed in. "They're quite militant about proper working conditions. Last century, they managed to negotiate mandatory velvet-lined coffins for all employees."

"I...see," Rosemary said, though she wasn't sure she did at all.

30

ATHENA

Athena began the preparations. She had all the ingredients she needed for the potion. At least she hoped she did.

She went over the instructions once more, hoping that Marjie was asleep as she made her way up to the tower.

Wind rattled the windows and a storm seemed to be brewing outside. Lightning crashed through the sky followed immediate by thunder. Rain sounded heavy on the roof.

Athena took a moment to enjoy the sound.

She'd always found storms relaxing – when she got over the fear of them, at least.

She looked out the dark forest near the house. It looked really ordinary at night. But then again there wasn't much to see through the stormy weather and she knew whatever was lurking there was far from ordinary.

She'd talked to Marjie about it, of course, earlier that afternoon. Marjie felt the need to message Neve to update her. But Athena suggested not telling her mother, at least not yet. Rosemary had enough on her plate as it was.

It was Athena's job to hold things together while her mother was away. In some ways, she'd always looked out for Rosemary. For most of her life Athena had to be mature and responsible for the sake of her wayward parents, and then of course, she also resisted it. For most of her life, her father was hopeless and her mum hadn't gotten her act together. Athena felt that she had to take on responsibility that she'd never wanted to.

She also knew that neither her mother nor Marjie would like what she was doing right now. They would tell her to stop. They'd tell her not to rely on a potion to get through the day, not to depend on it to have the energy to do work that she desperately had to catch up on.

They'd tell her to take it easy, to rest and relax...and just do her best. But that clearly wasn't going to be enough to face the heaviness and pain...not without magical help.

Her grief for Elise was so draining it made her want to sleep all day, yet she couldn't really sleep. Athena felt like an abject failure, unworthy of existence, not worthy of living...she'd find herself moping around in a miasma of self-pity.

This was not the kind of cycle she wanted to be stuck in.

At least the potion helped her to get her out of bed.

Athena prepared the mushrooms as instructed in the recipe and then began the first steps of the potion.

The cauldron bubbled merrily as she added other ingredients, hoping against hope that she'd prepared and gathered the ingredients properly. She'd struggled with potions at school, except for an occasional fluke. On some level, Athena realised she was as impulsive as her mother.

She said the incantation and added the final drops of enchanted colloidal gold.

A mist appeared over the cauldron. She ladled some liquid. It looked more purple-tinged than gold. It was supposed to be gold...

"Close enough?" Athena mumbled. It was more of a question than a proclamation as she decanted the potion into bottles from the store cupboard.

If she was being completely honest with herself, she knew something wasn't right. But she'd already gone to so much effort making a fae potion in the earth realm, with ingredients from both worlds...it wasn't *exactly* the same as the one her grandmother had given her.

Perhaps there was some fae magic she didn't understand, or the ingredients had mutated before arriving. What choice did she have?

She'd been using the remaining potion sparingly. She only had one drop left, not even enough to get through the night.

She took a deep breath as more thunder sounded outside. She lifted the vial to her lips, taking a sip of the new potion.

Radiant joy spread through her, followed by dizziness and bliss. Thank goodness it worked. She slipped the remaining bottles into her old hat box, which she placed on top of Granny's bookshelf. Surely nobody would find them there, and hardly anybody could find this room anyway.

She slipped downstairs, ready for another evening of studying. Her potion worked brilliantly, perhaps even better than the one her grandmother had given her. Athena managed to finish her history essay and race through the latest astrology transits report, as well as weaving some traditional items and preparing for the Imbolc feast. It was the most productive night she'd had so far.

She felt quietly pleased with herself. Perhaps her own magic had added something extra to the potion, she mused.

It wasn't until breakfast time, when she slipped downstairs to greet Marjie in the kitchen, that she realised something was amiss. The look of shock on Marjie's face said it all.

"Athena, what's happened to you?" Marjie asked.

"What do you mean?" Athena replied, confused.

"Haven't you looked in the mirror this morning? You're bright pink!"

Athena shook her head. "What are you talking about?"

Marjie spoke more seriously now. "What have you been doing, love?"

"I don't know what you're talking about," said Athena, rushing to the sideboard to check her reflection in the mirror. Her skin was indeed pink, or perhaps fuchsia was a better word for it.

"What's this about?" Marjie asked. "Athena?"

"I don't know. Maybe it's an allergic reaction?"

"No, Athena," said Marjie. "Look at your feet. You're floating!"

31

ROSEMARY

Rosemary's eyes fluttered open. She was momentarily disoriented by the unfamiliar stone ceiling above her. The events of the past few days came flooding back – the vampire research facility, the endless tests, the strange mix of ancient lore and cutting-edge magical science. She sat up slowly, her body aching from the rigorous examinations.

A soft knock at the door preceded Azalea's entrance. Burk's mother glided in, a vision of gothic elegance in a flowing black gown. "Good evening, dear," she said, her voice like velvet. "I trust you slept well?"

Rosemary nodded, stifling a yawn. "What time is it?"

"Just past sunset," Azalea replied with a smile. "The researchers are eager to begin today's tests, but I insisted you be allowed to rest properly. Now, shall we get you some breakfast?"

They entered a grand dining hall where Charles and Burk were already seated. Rosemary's heart leapt at the sight of Burk, and she rushed to embrace him.

"I've missed you," she murmured into his chest.

"And I you," he replied, pulling back to look at her with concern. He'd been held up in an all-night experiment to test if simulated sunlight would burn him in the darkness. "How are you holding up?"

Before Rosemary could answer, Dr Drake burst into the room, his lab coat billowing behind him. "Ah, Ms Thorn! Excellent, you're awake. Eat up! We have much to cover today."

Rosemary breakfasted on an odd mix of traditional Scottish fare and more exotic dishes. As she ate, she couldn't help but notice the vampires watching her with intense curiosity.

"I hope you don't mind," Dr Drake said, noticing her discomfort. "It's just so fascinating to observe human eating habits. Especially those of a witch as powerful as yourself."

Rosemary swallowed a bite of haggis, feeling self-conscious. "I'm hardly that powerful," she protested.

Charles chuckled, a rare sound. "My dear, you've managed to alter vampire physiology in a way we've never seen before. I'd say that qualifies as rather powerful indeed."

After breakfast, Rosemary found herself once again in the Grand Atrium, surrounded by whirring machines and excited vampire researchers. Today's tests focused on the emotional component of her magic – how her feelings for Burk had influenced the spell that allowed him to walk in sunlight.

This part of the testing was run by Dr Verge, a young-looking vampire wearing a lab coat and thick round glasses, her blonde hair pulled back in a tight bun.

She considered the results carefully. "It appears that your affection for Perseus Burk created a unique effect that allows him to withstand sunlight and enjoy human food."

"Can it be replicated?" Dr Drake asked eagerly, practically bouncing on his toes.

Dr Verge shook her head, her bun wobbling slightly. "Not directly, no. This isn't a spell or potion that can be reproduced. It's a natural phenomenon born from Ms Thorn's particular magical signature and her emotional bond."

Rosemary felt a warmth spread through her chest at these words, thinking of Burk's sparkling skin in the sunlight. She's saved him because of her love for him. There was something sweet and beautiful about that.

"However," the vampire continued, her eyes gleaming with excitement, "understanding this interaction between emotion, magic, and vampire physiology could lead to groundbreaking advancements in magical science. Ms Thorn, your contribution here today may change the future for vampires and witches alike. It will make excellent contributions to the sanguinarian literature."

"Love is such a curious thing," mused an ancient vampire named Eustace as he examined a parchment covered in runes. "So powerful, yet so unpredictable. It makes for rather frustrating scientific study."

Rosemary couldn't help but agree. As the day wore on, she found herself growing increasingly exhausted. The constant probing of her emotions, combined with the intense magical exertion, left her feeling drained and raw.

During a brief respite, Burk found her slumped in a corner of the library. "Are you alright?" he asked, his voice laced with concern.

Rosemary managed a weak smile. "Just tired. It's a lot, you know? All this poking and prodding."

Burk nodded, his expression darkening. "I know. I'm sorry you have to go through this. If there was any other way—"

"No, it's fine," Rosemary interrupted. "I understand why it's necessary. It's just..."

As if on cue, Dr Drake appeared, practically vibrating with excitement. "Ms Thorn! We've had a breakthrough. Come quickly!"

Rosemary sighed, pushing herself to her feet. Burk squeezed her hand reassuringly before she followed Dr Drake back to the Atrium.

The room was abuzz with activity. In the centre, a large, ornate mirror stood on a pedestal, its surface swirling with strange, smoky images.

"This," Dr Drake announced proudly, "is the Mirror of Veridian. It's an ancient artifact capable of revealing hidden truths. And it's just shown us something remarkable about your magic, Ms Thorn."

Rosemary approached the mirror cautiously. As she gazed into its depths, she saw flashes of images – herself and Burk, bathed in sunlight; strange, shadowy creatures lurking in the background.

"What does it mean?" she whispered, unable to tear her eyes away.

An elderly vampire with spectacles perched on her nose stepped forward. "It appears, my dear, that your magic is intrinsically linked to the balance of light and dark."

Before she could process this, Dr Drake cleared his throat. "In light of these findings, the High Council has…requested that you remain here for further study. Indefinitely."

Rosemary felt the blood drain from her face. "What? No, I can't – I have to get back to Myrtlewood. My daughter—"

"I'm afraid it's not a request," Dr Drake said, looking uncomfortable. "The potential implications of your magic are too significant to ignore."

Panic rose in Rosemary's chest. She looked around wildly, feeling suddenly trapped. The walls of the Atrium seemed to close in around her, the excited chatter of the vampires becoming a deafening roar.

Just as she felt she might collapse, a familiar voice cut through the chaos. "That's quite enough."

Azalea strode into the room, her presence immediately commanding attention. Charles and Burk flanked her, their expressions fierce.

"Rosemary Thorn has fulfilled her part of the agreement," Azalea said, her voice carrying a hint of steel beneath its silky tones. "Anything further would be…voluntary."

Charles nodded, his eyes glinting dangerously. "Specifically as she is only contracted to stay several more hours, and believe me when I say that contract is water-tight. And I'm sure you wouldn't want to be seen as coercing a guest, would you?"

Dr Drake paled slightly, if that was possible for a vampire. "Of course not," he stammered. "I merely thought—"

"Your enthusiasm is commendable," Charles cut him off. "But perhaps misplaced in this instance. Rosemary will be leaving with us. Now."

The dismissal was clear. The other vampires quickly dispersed, leaving Rosemary alone with Burk and his parents.

"Thank you," she said softly, feeling tears prick at her eyes as Burk wrapped his arms around her.

Azalea's expression softened. "Think nothing of it, dear. Now, let's get you out of here."

32

ATHENA

The rolling waves rushed in. That was the only sound. Athena opened her eyes, wondering whether she was somehow by the sea. She blinked. "What's going on?"

Marjie was there, and so was Dain.

"Dad?" Athena asked. "Why..."

Athena was in her bedroom, and Dain and Marjie were both staring at her, concerned.

"We're here for you, Athena," Dain said softly.

"Mum?" Athena asked, disoriented, before remembering Rosemary was still away.

"I've called her and left a message," said Marjie. "I'm sure she'll be back as soon as she can."

Athena shook her head, pushing herself up to sitting. "No, it's fine. You've got it wrong. Everything's under control. I just need—" That was when the guilt hit her. She wasn't supposed to be doing what she was doing. Even though it seemed harmless, a part of her knew that if other people, her mother and father included, had heard the full story, they would have told her to stop.

The weight of exhaustion washed over her. Tears welled up in her eyes. "It's too much," she said. "Too much. I can't do this right now. Please, please leave. I don't want to yell at you, but please leave me alone."

"Leave you alone for a few minutes…or for an hour or two if you need to sleep," said Marjie. "But Athena, we're not going to let you go through this alone."

"That's right," Dain added. "Whatever it is, you're going to tell us. Okay?"

Athena nodded. How could she say no to Marjie, who was always so caring and so nurturing?

"You've got this, kid," Dain said, giving her a wink. "I'm here for you. I think I know what you're going through, or at least I can try to understand."

Athena collapsed back into bed with a heavy sigh, followed by more tears. "It's just trying to make everything work, that's all."

"Of course, my love," said Marjie. "We'll leave if you want us to, but we won't leave you for long, because we love you and we want to be here for you. And I think it's time for you to admit that right now, you need someone."

33

ROSEMARY

Rosemary glanced at her phone as the helicopter lifted off. Burk gave her hand a squeeze. He was sitting next to her. Charles had stayed behind to take care of some Vampire Council business with the research facility. Rosemary was so glad to be getting away from that strange, ancient place that she wasn't even worried about Azalea's helicopter piloting.

"No messages from Athena," said Rosemary, frowning as she stared at the bottom of her phone screen.

"The reception's not great up here, for some reason," Burk offered before giving her a reassuring smile. "I'm sure it'll be fine. They're probably having a wonderful time and just haven't bothered to check in."

Rosemary shook her head. "I don't like it. Maybe we should just go back to Myrtlewood."

"If that's what you wish," said Burk, "but didn't Athena talk you into having a nice, relaxing holiday?" He grinned. "How do you think she'd feel if you showed up now and spoiled her fun?"

Rosemary sighed. "Maybe my phone's broken. I wonder..." she

trailed off. "When they took it while I was doing the tests, do you think they tampered with it somehow?"

"Hard to say," said Burk. "You can use mine." He handed over his phone. It was so new and shiny that Rosemary was almost afraid to touch it in case she broke it, but he insisted. He seemed to be getting perfectly fine reception. She dialled Athena's number.

"Hello, Mum," Athena answered, sounding slightly anxious.

"How are you doing, love? I haven't heard from you."

"Oh," said Athena, "I thought Marjie called you."

"My phone's playing up," said Rosemary. "Is everything all right? Should I come home?"

"Of course not," said Athena, though she seemed to hesitate for a moment. "Everything's going well."

"Then—" said Rosemary.

"Everything's fine," Athena interrupted. "It's just—Marjie is quite busy at the moment. You might not get a chance to talk to her until you get back, but definitely go and have a lovely holiday. I'm doing really well. Catching up on all my assignments. Everything's fine."

"Are you sure?" Rosemary asked. "I really don't mind coming home. Marjie might need a break."

"Oh no. You know Marjie. She's loving every moment. You should go and have fun, relax for a change. Have a holiday. Remember?"

"All right, if you insist," said Rosemary. "I'll be home in a few days, though."

"Take as long as you need," said Athena. "Just make sure you look after yourself."

"You too," said Rosemary. "Don't get into too much trouble without me."

Rosemary hung up, still feeling a twinge of anxiety.

"What is it?" said Burk. "Do you want to go home?"

"Part of me does, but I'm sure Athena won't have a bar of it. She insists we should carry on and have a little holiday."

"And what do you want to do?"

"I'm in two minds," Rosemary admitted. "On one hand, my anxiety is telling me I should be at home, worried that something bad is going to happen. You know, there were those deaths in the forest, and Athena's organising the seasonal festival for Imbolc, and the risks of that are worrying me...But on the other hand, she clearly doesn't want me there and the festival is still a few weeks away. Maybe I can let her figure some things out for herself. She sounded okay."

"So you want to continue on to Portugal?"

"I suppose so," said Rosemary. "Give me time to process my anxiety, maybe even relax a bit."

"On to Portugal it is," said Burk.

～

AS THE CAR rolled to a gentle stop, Rosemary stepped out, her feet finding the gravel path, a hanging iron sign reading *Casa da Bruma*. The air was thick with the scent of the ocean, mingled with the sweet, earthy aroma of wild lavender and rosemary. She took a deep breath, letting the peace of this place wash over her. The house was old, weathered by centuries of salt and sun, overlooking the sea. Its whitewashed walls and red-tiled roof blended with the landscape.

Burk moved towards the house, unhurried, relaxed in a way she rarely saw him. As they approached the entrance, she noticed the way his hand brushed the worn wood of the door with familiarity and fondness.

"Welcome to Casa da Bruma," Burk said, his voice rich with the warmth of a place long cherished. "My mother found this spot centuries ago, during one of her travels. She said the moment she set eyes on it, she knew she had to make it ours."

Rosemary smiled, picturing Azalea, with her striking beauty and insatiable curiosity, discovering this tranquil haven by moonlight. It wasn't hard to imagine why Azalea had been captivated; the place had a serene, mystical quality to it.

Burk pushed open the door, revealing a cosy, sun-dappled living room. The stone fireplace caught her eye, its hearth worn smooth by countless fires over the years.

"Azalea brought my father here for their hundredth honeymoon," Burk continued, his tone light, "and they ended up spending decades here, just the two of them, away from the rest of the world."

As he spoke, Rosemary could almost see them, Azalea and Charles, living a life removed from the world's relentless march of time. It was easy to imagine them in this room, perhaps sitting by the fire as the sun set, the warmth of the flames casting a golden glow on their faces.

They moved into the kitchen, a small but charming space with open shelves displaying rustic pottery and copper pans that glinted softly in the light. A large window above the sink framed a view of the rolling waves beyond, the sea a constant presence, calming and eternal.

"This kitchen has seen more than its share of history," Burk said, running his fingers over the wooden countertop. "During the Age of Exploration, when Portuguese ships were setting sail to discover new worlds, this house was already standing, watching it all unfold."

Rosemary looked out at the ocean, imagining those ships on the horizon, full of dreams and ambitions. But her thoughts inevitably turned darker, reflecting on the endless cycles of conquest, the thirst for power that had driven humanity throughout the ages. She felt the weight of it, the knowledge that while some sought to explore, others sought to dominate.

But as Burk continued to speak, sharing stories of his own experiences with the house, that weight seemed to lift.

"I've come here during some of my darkest times," he admitted, his voice softening. "When the ennui of eternal life was too much, this place became my refuge. There's something about the sea, the way it never changes yet is always moving, that brings a sense of perspective. It's here that I remember who I am, and why I continue."

Rosemary glanced at him, seeing the flicker of vulnerability in his eyes. Burk had always been a pillar of strength, but here, in this house, she saw a different side of him – a side that wasn't afraid to show the burdens he carried. Her heart warmed as he shared these personal details, and she felt her love for him deepen, blossoming in this place that held so much of his history.

They moved through the house, Burk pointing out small details that told stories of the past – how the beams in the ceiling had been replaced after a storm in the seventeenth century, how the garden had been planted by Azalea herself, filled with plants she'd collected from around the world.

"She's always loved to garden," Burk said, a hint of a smile on his lips. "Even when the world around her was changing rapidly, she found peace in the simple act of nurturing life."

Finally, they reached the bedroom which was Burk's personal sanctuary. The room was as simple and charming as the rest of the house, with a large bed framed by soft, white linens, big windows, and a balcony that opened to the sea. The light was golden here, softened by the late afternoon sun, and the air was filled with the gentle sound of the waves.

"This has been my room for as long as I can remember," Burk said, stepping inside. "I've watched empires rise and fall from that window, seen wars fought and peace brokered. But I've never seen it in the daylight before…"

Rosemary clutched his hand.

"It's magnificent in the sunlight…" His voice strained slightly as he gestured around. "This place remained a constant. A reminder that not all is lost, that some things endure."

Rosemary stood beside him, feeling the truth of his words settle in her chest. Here, in this house, there was a sense of continuity, of something larger than the endless pursuit of power. It was a place where love, peace, and solace could be found, even in the face of eternity.

She reached out, taking Burk's hand in hers, feeling the solid warmth of him. "Thank you for bringing me here," she said, her voice filled with a quiet reverence. "For sharing this part of yourself with me."

Burk squeezed her hand gently, his eyes meeting hers with a look that spoke of centuries of experiences and emotions, distilled into this one, perfect moment. "I wanted you to see it, to understand what this place means to me. To us."

As they stood together, the golden light of the setting sun filling the room, Rosemary felt her love for Burk bloom fully, like a flower finally opening its petals. This house, with its rich history and quiet beauty, had shown her a side of him she hadn't seen before, and in doing so, had brought them closer than ever. He sparkled softly under a beam of sunlight, and she pulled him closer to the window, letting the sunlight wash over him.

He smiled. The way the light touched his skin, warming it, was still a new sensation – one he hadn't yet fully grown accustomed to. He turned to Rosemary, a small smile playing on his lips. "It's hard to explain knowing a place like this for hundreds of years and never seeing it in the sunlight before," he said, his voice filled with quiet wonder. "Candlelight and moonlight are beautiful, but in the sun...it's spectacular."

Rosemary watched him, captivated by this man who had spent so many centuries in the shadows now standing fully in the light. There was a radiance to him, a softness that she rarely saw, and it stirred something deep within her. "It suits you," she said gently, stepping closer to him. "This light...it's like it was made for you."

Burk chuckled, a low, rich sound that seemed to resonate with the very walls of the house. "It's strange, isn't it? To have lived so long in the dark, only to find that the light feels...like coming home." He glanced around the room, his eyes lingering on the worn wood of the floor, the simple elegance of the bed, the soft white linens that caught the golden glow of the sun. "This place has seen so much – so many centuries of history, so many lives passing through. And yet, it endures. Just like us."

Burk's voice broke into her thoughts, grounding her in the present. "I've found refuge here, especially during the darker times. There were moments when the weight of eternity became too much, when the nights felt endless, and the thought of facing another century was unbearable. But this place...it's like the house knew. It offered me comfort, Even in the darkest of times, there's still light."

He turned to her, his eyes meeting hers with an intensity that sent a shiver down her spine. "And now, being able to stand here in the sunlight, it feels like a new beginning. Like I've been given another chance to find joy, to find peace."

Rosemary squeezed his hand, feeling the connection between them deepen. "You deserve that, Burk," she said softly. "You deserve happiness, to be in the light."

He smiled, a genuine warmth in his expression. "You've been a part of that, Rosemary. You've brought a light into my life that I didn't know I needed. Being here with you, in this house that has meant so much to my family, it feels...right. Like everything has led us to this moment."

She leaned into him, resting her head against his chest, listening to the steady beat of his heart. The sunlight bathed them both in a golden glow, the warmth of it wrapping around them like a comforting embrace.

As his words settled in her heart, Rosemary felt her love for him deepen, blossoming in the warmth of the sunlight that streamed through the window.

Rosemary could feel the energy of the house, a subtle hum

beneath the surface, as if the walls themselves were alive with the stories of those who had lived and loved here.

"This room in particular...it's where I've spent countless days and nights, trying to find a sense of peace. I've watched the world change from that window."

Rosemary's breath caught as she stepped closer to him, the tension between them thickening. The room seemed to shrink around them, the walls pressing in as the air between them crackled with unspoken emotion. She could feel her heart beating faster, her skin tingling with anticipation.

"Burk," she whispered, her voice trembling slightly, "I'm so glad you brought me here."

He reached out, his fingers brushing her cheek, sending a shiver down her spine. "You're the first person I've ever brought here, Rosemary," he confessed, his voice low and intense. "It has been my refuge, but I wanted to share it with you. I wanted you to see this side of me, to understand..."

His words trailed off as their eyes locked, the space between them filled with the weight of everything left unsaid. Rosemary could see the depth of his feelings in his gaze, the way he looked at her as if she were the only thing that mattered in the world.

She closed the distance between them, her hand reaching up to rest on his chest. She could feel the steady thrum of his heartbeat beneath her palm, a rhythm that matched her own. Slowly, she tilted her head up.

Burk didn't hesitate. He leaned down, capturing her lips in a kiss that was both tender and hungry, a release of the tension that had been building between them. His arms wrapped around her, pulling her closer as if he couldn't bear to let her go.

The kiss deepened, the taste of him intoxicating, as if she could drink in centuries of history and passion with every touch. The world outside faded away, leaving only the two of them, entwined.

34

ATHENA

Athena felt as though she was looking at life from behind a thick pane of glass as she finally dressed and plodded slowly downstairs. She was no longer pink, at least physically, but she felt the humiliation crawl across her skin like a painful blush.

At the bottom of the staircase, she was ambushed by a flurry of hugs.

"Finnegan, Cedar? Why are you here?"

"Thought we might be useful," said Finnegan.

Athena smiled back, though she was aware that she didn't feel it... and that he would know.

"Whatever's happening," Finnegan said, "we've got your back."

"I'm not gonna pretend I know you very well," said Cedar, "but I'm here to offer my support if I can."

"Thank you. That's sweet of you, but not needed. I'm fine, really," Athena replied.

The two looked at each other as though they did not believe Athena at all – as though they were entertaining the musings of a young child.

She rolled her eyes. "Just leave me alone."

"Okay, if that is what you wish," said Finnegan. He lifted the little felt hat he wore and tipped it. "We'll see you later."

"There you are," said Dain. "Are you ready?"

"I'm told I have no choice in the matter," Athena replied.

"Come on." Dain ushered her into the car. They drove towards the beach.

"You know, I can only drive for short periods because of the iron in the steel. At the moment, sitting in it gives me a headache, especially when I'm used to being in the fae realm," Dain explained.

Athena shrugged.

"Athena, I know what's going on."

"How could you possibly know?" she said, pain coming through in her words. "I'm sorry. I'm not very pleasant to be around at the moment. I don't feel good. I need—"

"You need the thing that's been helping you get through the darkness," said Dain.

"What? How do you know about that?"

"I might have called in to pay a visit to my mother briefly on the way here. I had a feeling she had something to do with this."

"That's awfully intuitive of you, Dad," said Athena, crossing her arms.

They'd arrived at the beach. Dain parked the car and walked around to open Athena's door. Reluctant as she was, she knew she had to go along with this. He scooped her arm into his and they walked along the sand, linked together.

Athena allowed herself to soften just a little bit. Dain was being a good dad. It was always nice to know that he could have been all along, yet somehow also painful. She'd never been able to rely on him as a child.

"You know, I can hear your thoughts," said Dain. "You aren't guarding your mind properly. And you know, the reason that I couldn't be a great dad to you was because I had problems..."

"That was different," said Athena, looking out to the horizon as the waves crashed along the shore. "You had a cream addiction that meant you couldn't function, and you gambled...You made stupid decisions, you gave away your money. You lost all sense of self-control. This is the opposite. When I take the potion that your mother gave me, if feels like I can fly! I can do all the things. The emotional stuff doesn't bother me anymore. I just—"

"You've been through a lot, Athena," said Dain, patting her on the shoulder. "You've been through so much, but you haven't grieved—"

"You sound like Marjie. How did you get to be wise?" Athena asked, shooting him a dark look. "You know...with your track record."

"I know. I know I'm the last person who should be giving you advice. I'm well aware of that, and yet here I am, because sometimes the people who can give you the best advice are the ones who've been there. They've ruined things. They've lost the most important people to them."

"Did you feel like that was Mum? Was she the most important person?"

"Of course, I did," said Dain. "Rosemary was everything to me. You probably don't remember, but there was a time when we were so happy together. And then there was you..."

"And then you messed with her memory," said Athena. "I suppose you couldn't help that."

"I might have been able to help it if I'd really tried," said Dain, "but it was convenient for her to forget all of the bad things I'd done. Magic can be awfully convenient like that."

"I want to forget myself," Athena admitted, tears springing up. "I don't want to mess with anyone else's head. That's why I couldn't resist the potion; it helps me, Dad."

"It wasn't until you and your mother performed that healing spell that I felt I could finally get control over my life, and now I don't crave it."

"Really?" said Athena.

Dain shook his head. "I even tested myself once. I was here on a date with Juniper, and after she left, I summoned one of my heralds from the fae realm. I told him to do whatever he could to restrain me if I lost the plot. I bought a tiny cream cake and took one look."

"Wouldn't it make you nauseous because of the spell?"

"Yeah, I was quite sick," said Dain. "That was probably a bad move to test it like that, but I didn't crave it either. I didn't miss it. I don't miss it. I don't miss not being in control of my life."

Athena sighed. "The problem is that this potion gives me control of my life."

"And maybe it's not the worst thing for you in the long run, but for now, you're losing control, kid," Dain replied.

Athena shook her head. "It helps me. You don't understand. It helps me to function. I don't—I can't do anything in this mental state. I'm in so much pain."

Dain sighed. "Even if you dropped out of school, none of your friends talked to you for a few years, and you hid in a cave in the forest for that whole time, you wouldn't ruin your life. School's not the end of the world. I didn't do it at all. As far as I recall, various foster homes would send me to several schools, but I could never perform, and I never got my act together. Look at me now."

"You're fae royalty," said Athena.

"Yes, and I have a budding career as a magical consultant, I have a life," said Dain. "Besides, you are fae royalty too. But even if you weren't, you could still make so much of your life regardless of what any institution thinks. It's you that's important, not anything else. There are people who struggled at school and went on to become the most brilliant scientists and magical practitioners in the world.

Einstein, for instance, was a terrible student because he was an original thinker."

"This is different," said Athena. "And I'm not Einstein, anyway. I'm nothing..." *I'm nothing without Elise*, her mind echoed, but Dain could hear it.

He put his arm around her and pulled her in tightly. He breathed slowly with her as she sobbed.

"It's horrible," said Athena, "but part of me feels like it would be more understandable if she died, because then she would have no choice in the matter. But she left us. She left this entire world, she left me. She chose that. Even though I love her, even though she says she loves me, how could she love me if she was going to leave me? How could she make that choice and destroy what we had? I went to hell and back, literally, to try to save her, and she didn't even need saving. I put everything at risk, and it's all my fault."

"Hey, hey," said Dain, patting her on the back. "It's no one's fault. It's never anyone's fault. We don't have enough knowledge or enough power most of the time to take that kind of blame, and the blame is not useful anyway."

"Seriously, how did you get so wise?" Athena asked again, glaring at him.

35

ROSEMARY

Portugal was a dream. Burk had cooked Rosemary the most exquisite meal, and they'd shared it together in between enjoying their pleasure of their intimacy. Rosemary had fallen asleep to rolling waves, only to find herself sitting in Thorn Manor at the table, Marjie next to her, a cup of tea in hand.

Rosemary looked around and blinked, confused. "What's going on?"

"You're here. Finally," said Marjie. "I didn't know if this would work."

"Am I in a dream?"

"Of course, you are, dear. I was waiting until you were asleep so I could get a message through. Your phone doesn't seem to be working."

Rosemary had wondered about that. She'd thought she might go into the local township to buy a new phone that day, just so she could get in touch with Athena if she needed to.

"I've been trying to call you," said Marjie. "Since that didn't work, I figured I might as well give this a try."

"And what is this?" Rosemary asked.

"I've been working on my intuitive talents, as you know," said Marjie. "I tried scrying...err...I tried to catch you earlier, but it looked like you were having far too much fun. Besides, I figured this would be better if you were asleep, less chance of a vision interrupting you."

Rosemary blushed. "So you're really talking to me right now? My mind's not just making this up?"

"Yes, dear, and you must come home as soon as possible. Athena—"

"I just spoke to Athena yesterday. She said everything was fine."

"Of course, she would say that. She doesn't want to worry you. She wants you to have a nice holiday, but I insist that you're needed at home. I'm sorry to interrupt you when you're having such a lovely time," Marjie said with a slight smile.

"Marjie, it's a bit invasive to know that you can spy on me like that with your scrying."

"I didn't see any details," said Marjie. "As soon as I realised you were busy, I poured the water out of my scrying bowl and decided to try again later. Gave you a good amount of time too. I figured you'd be asleep by now."

"Well, apparently I am."

"Drink your tea, dear," said Marjie, handing Rosemary a cup.

"I don't need your dream tea, Marjie. I need to know what's going on with my daughter."

"It's complicated," said Marjie. "I'm not entirely sure what it is, but I think she's developed some kind of addiction, a magical one."

"Oh, not again," said Rosemary. "I thought she was desensitised to the fae realm magic by now."

"It seems she's been taking some kind of potion from Queen Áine to cope with the emotions...the heartbreak over Elise. And now Athena is...Well, how can I put this? She's not coping."

Rosemary sighed. "Right. I'll come back as soon as I can. Is there anything else you want to give me a heads up about?"

"Dain's here."

"Oh no," said Rosemary. "Is there something wrong with him, too?"

"No, he's just being a good parent for a change," said Marjie with a wink. "You know, he really does get better as he ages. I would say he's like a fine wine, but I suspect he's more like a cheap wine that was atrocious at first and happens to be good when it gets older."

"I couldn't have put it better myself," said Rosemary. "And I'm glad he's doing some good parenting. I feel terrible for not doing it myself, for not being there."

"It's not your fault, love. You had other things to attend to, but Athena needs you."

"Athena is the most important thing in the world to me," said Rosemary. "She always has been, even when I haven't been that great at looking after her. I'm trying."

"I know you are," said Marjie. "That's all we can ever do. Don't be too hard on yourself. She's fine. We're all going to be fine. But I thought you'd want to know."

"Thank you so much. I'll be back there before you know it. Make sure you keep an eye on her."

"We're all taking turns at sitting vigil so she doesn't escape," said Marjie. "She's got her friends here too. Now she's going to have to face her grief over everything that's happened, and we'll be here to support her."

"What would I do without you?" said Rosemary.

"You'd be wasting away to nothing but Jaffa Cakes and beans on toast, I'm sure of it," Marjie said with a cackle.

"That's for certain," said Rosemary. "I'd better wake up, I suppose. Do you know how I can do that?"

"Wake up, Rosemary dear," said Marjie.

The dream faded out, and Rosemary found herself amidst the

waves again. They were lulling her, soothing her, and yet a part of her was endlessly restless. She woke with a cry as though she was being pulled under by the churn of the ocean as the waves became heavier.

Burk was next to her, resting up on his elbow as he gazed at her with adoration and concern in his eyes.

"It's Athena," said Rosemary. "We've got to go."

36

ATHENA

Everything felt so heavy. Athena could barely get out of bed. The pain, the anguish, the crushing sensation – how could she possibly function? It all came back to haunt her: her anxiety about ruining her life, her pain and anger about the situation with Elise. Everything went round in circles in her mind, over and over again. She needed the potion. She needed it so she could function.

And of course, she needed her mother. But she had pushed her away, told her to go on holiday. And now, even when Rosemary had called, Athena had told her everything was fine when it wasn't.

If Mum was here, it would be harder to do what I have to do next...

She took a deep breath, knowing that Dain or Finnegan were sitting outside her door. Knowing that she was causing all of this work, all of this stress for so many people, was only making it worse. Marjie, of course, had put a charm on the balcony door of her room to stop her from leaving without letting them all know.

But Athena knew that she didn't have to go to the forest to get to the fae realm. She could bring the fae realm to her. She just needed to figure out how to get through Thorn Manor's protections first.

She selected four clear quartz crystals and placed them around her in a circle. They were just to protect her, to put up a kind of shield, an energetic barrier, so that nobody would know what she was about to do next.

She focused with all her attention on the fae realm, on the feeling of home, recalling how at one point, she had so craved that feeling of homecoming, that fae magic, that she would do anything to access it again.

Athena knew that she had caused havoc and chaos; she didn't want to do that again. She'd already created so many problems for so many people, she was surprised they didn't all hate her and hadn't all thrown her out of town. Perhaps they were just too polite to show it.

Unless she could get her life back on track and become independent, how on earth was she going to repay anyone? How was she going to stop being a burden, to stop being the one who was always messing everything up?

She'd run away to the fae realm not long after arriving in Myrtlewood. She'd let the fire sprites in, in her attempt to get back to the feeling of glee. She'd been entranced by the bard with the magical music. If people hadn't rescued her, who knows what might have happened? She'd almost married him. She'd dragged her mother to the underworld that almost ended the entire world, and she hadn't listened to Elise. She hadn't been around when things started to get bad, and not when they'd gotten worse. If she'd been there for Elise, then perhaps things would have been different, but the guilt was doing her no good at the moment. The feeling that she was somehow achingly wrong drove her onwards.

From inside the circle Athena created she focused intently on the fae realm. She reached out, and instead of cutting a door, she simply spun her arm and spun into the realm that was her natural other home. She didn't go to the path of the forest that usually intersected with Myrtlewood. No, she went deep, spinning three times until she was in the very heart of the palace, surrounded by trees, looking at the sacred pool in which only the Queen bathed.

Her grandmother lay before her in the water, tranquil as always, without even a hint of surprise on her face. Queen Áine's lack of reaction gave Athena pause. There was such intelligence behind those golden eyes.

"Did you do this to me on purpose? Were you watching me as I took the potion? Did you know about me all along?" Athena asked.

Queen Áine broke into a smile, punctuated by musical laughter. "Oh, how clever you are, my sweet princess, my delightful granddaughter. Of course, I knew you, not at first – your father made sure of that – but from the first time you made contact with our realm, with our powers. Of course, we could feel you there. We could sense you. What is it to be the fae Queen? What is it to rule this realm, if it is not to recognise our kin trapped in a world where you have no power, where you can never feel quite right? The Earth realm is so harsh, is it not?"

Athena nodded, choking back a sob.

"You know you belong with me," Queen Áine said. "If I've interfered along the way, I have kept you safe."

"You know, they say never to trust the fae," said Athena. "And I think there's a good reason for that."

"Of course there is, my love," said Queen Áine. "But won't you join me in the wisdom pool? Won't you see what I can see, that the challenges you face would all melt away?"

Athena shook her head. "I don't think so."

The Queen gave her a dangerous look. "I'm offering you a gift."

Athena held her ground. "And it's dangerous to accept gifts from the fae, even if you are fae."

"Perhaps it is..." Queen Áine said, resigned.

"I don't like the idea that you've been pulling these strings all this time," said Athena, "that you've been manipulating me."

"Sweet child," said the Queen, "sweet child, I've only done what is in your highest good."

"I need to know how far that goes," Athena replied. "If you want me to trust you, you have to show me everything you've done."

"Step into the wisdom pool, and I'll show you."

Athena hesitated. She didn't want to step into the wisdom pool. Something told her to hold back. She didn't think her grandmother was evil. She also didn't think that she was good in a benevolent sense, even if she had divine powers. Perhaps all powerful beings were all the same. They had many powers, but were they necessarily good, or were they complicated? What was good anyway? It was all rather a lot to process.

"Athena, you've come here now for a reason," said Queen Áine. "Are you going to tell me what it is?"

"I think you know what it is," said Athena. "You gave me a magic potion that made everything better, that made me function, that made the pain go away."

Queen Áine nodded. "I gave you a gift, a gift that you asked for, a gift that you sought."

"And I suppose now I'm paying the price," said Athena. "I feel like I can't live without it, at least not right now. I need to get through my schooling. I need to organise a ritual. I need to function so I don't throw my life away."

"Your life's far more valuable than that," said Queen Áine. "It doesn't matter what you do at this particular point. It doesn't matter what path you go down in the mortal world. You belong here. You belong to us. You are royalty, and you will help to bridge the world as a witch and fae."

Athena shook her head. "I'm not going to go into some kind of role that you push me into. I'm not a puppet."

"Why have you come here?" said the Queen. "What is it I can do for you right now? What will make everything better?"

"You know that I've come here because I need the potion," Athena replied.

The Queen smiled sadly. "Don't you see that I've helped you? Don't you see how far you've come because of me?"

"I would thank you for your help," said Athena, with a hint of dry sarcasm, "but I hear it's not culturally appropriate."

The Queen's laughter echoed, the sound of bells rang through. "When I bathe here, I'm connected to all my kin and all my realm," said the Queen. "It is hard to hide from me. I can feel all your feelings, especially as you are so close. You know, you've made a deal with me, Athena."

Athena nodded. "I suppose I can't run from that."

"So this is my offer to you," the Queen continued. "You must not attempt to replicate the potion. Not again. I will give you a different potion, one that won't get in the way. It won't make all the pain disappear, but it will ease you in your emotional state. This one, you can only take in the most minuscule amounts. I will enchant it so that you cannot take any more than that."

"That sounds...frustrating and also relatively wise," said Athena.

"It will ease your suffering for a short time and help you to focus."

"Please help the pain to go away."

Queen Áine nodded. "In return, you will be a diplomat for me, traveling between my realm and yours. You've committed to staying in the realm of your mother. I will respect that for now, but you also have a role here, whether you're ready to admit that or not."

"I need to know what I'm signing up for," said Athena. "What will it entail?"

"Before the spring equinox, when the treaty comes into full force, you must come here and bathe in the wisdom pool. You must connect with the power and responsibility over your people that fae royalty share. Our systems haven't always worked. The countess was rogue.

She was amassing her own power, and as you know, others have sought to battle against me."

Athena sighed, expecting this might be the case. She was being roped into fae politics whether she liked it or not.

"I will not deceive you, my dearest," Queen Áine said.

"How can you say that when you already have?" Athena retorted.

"I will not deceive you further than I have to," the Queen amended.

"That is not exactly reassuring," said Athena.

"What choice do you have?" Queen Áine asked. "You came here because you needed something from me, and I am generously offering to give it to you. I'd move the stars for you, my darling."

"Please don't," said Athena. "It's complicated enough trying to learn astrology when they're all in the places they should be."

Queen Áine laughed. "You are brilliant, my little one. You will be a magnificent leader. No doubt you're unique on both sides of your lineage. I'm merely seeking to bridge that gap, to bring you further into connection with your father's side, with my side, with our power."

"I can understand that," said Athena, "but why does it feel like I'm being coerced?"

"Coercion sounds like a terrible word," said the Queen. "It's not one we use in our realm, because we know that everyone has will, and everyone tries to enact that will."

"You mean it's not a term you use because it's just as normal as breathing to the fae?" Athena asked.

"Exactly," said Queen Áine, quite unapologetically.

"Now, as you say, what choice do I have?" said Athena. "I want to make everything right, but I can't function under all this pain. My mind, my heart, my body, it's like nothing is working. It's like everything is too heavy."

Queen Áine rose from the pool, wrapping herself in a silky robe. She approached Athena with gentleness in her expression that put Athena off guard.

"I want to take your suffering away," said Queen Áine, "and I know I have the power to do that, at least temporarily. But you must know, my dear, that you need to face all your feelings eventually. You might not be ready for it yet, and that is okay. You can distract yourself. You can enchant yourself. You can potion yourself as much as you want, but eventually you will have to return to the Underworld, even if it's in your own mind, in your own being, in your own soul. You will have to process. You will have to grieve."

"And I know this," Athena said. "I do. I just...I'm not ready. I need the release. I need the bliss. I need something to get me through just the next few weeks."

Queen Áine exhaled slowly. "My son will not be happy about me doing this, and nor will your mother, but perhaps one day they will see that what you are doing right now is a kind of therapy, a kind of medicine, and it will get you through. It's okay to take what you need for now when you're not hurting anyone. Is it not?"

Athena nodded. "It's just they're afraid of addiction."

"Isn't everyone in your world afraid of addiction?" said the Queen. "Because of the harsh limitations of the realm, because of the ease of falling into spells and enchantments just to escape the ever so challenging realities."

Athena nodded. "Do we not have that problem here?"

"Well, of course there's cream. We do not have it here. Cream is very different when fae are under its spell. It changes us. We lose our grip on reason. We lose any values we might have had before. The world flips upside down, and it is delightful fun, but it is terribly, terribly dangerous."

"Well, cream doesn't do that to me," said Athena.

"No, and this potion is not the same," the Queen replied. "This potion merely gives you a reprieve. It can't be a long-term crutch. You are strong enough and brave enough and wise enough to overcome all of the pain, my darling. You will face your problems, I can tell. You will rise above them, and you will shine."

"Thank you," said Athena. "I know I'm not supposed to thank you, but I feel like you've seen something of me that nobody else has."

"I've seen your brokenness and your pain," said Queen Áine. "You are not to blame, but you will not understand that yet. In time...in time, you will."

A tiny purple potion bottle materialised in the Queen's hand, studded with gold in a similar shape to a chrysalis. "You must not show this to your father or your mother or the other sweet, plump one who cares for you and feeds you cakes."

Athena shook her head. "I don't think they'll understand. I'm scared that I'm doing something wrong, that I'm making it worse, but I just don't know how to be at the moment. I don't know how else to do what I need to do, and I know that I need this right now. I just hope that I'm not falling into a devil's bargain."

"I'm not familiar with this term," said the Queen.

Athena shrugged. "I think it's when you make a deal with some sort of demon."

"Oh, that's not a good idea. Demons tend to be pests."

Athena smiled. "Some would say the same for the fae, that you're never really making the deal that you think you are."

"Can you not tell," said Queen Áine, "that I care for you?"

Athena looked her in the eyes, seeing such glowing warmth. "I do not doubt that you care for me, grandmother, but at one point you tried to marry me off to my cousin who I just met. So something tells me we don't quite have the same ideas about what's right or appropriate."

"It would have been a good match," said Queen Áine with a twinkle in her eye.

"Oh yeah, tell that to Finnegan and Cedar," Athena retorted.

"Now it's time for you to go," the Queen said. There was a slight sharpness in her voice. She clearly did not enjoy being wrong, but that was a feeling Athena could understand.

"I'll see you before the equinox, I suppose," said Athena.

"You will take your place, but you will not have to leave your world. That is the bargain we agreed," said Queen Áine.

Athena took the potion and slipped it into her pocket. The quartz crystals lay scattered on the floor. She quickly picked them up just as there was a knock at the door.

"Athena?"

"Mum?" Athena gasped. "You're back."

The conversation was a blur. Rosemary had been full of apologies and concern. As soon as her mother had left the room, Athena retrieved the bottle of potion Queen Áine had given her. It wasn't the same – it wasn't the same thing at all. When she looked at it closely, the liquid had a purple sheen, not just gold, although there was gold amongst it too. She could only have it in small doses or it would lose its effect.

Athena let one drop of potion fall onto her tongue, as her grandmother had instructed. She was hoping for that good feeling again, for the pain to fade away. Instead, she felt herself pulled into a vortex, and as she surrendered to sleep she could still feel the pain, the agony, but there was something more. There was so much complexity; everything was connected.

So instead of getting up and doing all the productive things she needed to do, she let herself surrender to deep, deep rest.

In that deep, deep rest she let herself feel a little of the enormous pain. She wrapped her arms around herself, she cried, and then she drifted away into sleep, knowing that the journey ahead was long, knowing that there were no quick fixes, knowing that she had to deeply face this pain, knowing that even though she wasn't ready yet, she would do what she could to make up for everything she had ever done wrong.

37

ROSEMARY

As Rosemary unpacked, a chill ran down her spine. She glanced out the window towards the forest. The usual vibrant greens seemed muted, as if a thin veil of shadow had been cast over the leaves.

Rosemary went to her bed, feeling the weight of guilt. She hadn't been there when her daughter needed her, and though Athena was growing up and pushing her away, insisting that she needed to live her life on her own terms, Rosemary couldn't help feeling her own guilt for all the years where she couldn't get her act together. She'd been confused and hadn't had the energy, money, or competence to give them the life that they needed – to give Athena everything she needed to thrive.

The tears came as she curled up under the covers. A gentle tapping sensation repeated on her back, reminding Rosemary much of Granny's tapping on her back when she was a little child.

"Granny, is that you?" Rosemary asked, her voice coming out sounding so young.

"Of course it is, my love," her Granny Thorn's ghostly voice reached out to her. Rosemary looked around and caught a glimpse of her grandmother in the dresser mirror.

"Why did you come?" Rosemary asked.

"I came because you needed me."

"I can't get over this guilt," said Rosemary. "I feel like the most important person in the world to me is struggling, and I don't know what to do about it. I know there are no instant magical fixes for pain and grief. And I think Athena is falling into traps, into addictive patterns, because she doesn't know how to deal with reality, and I don't know how to help her."

"Sounds familiar..." said Granny. "I myself was far from a perfect parent. I made all the mistakes."

"I never figured out what I was doing as a parent. I was in my early twenties when I had Athena," said Rosemary.

"I was well-past normal reproductive age for a human when I had my children," said Granny. "I didn't even want to have children at all when I was younger. Turned out I was no better at having them when I was older, either. So perhaps age doesn't have that much to do with it. After all, I tried my best, and my children are who they need to be, even if they're not who I might have expected them to be. They've done their best. You've done your best. That's all we can ever do. We can try. We can learn to heal. We can learn to listen and pay attention, and we can listen to any guidance or intuition. That's all we can really do here. You know, we can try to make each generation just a tiny bit better than the one before."

Rosemary burrowed into the blankets, not feeling any better.

"You were let down by your parents, Rosemary, just as I felt let down by my own children," Granny continued, then laughed. "Which sounds a lot worse now that I say it."

Rosemary laughed. "Well, I don't know if my father was ever going to be a well-rounded part of the magical community."

"I couldn't connect emotionally with either of my children,"

Granny mused. "I felt that they were always pushing me away, and I didn't like to be pushed away. I didn't like to be wrong. So I pushed them away. I gave them a taste of their own medicine, and we never got to grow and heal together, unless you count last Samhain, when I was already technically dead."

"Life is wasted on the living, as they say." Rosemary chuckled.

"Sometimes families are just what they are," Granny said. "We can't always control or affect what happens to them. We can't coddle them. We can't manipulate them. We can only love them...and that is doing our best."

38

THE DEVOURER

The Devourer surged through the forest, a roiling mass of darkness and insatiable hunger. Trees withered in its wake, their life force greedily consumed, leaving nothing but twisted, blackened husks. The air grew thick with the stench of decay and the sickly-sweet aroma of corrupted magic.

It could sense every living thing around it – the terrified heartbeats of fleeing animals, the silent screams of the trees as their roots were torn from the earth. Each life it devoured only stoked its hunger further, an endless cycle of consumption and craving.

The forest floor squelched beneath its ever-shifting form, a mixture of tarry ooze and writhing tendrils. Leaves crumbled to ash at its touch, and flowers wilted before they could release their final fragrant gasps.

As it approached the edge of the forest, the Devourer felt the resistance of the magical boundary.

It pressed against the shimmering barrier, feeling it bend and warp under the onslaught. Flashes of the town beyond flickered in its countless eyes – quaint buildings ripe for destruction, streets waiting to be flooded with darkness, and most tantalisingly, people brimming with life force to be devoured.

The barrier crackled and hissed where the Devourer touched it, sending jolts of pain through its amorphous body. But pain was nothing compared to the gnawing emptiness within. It pushed harder, feeling the magic start to fray and unravel.

Visions of carnage danced in the Devourer's fractured mind. It saw itself looming over Myrtlewood, tendrils of darkness snaking through every street and alley.

It imagined the satisfying crunch of buildings collapsing, the sweet melody of screams filling the air, the intoxicating rush of countless lives snuffed out in an instant.

The boundary pulsed, weakening with each assault. The Devourer's hunger rose to a feverish pitch. Soon, so very soon, it would break free. And when it did, nothing would stand in its way.

With a sound like tearing reality, a small crack appeared in the magical barrier. The Devourer focused all its ravenous attention on that tiny flaw, pressing against it with all its might. As the crack began to spread, a single thought echoed through its chaotic mind:

Myrtlewood would fall, and the feast would finally be ready.

39

ROSEMARY

There was a knock at the door.

"What is it?" said Rosemary, wiping her eyes.

The door gently swung open, and Burk's handsome face appeared.

"Oh, you don't want to see me when I'm like this. I'm just having a minor meltdown," said Rosemary.

"I'll leave if you want me to," said Burk, "but I do want to see you like this and every other way. Just so you know...I don't just want to see the good stuff, Rosemary Thorn. I want to see and know and love all of you."

Rosemary smiled at him suddenly. A puffy, tear-stained face didn't seem so terrible, after all. He had a way of making her feel beautiful, even when her natural inclination would be to bury her head in the blankets, feeling anything but.

"Come here, you," she said, reaching out a hand. Burk took her hand and climbed into bed next to her, holding her. Rosemary exhaled slowly. "I feel like I failed Athena again."

"Maybe you had to," said Burk. "Maybe she needs you to let her fail, to let her figure things out on her own."

"Nobody should have to be alone, especially not when things are bad," said Rosemary.

"And you didn't leave her alone."

"She pushes me away when I try to help." Rosemary frowned. "Maybe I need to find someone else to help her. Do you know of any magical counsellors?"

Burk chuckled.

"No, I'm serious," Rosemary said. "I couldn't send her to a regular mental health professional. They'd lock her up if she let slip any details of her present life at all. Surely there must be people who specialise in therapy for the magically inclined."

"I wasn't laughing because it was a silly idea."

"Then what?" Rosemary asked.

Burk looked her in the eye. "I do happen to know a very good magical counsellor. She specialises in vampires. She's highly trained in over forty different techniques. Sometimes she'll take on non-vampire clients, including witches, on special request."

Rosemary narrowed her eyes at him and waited. Burk just looked back at her with a half-smile.

"It's your mother, isn't it?" she said eventually.

"How did you know?" Burk asked.

Rosemary shook her head and sighed. "Something about the tone of your voice," she said, "and the fact that you laughed just before. There was something absurd about the whole situation that reminded me of Azalea...I don't know if she'd be the right person to talk to Athena."

Burk shrugged. "Perhaps not, but she is highly skilled, and she's helped a lot of people. She mostly specialises in helping new vampires to adapt. I'm sure there are plenty of other therapists out there that you could find, but—"

"But what?" Rosemary asked. "Do you really think your mother would be better than some kind of witch therapist?"

"That depends," said Burk, "but the reason that I think she might be helpful in this situation is that my mother understands the darkness. Athena's been to hades and back. She's had a broken heart to show for it. She needs to talk to someone who can be there with her, who can help her through her own feelings. I don't know anyone who can do that better than my mother. As strange as it is to say that. I've just seen her help so many people over the last few centuries," he continued. "She got to a point herself a long time ago where her endless existence felt hopeless. She was lost in ennui, and at that point, she stumbled upon a young vampire who was not doing so well. She hadn't been able to help Cyrus, my brother. He never wanted any help from her at all, but a newly made vampire needed her, and so she helped him. She probably saved his life, and that made her curious. She started learning different therapeutic arts long before the invention of modern psychotherapeutic techniques. When the first psychologists came along, she studied with them. Freud became obsessed with her…"

"Projecting his own mummy issues onto her, no doubt," Rosemary added.

Burk nodded. "She had to cut him loose. Then she studied with Jung for quite some time, exploring the magic of the unconscious. And when she went on to learn new techniques as they arose, it's really kept her going, kept her busy, all the learning that there is to do, how to heal trauma, how to feel all the difficult feelings. There's no one quite like Azalea for that."

"We can give it a shot," said Rosemary, "if Azalea's willing to take on a non-vampire client at the moment."

"I'll put in a special request. I'm sure she won't say no," said Burk.

"I'm not sure if Athena will like the idea, but she's got to admit that she needs some help, that she's not totally fine, even if she's been pretending to be all this time. I keep tracing it back. You know, she seemed fine once we got back from the Underworld, but—"

Burk looked at her slowly. "She probably was, you know. She was probably caught up in the excitement of returning to the world of the living, the house rebuilding itself, of reconnecting with everyone here. Maybe everything that she's facing now are feelings that were just lingering then, or that she's suppressed in favour of dealing with other things, and then when reality hit, well, that's when the grief came back in waves, I suppose."

"Because it is grief, isn't it?" said Rosemary. "She's lost someone so important to her. And yes, grief comes in waves. I suppose it did for me with Granny, at least. Sometimes there's numbness for a while, and then it's there, and it takes over your whole system. And Athena's been trying not to feel it. She's been so stressed about school, she's so convinced that if she doesn't pass everything and get into a good university programme, that she'll be throwing her life away, ruining it, and I suppose she's scared of turning out like me, how I was when she was growing up, just going from dead-end job to dead-end job without any aspiration, just coping, just surviving. I was a great example of what not to be."

Burk ran his hands through her hair, gently caressing her forehead, and Rosemary relaxed back into her own mixed feelings.

"There's no point in blaming yourself. All we can do at the moment is speculate about Athena. We don't really know what's going on. She probably doesn't either."

"Well, if your mother will have her and Athena will try counselling, then why not?" said Rosemary. "I'll let Athena know after I've tidied myself up and had a good cup of tea."

"Tea," said Burk with a contented smile on his face. "You know, it's quite a novelty to enjoy tea again without it having to taste like blood."

Rosemary chuckled. "I certainly prefer my tea that way."

40

ATHENA

After a rather long nap, Athena woke up slightly more energised. She couldn't remember her dreams – perhaps the potion had made her forget them – but something had happened in that night, in that restful state, because she felt different, slightly more restored. Even if she was still aching and broken, even if she still missed Elise terribly and felt guilty, at least it wasn't too painful to get up, have a quick shower, put on a fresh change of clothing, and make her way downstairs.

Her mother, Dain, Finnegan, Cedar, and Marjie were all sitting around the table. It wasn't just them either. Felix, Ash, Sam, and Deron were lounging on the window seats.

"Is this an intervention?" Athena asked warily. "Because I have study to do."

"Not exactly," said Rosemary, "but we thought it might be nice for you to see your friends, help you study."

"Look, I'm okay. I don't know what's going on, but I'm fine," said Athena, realising how defensive she sounded just as she said it.

"We know you've been through a hard time," said Ash. "We're just here to help. Okay? Even if you don't think you need our help, just at least tolerate us for a little bit."

Athena sighed. "I suppose I do need to study, and it might be good to have some company."

"Why don't you go into the living room, dear?" said Marjie. "I'll whip you up some scones and tea."

Athena shrugged. "Okay, that would be lovely. Thank you." She gave her friends a hug and smiled apologetically at them. She wasn't sure exactly what her mother or Marjie or Dain had said to them, but she was going to find out.

"Could I have a word?" Rosemary asked her. "Just for a minute."

"Yes, Mum," Athena replied.

"We'll meet you in there," said Ash, heading towards the living room, dragging Derron and Felix along with her, while Sam followed.

"What is it, Mum? This is a really weird situation. I hope you know that. I hope it's not making you too anxious," said Athena.

"There is something else," Rosemary began.

"What?"

"Well, I thought it might be helpful for you to talk to someone."

"You mean a shrink?"

"Yes," said Rosemary, "but also not."

Athena bristled. "What are you talking about? I'm not mentally unstable."

"But you're also not a hundred percent fine, are you?" Rosemary countered.

Athena shrugged. "What am I going to do? Go tell some poor counsellor about my ex-girlfriend, who's now a goddess of the underworld? Do you know any mental health professionals who can handle that kind of bizarre situation?"

"As a matter of fact, Burk does," Rosemary replied.

Athena squinted at her mother. "Does he now?"

"Do you remember Burk's mum? Azalea?"

"The Morticia Addams lookalike?"

Rosemary smiled almost maniacally. "That's the one. It turns out, she's an incredibly skilled psychologist. In fact, it seems like she's the most qualified therapist in the world, given the fact that she trained with the founders of psychotherapy, hung out with them, and then went on to learn every new technique under the sun that suited her fancy."

Athena laughed. "Can you get any more weird than this?"

Rosemary patted her daughter on the shoulder. "Given that I've invited one of the scariest goddesses for cocktails in a couple of weeks, I'd say our life probably couldn't get that much stranger. But I'm afraid of saying it, actually, because now that I have, you know things are going to get even weirder than this."

"I hope it's weird in a good way," said Athena. "As Granny says, only use the term 'weird' to talk about the amazing and strange interconnectedness of all things in magic, not as a derogatory term, because that's apparently rather offensive."

"You know, as bizarre as everything is," said Rosemary, "there's a part of me that wouldn't want it any other way. Whatever you're going through, darling, it's a process, and I want to help in any way I can, even if the only thing I can do is give you somebody to talk to who might be able to help you sort through things."

"You're not going to shut up about this until I do it, are you?" said Athena. "Fine. I'll see the evil queen in her lair and have her meddle with my mind. I'll do that just for you."

Rosemary pulled Athena in for a big hug, and they both sighed, resting in each other's arms for a moment.

"Thank you, Mum. It's good to have you back, even if I was handling everything totally fine on my own."

"We'll see about that," said Rosemary, "but I'm willing to give you a little bit more freedom and help you wherever I can, while letting you figure things out. I know trying to control you doesn't work from experience, so at least let me help when you think that it will help."

"Deal," said Athena. "Now I better go and deal with the unruly teenagers in the living room. Maybe I'll even get some studying in."

As much as Athena hated to admit it, the adults in her life were right. It was good to see her friends, and it was good to relax, and maybe, just maybe, it'd be good to have someone to talk to.

There was something powerful and inspiring and slightly terrifying about Azalea Burk. Athena had always somewhat admired her. She couldn't help it; Azalea was as close to a goddess as Athena had met, other than actual goddesses. Azalea had so much power that her presence in any room was magnetic. She seemed to enjoy even discomfort with glee. The only thing she didn't seem to like was things that were too nice, things that were pretending to be good but weren't really – and perhaps pastels tones, which were another thing that Granny couldn't stand, apparently.

Two days later, Athena got out of the car in front of the Burk family castle. She'd not visited this magnificent home very often, given that she'd rather stay out of her mother's romantic life as much as possible, and this was where Burk lived. But this time, she was coming here not specifically because of Rosemary or Burk, but because of her own needs.

She had been taking the potion every night, just one drop of what her grandmother had given her, and it hadn't made the pain go away, but it had helped her to properly rest. When she properly rested, her mind was able to function just a little bit better. So after three night she felt stronger.

She walked up the steps, leaving Rosemary behind in the car because she wanted to do this alone, having been assured that she would be perfectly safe by Burk, who was apparently at home.

In a flurry, the door flew open, and Azalea stood there, resplendent in a tight-fitting black, shimmery dress with long, drooping sleeves.

"There you are, powerful witch and fae royalty. How would you prefer to be addressed?"

"Athena's fine." She didn't know quite how to greet Azalea Burk, either. "Err, how would you like to be addressed?"

"Azalea is fine. Now come this way." She turned and, with a wave of her hand, led Athena down a dark stone corridor lit only by torches.

"I practice down here when I work from home. New vampires tend to prefer the darkness, after all. It makes them feel slightly safer, even though, of course, we have specially tinted windows. We were one of the first buildings in this part of England to get them when the magicians invented them. Charles missed the sunlight."

Athena smiled politely, not sure how else to contribute to the conversation as she followed Azalea. Her voice, in itself, was spellbinding and enchanting.

"This is a portrait of me and Queen Elizabeth when we were good friends, before things turned a little sour, I'm afraid," Azalea said, pointing to an old oil painting of the first Queen Elizabeth next to a dark haired woman with Azalea's striking bone structure in an Elizabethan gown. "And this is a suit of armour that Charles had specially made to guard this corridor. It's enchanted, you see. If anything goes wrong, it will leap to attention and defend the innocent – and also us, even if we're not being innocent. That's the perk of being one of the owners of the house. We get to set it up our way."

Athena smiled politely again. Azalea opened the door to a room where the walls were a deep forest green, and the furniture was midnight purple velvet studded with stars.

"I have to say, you have beautiful taste in interior design," Athena remarked.

"Thank you very much, my dear. Now take a seat and tell me what's going on for you right now."

"There's not much to say," said Athena. "I've just been struggling a bit, I suppose. And my mum's really worried. I may have taken some potions that they think I might be addicted to. It's a little bit messy."

"And are you addicted?" Azalea asked.

Athena shrugged. "Apparently, I have to deal with my emotions. Not hide from them."

"It sounds like you're in a delightful conundrum," said Azalea with a smile. Athena felt a sudden lightness, a curiosity as she looked into the eyes of this powerful and very wise woman in front of her, a creature of the darkness and of the night, who had experienced so much over so many centuries. She felt something within her relax just slightly, and then the whole story came spilling out.

It came out in fragments. The story about Elise, meeting Elise for the first time, came after the story of the last time they met. The betrayal was all in different pieces. The pain was like sharp shards of glass. Tears flowed as she began to talk about Sally and Elise's possession, and how even before then, there were signs. Athena had known that something wasn't quite right with her girlfriend, and she still felt guilty about that. She'd been so caught up in her own budding powers and her own adventures because she hadn't really seen Elise's pain. She hadn't really seen how Elise needed to be the main character of her own story, not just Athena's sidekick girlfriend.

The pain tucked in her chest, and more words spilled out – more regrets, more hopes and fears, and more and more pain.

"You've been through a lot, darling," Azalea said. Athena felt the acknowledgment like a warm blanket on a cold night, wrapping around her shoulders, allowing them to loosen just slightly. She'd been through a lot. It felt good – maybe not good, but it felt like a gentle easing – just to have someone say that and listen and not try to fix things.

"Is this what you do?" Athena asked. "You just listen to people, and they tell you their stories and they fix themselves?"

Azalea nodded solemnly. "Sometimes, all people need is to tell their stories."

"I feel like I've told you everything already, and it's only been twenty minutes or more. What else do you do? Since you're such a skilled practitioner of therapy, so I've been told, I'm curious what works the best, what kind of psychological magic that's going to help me to feel good again."

"It's an underworld journey, my dear," said Azalea.

"I've already done that," said Athena. "I went to the underworld and came back."

"Yes, we've only touched the tip of the iceberg of what you've already been through, and yet healing can be an underworld journey of itself, not in the outer world, in the actual underworld, like the one you've already been on, but an inner journey."

"You want me to go into the underworld? In my mind?" said Athena.

"Only if you want to," said Azalea. "The metaphor is useful, you see, and I can guide you."

"Like a guided meditation? Like hypnotherapy?" said Athena.

"A little," said Azalea. "And yes, it's a technique I've developed, blending together many others that I've learned over the years, and it is very productive and useful, if I do say so myself. I find that our rational minds are so powerful at keeping us stuck exactly where we are, because that's a safe place to be, and so the only way to loosen some of those stuck patterns is to go into the unconscious, which is the metaphorical underworld of the psyche."

"Oh yes, that makes sense, I suppose."

"Would you like to?" Azalea asked.

"Right now?" said Athena, slightly terrified.

"There's no pressure," said Azalea. "This only works if you want it to. I'm not going to take you anywhere that you're not ready to go."

"I want to," Athena said finally. "Is there anywhere that you can take me that will take away this pain?"

"You want the pain to go away?"

"I do," said Athena. "Of course I do. Who wants to be in pain?"

"That is a question that has plagued humanity for its entire existence," said Azalea.

"Or at least as far as you can tell," Athena added. "And you would know more than most people."

"Indeed," said Azalea, "but it's been a long time since I've been human. The paradox is that avoiding pain inevitably leads to more of it. So when you tell me you want the pain to go away, that is somewhat of a red flag."

41

ROSEMARY

Rosemary watched the Burk family castle nervously for a few moments before convincing herself to go back to Thorn Manor. Athena had asked her just to drop her off and leave her there. She'd been very specific about it, but that didn't stop Rosemary from feeling uneasy, even though, for some reason, she did feel a deep trust when it came to Azalea Burk.

She took a moment to check in.

If I trust Azalea, what's making me feel so uneasy?

The answer came instantly: *I don't trust myself...*

She'd made a lot of bad moves. She hadn't been there to support her daughter when Athena had needed her, and she couldn't seem to find the right words, even when she was around.

Rosemary took a deep breath and exhaled.

I'm going to find Marjie, have a cup of tea and a nice chat...

The tea shop must have been in an afternoon lull, which suited Rosemary perfectly.

Marjie lit up when she walked in.

"How is she, dear?" Marjie asked, obviously talking about Athena.

"She went off to her vampire therapy session with no apparent difficulty," said Rosemary. "I only hope that this is a good move, that it's helpful. I trust Burk and Azalea. It's just...you just don't know...There's so much uncertainty."

"Exactly," said Marjie. "That is one of life's key frictions, I find. Uncertainty chafes us, doesn't it?"

"You're telling me," said Rosemary.

"Come on, take a seat by the window, my dear." Marjie ushered her to her favourite table and brought over tea laced with a special blend to uplift the mood, along with a lemon and cream sponge cake that was so light it was almost like a meringue and melted in the mouth like heaven.

After several bites and a few more sips of tea, Rosemary felt herself relaxing a little. Marjie came back to the table.

"What would I do without you?" said Rosemary, as Marjie sat down with her own cup of tea for a well-deserved break.

"I was a little worried about that myself," said Marjie. "I had to go away for a little bit. Growing business, you know."

"Of course," said Rosemary. Marjie had been awfully busy with the crones recently, and yet, Rosemary had never seen her so energetic. She had a feeling that Marjie and Papa Jack were going to make their relationship public soon as well, and it warmed her heart to see two such lovely people who were so important in her life finally getting the happiness they so deserved and wanted.

"And are you going to be away for the Imbolc ritual?" Rosemary asked.

"Oh no, dear. I thought perhaps I could help you with that, actually."

"Please, please do," said Rosemary. "If you can. I hate to be a bother, obviously, after everything you've done for us, but I feel like I'm in over my head. You know, we've invited the Goddesses for cocktails, and I was hoping you'd do the decorations. And there's something nefarious happening in the forest..."

"That everyone's too scared to properly investigate," said a voice.

Detective Constantine Neve had appeared behind Rosemary.

"Oh, sorry, Neve. I wasn't meaning you in particular."

"No, you're kind of right about that," said Neve. "I have a few updates."

"Oh yes, come and join us," said Marjie. "Have a seat, dear."

"Sure," said Neve.

"What is it you've discovered?" Rosemary asked.

"Well, Athena was right. She sent me through some notes a while ago. Very detailed, elegant notes, I must say. I'm sure she'll have no trouble catching up on her schoolwork, even with the time pinch."

Rosemary smiled gratefully. "Let's hope so. She's really stressed about that."

"I know," said Neve. "Isn't school the worst for that kind of thing? It always feels like the end of the world."

"Sure does," said Rosemary. "I wouldn't go back in time, not for a million dollars. Being a teenager was the worst. Everything was far too intense."

"Part of the journey, I'd say," said Marjie. "We really should bring back more rituals from the old days, more rites of passage around youth. Celebrating kids turning seventeen is one thing, but it's almost like they're being reborn into the world as an adult."

"We've had quite enough being reborn for one year," said Rosemary. "Coming out of the underworld was a little bit like that. Anyway, what do you mean Athena was right?" she asked Neve.

Neve hooked out a little notebook from her front pocket. "Well, one of the creatures that Athena documented, which we didn't really pay much attention to at first, might actually be responsible for what's going on. We'd overlooked it because it's Irish."

"Oh no," said Marjie, shaking her head. "Never overlook the Irish. No good will come of that."

Neve chuckled. "No, I mean, we didn't think that they would stray so far from home. But apparently, it has been known to happen."

"What kind of creature?" Rosemary asked.

"It's called a fear gorta."

"A far goitre?" said Rosemary. "Like a growth where there shouldn't be one?"

"No, a fear gorta," said Neve.

"What's that?" said Rosemary. "You think it's responsible for what's going on in the forest?"

"Well, traces of the magic in the forest have the same signature, but there's a difference," said Neve. "This one sort of supercharged, like the original magic of the mythos of the fear gorta has been tampered with or amplified. I'm not sure exactly. It seems like it's a result of some kind of strange experiment."

"So," Rosemary said, "do you think we have a mad scientist creating bizarre mythic creatures?"

Neve shook her head. "I don't know. These sorts of things can happen organically. Like attracts like, you know. One powerful magical being with the same vibration can meld with another kind and create a sort of super monster. That's what I'm concerned about."

"Do you think this has anything to do with our other missing person?" Marjie asked. "Because my crone intuition is super powerful now. I just have an inkling. You remember Zade turned up at the house looking for his estranged husband?"

"You don't think Don June had something to do with this, do you?" said Rosemary.

"I wouldn't put it past him," said Marjie. "If he got out of jail like Zade said, maybe he's the one controlling the fear gorta. Maybe he's trying to get revenge on the town like some kind of evil scientist mad magician."

"It makes for a great story, don't you think?" said Rosemary ironically, as dread pooled in her gut.

Neve shook her head. "Not a great story that I'd want in my life, no."

"Maybe not," said Rosemary. "Well, he was always looking for magical amulets and using magic to enhance his power. So I suppose this is very on-brand. Do you think he's evil?"

Marjie shrugged. "I'd say it's rare, extremely rare, for somebody to be completely evil, but a lust for power and an inability to humble oneself, to surrender to the earth and to connect with other people... Well, that's what drives people away from the good side of their humanity and into an existence that's hardly worth living, where the only thing that matters is more power. I'd say he's very damaged, and I'm not sure there's any way of coming back from that."

"It's kind of sad, when you think about it, isn't it?" said Rosemary.

"Sad. Also twisted," Neve added.

"Well, thank you for the update," Rosemary said. "Why don't you swing by the house later, or we can come and visit you guys and the baby?" she said to Neve, as the detective was getting up to leave.

"That sounds good. I'd like to thank Athena," said Neve, "and maybe see if she has any other ideas. She's very intelligent, you know. Your daughter, she's a good one."

"I just wish I was better at being her mother," said Rosemary.

"There, there," said Marjie, patting Rosemary on the shoulder. "There's no such thing as a perfect parent, but I'll have you know that you're doing a brilliant job, and we can all only do the best that we can at this life business and hope that it's good enough."

Rosemary smiled. "I hope so."

42

ATHENA

Azalea leaned forward, her dark eyes locking onto Athena's with an intensity that was both unnerving and comforting. Her voice, low and smooth like silk, filled the room with a sense of gravity. "You see, my dear Athena, pain is not merely a nuisance to be banished. It is a guide, a teacher. Pain demands your attention because it has something important to convey."

Athena's brow furrowed slightly, and she fidgeted with her hands. "So you're saying I should just accept it? Embrace it? How does that help anything?"

Azalea smiled faintly, a glimmer of amusement in her gaze. "Acceptance is not defeat. Embracing pain does not mean you let it consume you. Rather, it means acknowledging its presence and understanding what it seeks to reveal. Pain is often the symptom of something deeper, something that has been buried or ignored. It is the signal flare of your psyche, calling for your awareness."

Athena shifted uncomfortably in her chair, feeling exposed and intrigued by Azalea's words. "But it hurts so much. How am I supposed to function when all I feel is this...weight?"

"By transforming that weight into something else," Azalea replied, her tone soothing, firm. "It begins with exploration – going deeper into the shadows of your mind, into that underworld we spoke of. There, you may find the roots of your pain, tangled and ancient, but once you understand them, you can begin to untangle them."

Athena sighed. "And you're sure this will help? That it won't just make things worse?"

Azalea tilted her head slightly, her expression softening. "There are no guarantees, my dear. But what I can tell you is that this journey is necessary. Whether you take it now or later, the call of the shadow will only grow louder. Facing it with guidance and support may allow you to find the strength you need to carry that weight differently – perhaps even to transform it into something that serves you, rather than burdens you."

Athena looked into Azalea's eyes, searching for something – perhaps a promise of relief or an assurance of safety. What she found instead was a reflection of her own determination, her own power. Slowly, she nodded. "Alright. I'll do it. I'll go on this journey, whatever it is, and I'll face whatever I need to face."

Azalea's smile widened just a fraction, a look of approval and perhaps even pride crossing her features. "Very well. We will begin when you are ready. And remember, Athena, the underworld is not just a place of darkness. It is also a place of rebirth. You may enter in pain, but you do not have to leave with it."

Athena nodded again, feeling a strange mixture of fear and hope. "I'm ready. Let's do this."

Azalea stood gracefully, offering her hand to Athena. "Then let us begin the descent, my dear. And remember – whatever you find in the darkness, you are not alone."

With a deep breath, Athena took Azalea's hand, ready to step into the unknown, hoping that, on the other side, she would find the light she so desperately sought.

Azalea Burk, draped in her resplendent black dress, leaned back slightly in her chair, her gaze never leaving Athena.

"Seeking to banish pain is very instinctive. But pain, as I see it, is a gateway – an invitation to explore the darker realms of your psyche, where the true transformations occur."

She paused, letting her words settle into the charged silence between them.

"You came here today because you are ready, though you might not fully realise it yet. Pain can be a potent teacher, but it is not one that can be ignored or wished away. It must be met, understood, and eventually, transformed."

Azalea's voice was as soothing as it was commanding, laced with a deep otherworldly wisdom. "You've already walked through the underworld once, Athena, but that was in the outer world. Now, you're being called to walk through the underworld within, where the echoes of Elise, and of all your past pains, reside."

She leaned forward slightly, a hint of a smile playing on her lips. "You say you're ready, but this journey is no trifling matter. So tell me, Athena, are you truly ready to step into that internal darkness and see what it holds for you?"

Athena struggled to find words to reply, but came up with nothing.

Azalea smiled, a slow, knowing smile that seemed to stretch time itself. "I understand your scepticism. It does sound too good to be true, doesn't it? The notion of transforming resistance, of embracing the darkness and finding bliss on the other side...It's a concept that defies our everyday logic. But let me assure you, it is not only possible – it is essential."

"I don't completely understand," Athena said, though she was starting to think that a part of her did.

Azalea leaned back, folding her hands elegantly in her lap, her dark eyes never leaving Athena's. "My therapeutic process is deeply effective, but it is challenging. We must confront our shadows if we are to open the door to transformation."

Azalea's voice was soft but resonant, carrying the weight of centuries of wisdom. "The guided journeys I offer are much like deep meditation, but they go further. They are journeys into the psyche, into the unconscious mind where the roots of your pain lie hidden. These journeys allow you to confront your shadows, the parts of yourself that you've buried or denied. And when you confront them, when you embrace them, they lose their power over you."

Athena listened intently, her scepticism beginning to waver in the face of Azalea's calm assurance. "It sounds...well, it sounds like it could be powerful. But how does that actually work? How do you take resistance and turn it into bliss?"

Azalea's smile widened, her eyes glinting with a secret knowledge. "It works because resistance, when faced with compassion and understanding, begins to soften. It no longer has to fight so hard to protect you, because it realises it is no longer needed. And as that resistance softens, as you release the grip of fear and control, you create space within yourself. Space for peace, for joy, and yes, for bliss."

She paused, letting the idea sink in. "This process is not about forcing change. It is about allowing it. It is about creating a safe space within yourself where your true self can emerge, free from the layers of protection you've built over the years. It is about trusting the process, even when it feels uncertain or frightening."

Athena nodded slowly, still trying to wrap her mind around the concept. "It does sound...transformative. But I'm still a bit afraid. What if I'm not ready? What if I can't do it?"

Azalea's gaze softened, and she reached out, placing a cool, reassuring hand on Athena's. "Darling girl, the fact that you are here, willing to try, tells me you are ready. And remember, you will not be alone. I will be here to guide you, to ensure you are safe throughout the process. We will take it one step at a time, only as far as you are comfortable. There is no rush, no pressure."

She squeezed Athena's hand gently before letting go. "Now, before we begin, I want you to understand a few things. This journey is yours and yours alone. It will be unique to you, shaped by your experiences, your fears, and your hopes. There is no right or wrong way to experience it. What matters is that you are open to whatever arises."

Azalea stood and moved quickly and gracefully to a small table, where a candle rested in a silver holder. She lit the candle, the flame flickering to life in the dim room. "We will use this candle as a focal point, a symbol of the light that exists even in the deepest darkness. As you focus on the flame, allow yourself to relax. Let go of any expectations, any doubts. Trust that whatever you encounter in this journey is there to help you, to guide you toward healing."

She turned back to Athena, the warm glow of the candle casting dancing shadows on her face. "This is not a journey of the mind alone. It is a journey of the heart, of the soul. And it is a journey that, once begun, will lead you to a place of greater peace and understanding."

Azalea returned to her seat with an ethereal expression. "Are you ready to take the first step, Athena?"

Athena swallowed, feeling a mix of fear and determination. "Yes. I'm ready. Let's do this."

Azalea nodded approvingly. "Very well. Let us prepare to begin. Remember, there is no need to force anything. Simply allow yourself to be guided, to follow where your inner self leads. We will begin slowly, gently, and as we go deeper, you will find that the resistance you feel will begin to dissolve, replaced by a sense of calm, of acceptance. And perhaps, in time, it will become a sense of bliss."

She leaned back slightly, her voice dropping to a soothing, rhythmic tone.

. . .

CLOSE YOUR EYES, Athena, and take a deep breath. Feel the air filling your lungs, cool and refreshing, and then slowly release it, letting go of any tension, any worry. Imagine yourself standing at the edge of a vast, ancient forest. The night is soft around you, wrapped in a velvet cloak of darkness, but it is a comforting darkness, one that holds you gently, cradling you in its embrace.

In the distance, you hear the song of night birds, their melodies sweet and haunting...life pulses even in the stillness of night. The leaves rustle softly in the breeze, whispering secrets of the woods, inviting you to step forward. As you do, the ground beneath your feet is cool and firm, grounding you, connecting you to the earth.

With each step you take, feel yourself moving deeper into the forest, deeper into relaxation. The darkness here is not frightening; it is welcoming, protective.

The trees stand tall and silent, their branches weaving a canopy above, through which the crescent moon and distant stars peek, offering their gentle light. This light is your guide, Athena, always present, always there to keep you safe as you journey into the unknown.

The sound of a stream reaches your ears, its waters flowing over stones with a soft, soothing murmur. Every note of its song carries you further into peace, into calm. Let the rhythm of the forest — its subtle symphony of night sounds — lull you into a deeper state of relaxation, where your body feels light, and your mind becomes open, receptive.

As you continue your journey, the path beneath your feet is easy, each step as natural as the breath you take. The deeper you go, the more the forest opens to you, revealing its mysteries, its quiet beauty. The air is cool against your skin, invigorating, soothing...the very essence of the night is flowing through you, relaxing you more and more with every moment.

Soon, the trees begin to part, and in a small clearing, you see a still pool of water, perfectly round, as if carved by the hands of time itself.

The surface is so smooth, so calm, that it mirrors the sky above, the stars twinkling softly, the crescent moon casting a gentle glow upon the water.

This pool is a mirror, Athena, one that reflects not just the sky, but everything you need to see within yourself.

Walk closer now, step by step, until you stand at the edge of the pool.

Look down into the water, and as you do, feel a wave of calm washing over you, relaxing you further, deeper. In this reflection, you will see what you need to see, the truths you carry within you. But there is no need to fear these reflections, for they are here to guide you, to help you understand and transform.

As you gaze into the water, let yourself relax even more. Breathe deeply, feeling the cool night air filling you with peace. Let go of any remaining tension, any resistance. This is a place of safety, of healing. The darkness here is not a void, but a space filled with potential, with the promise of transformation.

Allow the reflections in the water to show you what you need to see, Athena. Trust in this journey, trust in yourself. The stars and the moonlight are with you, guiding you, keeping you safe as you delve deeper into your own depths. Relax, and let the transformation begin.

As ATHENA GAZED into the still, dark pool, the first reflection that surfaced startled her. The image of Elise appeared, her face both familiar and strange, framed by shadows. Her eyes, once full of warmth and mischief, were now cold, distant – eyes that belonged to someone who had seen the underworld, who had been claimed by it. The sight of her, of what Elise had become, sent a chill through Athena, and her heart tightened with fear.

Do not turn away, Athena.

Azalea's voice floated through the air.

This reflection is not here to harm you. It is here to teach you, to show you what you have carried in your heart, hidden away. Breathe into it, soften into it. Let yourself be open to what you see.

Athena inhaled shakily, her eyes fixed on the reflection of Elise. As she continued to watch, the image shifted and rippled, transforming into another – a younger version of herself, eyes wide with hope and determination, stepping into the world with all the naivety of someone who hadn't yet faced true loss. The memory of who she was before Elise, before everything fell apart, pierced her deeply, filling her with a sorrow that was sharp and raw.

But beneath Azalea's steady guidance, Athena began to relax, to allow herself to see what these reflections were revealing. The initial shock gave way to something else, something warmer and softer. The pool began to show her not just the pain, but the growth – the moments of strength she had shown, the times she had persevered despite the odds. She saw the battles she had fought, not only with the forces around her but within herself, and how those battles had forged her into something stronger, more resilient.

Look closer, Azalea's voice urged. *Allow the pain to flow and wash over you so that you may feel it and so that you may see beyond it, too. See what you have become, what you are still becoming. This past year has not only been about loss; it has been about transformation. The darkness has not consumed you – it has shaped you, deepened you. Open to it, let it alchemise within you.*

Athena's gaze softened as she looked into the pool again, seeing herself as she was now – no longer the innocent girl she had once been, but a young woman who had faced the depths and had come through it, scarred but alive, stronger. The reflection shifted, and now the forest around her became part of the image, the towering trees that had silently witnessed her journey, the stream that had soothed her, and above, the endless sky, the stars twinkling like old friends, the crescent moon holding her in its light.

She realised, in that moment, how much she had grown. Even though losing Elise had shattered her, even though the guilt over the chaos she had caused still weighed heavily on her, she could see now how these experiences had pushed her to the very edge of herself, forcing her to expand, to become more than she ever thought she could be.

As she breathed deeply, something within her began to shift. The tightness in her chest eased, and in its place, a gentle warmth began to bloom. She felt it spreading, like a soft light, filling the spaces within her that had been cold and dark for so long. This warmth was acceptance – a quiet acknowledgment of all that had happened, of all she had lost, and of all she had gained. She could see now that this was the beginning of alchemy, the process of turning her shadow, her pain, into something else – something that could heal, something that could give her strength.

Yes, Athena. Azalea's voice was soft now, almost a whisper. *This is the alchemy of the soul. By opening to the darkness, by embracing it, you transform it. The energy you had cut yourself off from, the parts of you that you had pushed away – they are returning now, integrating back into the whole. This is the path of true healing, of true power. Let it happen slowly, gently, as the night turns to dawn.*

Athena's eyes filled with tears, not of sorrow but of release. She felt the warmth expanding within her, touching all the places that had been frozen, bringing them back to life. She knew this was just the beginning, that the journey of facing her shadow would take time, but she felt ready now, ready to embrace it, to let it change her in ways she could not yet fully comprehend.

As she stood there, the night around her felt less dark, the stars above seemed brighter, and the reflection in the pool no longer frightened her. Instead, it filled her with a quiet sense of peace. She was still herself, but she was also something more – someone who had faced the darkness and was beginning to find her way through it, towards the light.

This is your journey, Athena, Azalea said, her voice filled with pride. *And you are walking it with exquisite grace. Continue to open up to your* own pain. You are transforming, my dear, and the woman you are becoming is extraordinary.

Athena smiled faintly, the first genuine smile she had felt in a long time – even through the tears there was joy. She knew there was still much to face, much to heal, but she also knew she was not alone in this journey. And for the first time in what felt like an eternity, she felt a glimmer of hope, a sense of possibility, as she stood on the threshold of a new chapter in her life.

Go deeper now, child...

Athena's breath caught as the warm light she had felt within began to flicker, and the comforting images in the pool started to shift again. The reflection of herself as strong and resilient began to fade, replaced by something darker, murkier – an image that stirred a deep unease within her.

There, in the still waters, she saw herself not as she wished to be, but as she feared she truly was. Her face was gaunt, her eyes hollowed by guilt and loss, her posture hunched as if the weight of the world pressed down on her shoulders. The image seemed to mock the moments of strength she had seen just a moment before, challenging the hope that had begun to stir in her chest.

A surge of panic rose within her, tightening her throat, making her want to look away, to retreat into the safety of ignorance. The warmth that had started to spread through her felt fragile, vulnerable to being snuffed out by the darker truths reflected in the water.

Allow yourself to be present, Athena, Azalea's voice came again, more insistent now, cutting through her fear.

This reflection is not here to punish you, but to reveal what still lies hidden. These are the parts of yourself that you have yet to accept, the shadows that still hold power over you. This is where the true alchemy begins.

Athena's heart pounded in her chest, her instincts screaming at her to pull back, to retreat into the safety of denial. But there was something in Azalea's voice, something in the cold, calm certainty of it, that kept her rooted in place. She knew, deep down, that if she turned away now, the shadows would only grow stronger, more insidious.

Slowly, painfully, she forced herself to keep looking, to confront the reflection before her. The image of her broken, guilt-ridden self shimmered in the water, the details growing sharper, more defined. She could see the lines of exhaustion etched into her face, the haunted look in her eyes that spoke of sleepless nights and endless self-recrimination.

This is the reality of your journey, Athena, Azalea continued, her tone neither comforting nor harsh, simply matter-of-fact. *You cannot transform what you refuse to acknowledge. The pain, the guilt, the fear – these are all part of you. They have shaped you just as much as your moments of courage and determination. To truly alchemise your shadow, you must face it in its entirety, not just the parts that are easy to accept.*

Athena's eyes filled with tears once more, her chest tightening with the weight of the truth she was being forced to confront. She wanted to scream, to rage against all the unfairness of life. But she knew there would be no answers, no easy resolutions.

When you are ready, step into the pool...

Athena took a deep breath and stepped into the pool, and as she did so, something inside her began to crack – not in the comforting way it had earlier, but in a way that felt raw, jagged. The warmth she had felt before was still there, but it was now tinged with a cold, hard edge. The truth of her pain, of her guilt, settled into her bones, and she realised that this process of alchemy was not going to be a gentle transformation. It was going to be a battle, a fight for her own soul.

Athena's hands clenched into fists at her sides, the tension in her body growing with each passing moment. She felt as though she was teetering on the edge of a precipice, staring down into an abyss that threatened to swallow her whole.

But slipped into the cool, still, dark water, bracing against the weight of her fear and pain, something shifted within her. It wasn't the soft, comforting warmth she had felt earlier, but a different kind of strength.

This is the true alchemy of the soul, Athena. Azalea's voice was softer now, but still carrying that same note of unwavering certainty. *It is not about finding peace or comfort. It is about finding the strength to face the darkness, to confront the parts of yourself that you fear the most, and to emerge on the other side, not unscathed, but stronger, more resilient. This is not a journey that ends in bliss, but in transformation. And that transformation will be hard-fought, but it will be real.*

Athena took a deep, shuddering breath, the tension in her body slowly beginning to release. A small, but real, sense of peace revealed itself within her – not the peace of blissful ignorance, but the peace that comes from facing the truth, no matter how painful it might be.

"I'm ready," she whispered, her voice trembling but resolute. "I'm ready to face whatever comes next."

Very good, said Azalea. *Then let us continue...*

43

ROSEMARY

Athena was quiet on the drive home. Rosemary had barely gotten two words out of her other than "yes, the session was good" and "very helpful".

Rosemary had taken her daughter's lead and tried to enjoy the silence as much as possible. It was a good sign, she told herself...a good sign that Athena said the session went well, and she just needed a little time for processing.

After deliberately reassuring herself of this several times, it was a great surprise to Rosemary to arrive home at Thorn Manor, sit down with a cup of tea at the kitchen table, and to have the whole story pour out.

"I'm going to speak and I need some space...please don't try to interrupt, Mum," Athena said as soon as they took their first sips of their favourite afternoon blend.

Athena began to talk and talk and talk. She detailed the entire session with Azalea, and then she went further back, trying to share a story that seemed to now be emerging more coherently in her mind.

"I don't know what Azalea did, but I'm glad it's working so well," said Rosemary. "Maybe I should sign myself up for therapy with her."

"Oh, please do, Mum! She's amazing," Athena replied. "I had no idea that the thing I needed to do most was just to be open to my feelings, just to allow myself to experience everything, instead of closing off and going around in circles like I have been doing all this time."

"That sounds deceptively simple."

"Of course it is," said Athena. "It's not like it's easy to do, but she's got tools and techniques and visualisations and things. She just knows how to say the right thing, and her tone of voice just allowed me to open up and finally begin to process what I had been feeling for a long time. I felt so guilty about everything." Tears burst forth from Athena's eyes, and Rosemary got up to comfort her.

"Oh, my darling, you have nothing to feel guilty about. You're just doing your best."

"I know you say that, but that doesn't make it automatically go away."

"No," said Rosemary. "Azalea is right. You really have to feel it for it to be true, don't you?"

Athena nodded, wiping away her tears. "There's something else I need to tell you," she confessed.

"What is that?" said Rosemary.

"Please don't get annoyed. But you know how I got that potion from Queen Áine and I started relying on it too much to be functional?" Rosemary nodded. "Well, you're gonna hate this. But I went back to her, and I asked for another potion. Well, I asked for more of the same potion, actually."

Rosemary shook her head slowly. "Athena, I—"

"Wait. Just let me explain before you speak, please. Just listen to me." Rosemary took a deep breath and bit her tongue gently to stop herself from reacting.

"Okay," said Athena, taking her own grounding breath before continuing. "The potion that she gave me the first time, it made me feel so light, and I was avoiding my emotions. And I can see now that that wasn't a sustainable approach in the long run, but it wasn't the worst thing in the world, and I might have been slightly addicted to it, you know, because it made me feel good. But please, just trust me on this."

Rosemary gave her a questioning look.

"Okay, so when I went back, the Queen said she wouldn't give me the same potion, but she'd give me a different one." Rosemary's eyes widened, but she held back the expletives desperately trying to burst from her mouth. "I know you don't want me taking potions from the fae."

Rosemary shrugged and rolled her eyes, still trying desperately to maintain the silence and listen as Athena had requested, while struggling against her own nature to ramble on.

"So Queen Áine gave me a different potion. It doesn't do the same thing. Don't worry, I just take a drop every evening, and I have weird dreams. I feel a little bit lighter. I think it's helping me to process. I can't – if I take more of this potion, it won't have any more effect. And it's not addictive, I promise. But it's helping me. It's kind of helping me cope with the other situation. I'm not running from my feelings anymore. I think it's really allowing me to heal."

Rosemary shook her head in disbelief.

"Okay, you're probably thinking that it's just another substance I'm relying on, but it's not quite the same as that. I hope you believe me. I only take one drop every night, and I don't have to. In fact, I sometimes have forgotten, and I was fine. I know you don't want me to turn out like Dad, being a hopeless addict like he was. But I want you to know that this is not like that at all. And it's not the same as when I was obsessively going to the fae realm or any of those other things. It's just – I know you'll be mad at Queen Áine for giving me another potion. It looks like she's drugging me and coercing me, and I just—I needed to tell you before you found out another way. I want there to be trust between us."

Rosemary raised her eyebrows, still remaining silent.

"Yeah, I know being deceptive is not the best way of having trust between us, but I'm telling you now, okay?" said Athena. "Shouldn't that count for something? I'm really trying to do the best that I can."

They both sat in silence for a moment, sipping their tea.

"Aren't you going to say anything?" said Athena.

Rosemary burst into laughter. "Am I allowed to?"

"Yes," said Athena. "Thank you for being silent for once in your life. It was a lot to get off my chest, and I really appreciated you giving me the space for it."

Rosemary shook her head.

"You're not too mad, are you? You're still not speaking very much," said Athena.

With a deep breath, Rosemary gently said, "I'm not mad at you, darling. I wish you could have told me earlier about what was going on for you."

Athena looked down at her teacup and shrugged. "Sometimes I do want to work things out on my own, and sometimes I feel too ashamed to tell you." She wiped away another tear.

Rosemary reached out to put her hand on her daughter's arm. "This is a lot to deal with for you, and that means that it's a lot for me as well," said Rosemary. "I'm not going to be mad at you, but I must say I have a bone to pick with your grandmother."

Athena yawned. "You can do that if you want. I think I need a nap."

"Oh, go on then," said Rosemary, giving her daughter a gentle shoulder pat.

Athena got up, but paused before she left the room, gazing out the window towards the forest's edge. Rosemary followed her line of sight. The trees seemed to sway oddly, despite the still air.

"Mum," Athena said, "have you noticed anything else strange about the forest lately?"

Rosemary frowned slightly. "Now that you mention it, I haven't heard birdsong in days. This is getting extremely eerie."

44

ROSEMARY

Rosemary found Dain out in the garden. He was examining a magnolia that was starting to bud as though it was an interesting creature he was witnessing for the first time.

"What are you doing?" Rosemary asked.

"Communing with the trees. It's a fae thing. Don't worry," said Dain.

"Do they talk back?"

Dain smiled. "They're quite good conversation."

"Really? Sounds nice," said Rosemary. "On a slightly less nice note, I have an urgent issue to raise with your mother."

"You do?" said Dain. "Join the club. There's rather a long line when it comes to Mama. What is it this time?"

"Well, apparently she gave Athena another potion."

"What?" said Dain. Rosemary could feel the hair prickling on her arm as Dain bristled. "You're joking."

"I wish," said Rosemary. "But alas, Athena just confessed to me. Not only did your mother give her the first potion, she's given her another one. Apparently, this one's not addictive. Or so Athena believes. But I just—I don't have a good feeling about this. You know what the fae are like."

"Only too well," said Dain. "Well, what do you think?"

"You're the expert here. At risk of causing chaos and discord between our realms, what's the best approach?"

Dain gave Rosemary a sly look. "Look, if you have a bone to pick with my mother, then let's take this fight to her."

"You're serious?" said Rosemary.

"I'm happy to follow your lead," said Dain. "But when it comes to fae politics, sometimes a direct approach can cut through all the traps."

"All right," said Rosemary. "When shall we go?"

"How about now?" said Dain.

Rosemary looked down. She was wearing some old jeans, a bright purple top, and a green cardigan that she'd thrown on this morning, much to Athena's disapproval. "I'm not dressed to be entertained by royalty."

"It hardly matters, does it?" said Dain.

"I'm not sure your mother would share that opinion."

"Well, the element of surprise might be a good thing. If you're not coming in all pretentious and trying to pander to royalty, that can get their attention in a different way. Just make sure you don't show any signs of weakness."

"Given the rage that I'm currently feeling towards your mother, weakness is the last thing on my mind," said Rosemary. "How dare she meddle in our lives like this without even asking me?"

"All right, let's go," said Dain. He raised his arm and clapped a doorway into the garden.

"Don't tell me we have to go all the way through the fae realm to find her."

"Not this time. I've been working on my realm navigation and it's improved remarkably. I'm taking you right to the source. After me!" He dove through the gateway, and Rosemary followed behind, wondering if she knew quite what she was getting herself into.

As she passed through layers of mist between the realms, Rosemary found herself in an elaborate throne room. She didn't remember this one from their visit to the fae realm and figured they must not have had a reason to come into this particular space. Queen Áine sat resplendent on a throne, surrounded by subjects and courtiers.

"Prince Dain," she said, in a tone of mortification. "To what do I owe the *honour* of this surprise visit, and why have you brought such an unkempt guest with you?"

Rosemary bristled. "Ah, come on, Grandma. I'm sure you can figure out exactly why I'm here."

The Queen's mouth puckered into a tiny rosebud. The look in her eyes gave her away. "Leave us," she called. The throne room emptied of subjects and courtiers and even guards. Within a moment, they were alone.

"You know exactly why I'm here, don't you?" said Rosemary, allowing her rage to surface but still keeping herself in check, a feat for which she was incredibly proud. Sometimes one needs to bare one's teeth when one's boundaries are crossed, after all.

"I take it this is about my granddaughter," said Queen Áine, stretching languidly, as though a relaxed approach would diffuse the tension.

Rosemary wanted to assure her that it would not work. "Why, yes. Your granddaughter, my daughter, whom you drugged with a potion."

"Rosemary Thorn," said Queen Áine. "I understand that you're upset, but I'd caution you to be more easy on the accusations."

"All right," said Rosemary, taking a different tack. "How would you feel if somebody had given a potion that could be incredibly addictive to one of your children? What if they had given them cream?"

"This is not the same as cream," said Queen Áine. "Cream ruins lives. It makes us incredibly unreliable. You must see the difference in this situation."

"I do see part of the difference," said Rosemary. "But how would you feel? Be honest with me. Would you be all smiles and delight if somebody in another realm had given a potion to your child that had made them addicted?"

"I didn't know that that would happen with Athena. I was merely trying to give her support for the task ahead, something that you have clearly failed to do in your parenting."

Rosemary's eyes almost burst into flame as she shot daggers at the Queen.

"How dare you!" said Dain, jumping in with a ferocity that Rosemary had never seen in him. "This is the mother of my child. Don't you forget that. You might be my mother, and I will treat you with the respect that you deserve, but please do the same to Rosemary, or you put our whole family's relationships under threat."

Queen Áine's spine stiffened. "Very well. I take back those words. They were harsh and unkind. But I do mean what I said—"

"Excuse me?" said Rosemary.

"Not about you being a bad mother," said Queen Áine. "There's no such thing as a good mother, after all, is there?"

"That seems to be the theme of the present moment," said Rosemary.

"It's the hardest job in the world," said the Queen, "to shepherd an entire life to its fulfilment with all the pitfalls of growing up."

"You can say that again," Rosemary mumbled.

"What I mean to say is that I was only trying to help Athena by giving her the potion."

"And then you gave her another potion," said Rosemary.

"Yes," said the Queen. "And this one is most definitely not addictive. The earlier one made her feel too good, gave so much energy that she came to rely on it. This one has a subtler and deeper affect. I misjudged the earlier potion and the reaction with her witch powers, you see?"

"You gave it to her without telling me!" Rosemary snapped.

"She's an adult," said Queen Áine. "Magically, she's of age. She's seventeen years old. I don't have to go through her mother to give her medicine. You're not the guardian of her care anymore. She is."

Rosemary's shoulders slumped. "Fine. Athena's allowed to seek medical care –magical fae medical care – if she wants to. It's none of my business, is it?"

"I wouldn't say that," said Dain. "I'd say it would have been better if we all were on the same page, and you could have at least told her *father*." There was a sharp edge to his voice that was rare in someone who was usually so casual and flippant.

Rosemary smiled at him reassuringly.

"And I bet there are strings attached," said Rosemary. "Tell us, what fae bargain did you drive our daughter into?"

Queen Áine tossed back her hair and laughed. "Oh, come now. I just want my granddaughter to connect with our heritage. That's all."

Rosemary shook her head. "I don't think that's all. And don't believe for a second that this is the last you'll be hearing from me on this."

~

ROSEMARY LEFT Queen Áine's throne room with her heart still pounding in her chest. The conversation with Dain's mother had shaken her more than she wanted to admit. She hated confrontations, especially with powerful fae queens, but this time, it had been necessary. Now, as she stepped back through the misty doorway and returned to the mortal realm, her thoughts were fixed on Athena. Her daughter had been caught up in fae games, and Rosemary was determined to set things right.

She found Athena curled up in bed, staring out the window, lost in her thoughts. The look on her face broke Rosemary's heart. Without a word, she walked over and pulled her daughter into a tight hug.

"I'm sorry," Rosemary whispered into Athena's hair. "I'm so, so sorry I didn't understand sooner."

Athena stiffened at first but then relaxed, resting her head on Rosemary's shoulder. "Mum, I should have told you earlier. But I was scared. I thought...I thought you'd be angry."

"Angry? No, love, not at you. I'm angry at myself for not seeing how much you were struggling. And I'm angry at the fae for meddling in our lives again. But you? You've done nothing wrong. Not really."

Athena pulled away slightly, her face crumpling as tears welled up in her eyes. "But I *have* done something wrong! All I do is make a mess of things, and then you and Dad have to fix it. I don't see what the point of any of this is anymore. I'm just here making things worse, causing pain...The world would be better without me."

Rosemary's heart broke at the sound of those words. She took Athena's face in her hands, forcing her daughter to look into her eyes. "No, Athena. The world would not be better without you. The world would be a *lesser* place without you, and that's the truth. You're not broken, love. You're just human. We all are."

Athena shook her head, tears spilling down her cheeks. "But I *feel* broken. I mess everything up. I can't do anything right. And deep down, I just feel this constant guilt...like I should never have been born. Like everything is my fault."

Rosemary's throat tightened, but she kept her voice steady. "Oh, love, you were born an innocent baby. All you've ever done is try to navigate this chaotic, beautiful mess of a world the best way you can. That's all any of us can do. It's not your fault. Life is hard, and it's messy. But you? You're doing your best, and that's all anyone can ask."

Athena managed a small laugh through her tears. "You should be a poet, Mum."

Rosemary smiled softly. "Trust me, that's *exactly* not what the world needs."

"Why not?" Athena asked, her voice gaining a bit of strength. "You're actually quite articulate. You could be a great writer."

Rosemary sighed, brushing a strand of hair from Athena's face. "Maybe. I do want to write a book one day...even if it's mostly recipes."

Athena's eyes brightened for the first time in days. "Then do it."

Rosemary blinked. "Why? That feels like the least of our worries right now."

"Because," Athena said, her voice steady and sure, "the world will be a lesser place if your creation never exists. You sometimes say that to me. So now I'm saying it to you."

Rosemary felt tears prickling at the corners of her own eyes. She pulled Athena into another hug, holding her tightly. "Thank you," she whispered. "I'll think about it."

And in that moment, as mother and daughter sat together, wrapped in each other's warmth, Rosemary realised that maybe Athena was right. Maybe creating something – whether it was a book or a spell or simply a life well-lived – was worth it, no matter how chaotic or messy the world around them seemed. It might take time, but sometimes good things took time.

45

ATHENA

Athena felt exhausted after pouring her heart out to her mother, but there was also a sense of relief that came with the few tears shed and secrets shared. A weight had been lifted from her shoulders, and she felt lighter. As she finished her tea, she yawned, and Rosemary sent her upstairs for a nap.

Nestling down into the comforting embrace of her duvet, Athena fell asleep quickly. Soon, she found herself in darkness, a sense of fear permeating the air. As she looked around, she realised she was in the forest. A thumping sound ruptured the eerie silence, getting louder and closer. Something was moving towards her – something big, gnarly, and beastly. It was sucking the life out of the forest, leaving everything dead in its wake. A great gaping nothingness devoured everything in its path, consuming every ounce of juicy life and leaving nothing but barren wasteland.

Athena's heart beat a frantic rhythm in her chest as the creature approached. She screamed and woke up to the sound of her own voice echoing in her room.

"Are you all right, love?" Rosemary said, coming into the room.

"Nightmare...I guess," said Athena, her voice shaky. "I keep dreaming about whatever's happening in the forest, and I don't know if it's real or just my imagination."

Rosemary sat on the edge of the bed, her warm hand finding Athena's. "I keep having similar dreams. I wonder if they're the same, actually."

Athena shrugged, her brow furrowed. "They might be, but it's not good, is it? We've been so busy dealing with other things that we haven't really gotten any further on that front."

"Actually," said Rosemary, her eyes brightening, "Neve was going to drop by this afternoon. She has an update for you."

"Oh, really?" said Athena, sitting up straighter.

As if on cue, the doorbell sounded. "That might be her right now," Rosemary said. "In fact, it would be perfect timing, wouldn't it? Synchronicity is magic, you know."

"I bet it is," said Athena, a small smile playing on her lips.

"I'm going to go get the door," said Rosemary. "I'll see you down there in a minute."

As Rosemary went to answer the door, Athena lay in bed for a moment before getting up. She pulled a cosy jumper on over her checked pyjama pants. If it was just Neve or one of the other myriad people who called to ask for her mother's advice, believing that Rosemary could somehow help them, she didn't need to dress up.

When Athena got downstairs, she found not only Neve but also her wife, Nesta, and their beautiful baby Gwyn ensconced in the kitchen. Rosemary and Marjie were hovering around them, doting on the infant. The baby would have seemed fairly ordinary with her angelic smile and bright amber eyes, but on closer inspection, there was definitely something special about her. Though she didn't glow as much as when she was first born, there was still a shimmery quality to her complexion.

Athena got to have a cuddle, and as she held this miracle child –

conceived over the Beltane flames in a feat of mystical conception and deep magic from the love of both her parents – Athena felt a warm glow inside herself. "You really are a magic baby, aren't you?" she said, smiling down at Gwyn.

"Where's Little Mae?" Rosemary asked.

"With Una and Ashwin," Nesta replied with a smile. "She gets a little annoyed at the baby sometimes. She says she needs time to herself, and she toddles over to their house to play with the twins."

"Good for her," said Athena, impressed. "The girl knows what she wants." Turning to Neve, Athena said, "Mum tells me you have an update about what's going on in the forest."

Neve nodded, her expression turning serious. "I wanted to thank you. Those details you gave me about potential mythological creatures of relevance...it turned out you were right. It seems like we have something akin to an Irish fear gorta on our hands."

"Interesting," said Athena, rubbing her temple. "I didn't realise that they left Ireland. I thought it was a stretch."

"So did we at first," Neve admitted. "I contracted Juniper in to work on the case, and she's managed to help collect samples and used her connections with the magical authorities to get some complicated testing done. Basically, the signature of the magic is like the fear gorta plus something else, something amplifying it."

"Right," said Rosemary. "When I was talking to Neve before, she wondered whether Don June was also involved."

"How do you figure that?" said Athena, her mind racing. "Do you think he's trying to use a creature like that to get some sort of revenge or power? That seems to be his thing, right? Isn't that what Zade said?"

"Marjie's intuition," Rosemary explained. "Besides, it makes sense, doesn't it?"

"Indeed," said Neve. "What doesn't quite make sense is why he would be working with this particular creature. If he's plotting some kind of epic revenge, why now and why this way?"

"He's a strange guy," said Rosemary, shaking her head. "Remember all that stuff he did to compete with Ferg when they were both running for mayor?"

"Maybe it's not on purpose," Athena mused. "Maybe he's under the control of the monster."

Neve shrugged, her face a mask of concern. "It could be. We really have no way of knowing at this point, and it's too dangerous to get a closer look."

"I suppose." Rosemary sighed. "Everyone's been told to keep out of the forest, right?"

"It's all cordoned off and magically barricaded," said Neve. "The only people who can get in there at the moment would have to use some kind of magical teleportation."

"Although you could get in between the realms, I suppose," said Athena nervously, recalling what she herself had accidentally done not so long ago.

Neve nodded, her eyes narrowing. "Yes, that would do it, but I wouldn't recommend going in there."

"I've been in there enough in my dreams," said Athena.

"Me too," said Rosemary.

"You've both been dreaming consistently about the forest?" Nesta asked, her eyebrows raised. "That seems rather a coincidence."

"I'm afraid it's not really a coincidence at all," said Athena. "Our dreams tend to tell us things. We just don't know how much of it is actually happening and how much is our imagination."

"That's always my problem," said Rosemary, "just in general."

Athena patted her mother on the shoulder. "It makes you more interesting, though."

They smiled at each other, but Athena felt a creeping sense of unease as she contemplated the connections. If Don Juan was plotting revenge, then something terrible could happen at any moment. He could break out of the protections around the forest, not to mention the damage he was already doing.

"There must be a way to stop him," she said. "We can't just sit by and let this happen."

"We can't go in alone," Rosemary cautioned. "But he's destroying all the life in there. That is a huge concern."

"It is," Neve agreed. "Fortunately, we have access to magic that can revive the forest. It might take input from you, and maybe the Crones as well."

"I know somebody who knows a lot about magical forests and communicating with them," Marjie chimed in, her eyes twinkling. She'd been pottering around the house and had now sat down with them to join in the conversation.

"But we can't revive the forest until we've figured out what to do about the threat," said Rosemary, ever the voice of reason.

"And we can't do it all tonight," Marjie added. "We need good sleep and good nourishment. Rest is the best productivity at times like this, I find."

Neve and Nesta stayed for dinner, a nourishing stew that filled the kitchen with comforting aromas. It was a warm evening, filled with laughter and joy, especially in response to the adorable baby Gwyn, who seemed to enjoy being passed around for cuddles and smiled glowingly at every opportunity. Her laughter was musical, somehow both uplifting and reassuring.

As Athena went to bed that night, the warmth of the evening faded, and the cool dread returned. She quickly found herself back in the forest, this time with Rosemary beside her.

"WHAT ARE WE DOING HERE?" Rosemary asked. "And are we really here?"

"I can barely see you," Athena replied.

"Imagine a glowing purple teapot," Rosemary suggested. "That way, tomorrow we can find out if we both dreamed this together."

Athena nodded and imagined a purple teapot. She held it in her hands, and it floated and glowed in a brilliant lilac tone. She smiled and turned back to Rosemary, who had somehow morphed into a purple teapot herself.

"I didn't think that was what we were trying to do," said Athena, giggling. "You are a purple teapot."

Rosemary smiled in her teapot form. "I'm quite enjoying it though, aren't you?"

Athena couldn't help but laugh at her mother. "You are a very strange one, Rosemary."

"It's funny to hear you call me by my name," said Rosemary.

"I refuse to call a teapot 'Mother'," said Athena. "I shall have to turn myself into a teacup before anything like that happens."

A roaring sound cut through the air, dampening their laughter. "Maybe we can get a closer look, since we're dreaming. We're probably safe here," said Athena.

Rosemary turned back into her normal shape and nodded in agreement. "Take my hand."

They held hands and began to rise up over the town. It felt like slowly jumping on a trampoline as they floated into the air. Looking down in the pale moonlight, a devastating sight awaited them. The earth, caved in to darkness, festering with all kinds of terrifying monsters. In the centre was a gargantuan, pulsating void.

"What is this?" Athena whispered, her voice trembling. "Do we dare take a closer look, or is it too dangerous? Even in our dreams, it might not be totally safe. If this thing feeds on life force..."

She could feel the pull of the void and worried about her soul being sucked up, being devoured by the terrifying creature that seemed to feed on all life. With a start, Athena woke up, her heart racing. She lay in bed, contemplating everything she'd seen. It wasn't just one monster. There were a whole lot of monsters.

As she focused on them, she wondered what they were. Had they been corrupted? Or had they been magnetised into the forest by a force in the way that like seems to attract like? She had no idea how the former mayor was related to the situation, or whether he was at all, but she knew one thing for certain: the biggest threat was in the middle of that darkness, and it wasn't going to stay contained for long.

ATHENA SAT UP IN BED, her mind whirling with possibilities and fears. The threat in the forest was very real, and this posed a massive problem with Imbolc approaching. The axis points of the seasonal festivals always seemed to unleash magical chaos, and she was not ready to face the dark forces devouring the forest.

46

ROSEMARY

*R*osemary stirred, the echoes of a strange dream still lingering in her mind. The soft tapping of raindrops against her window slowly brought her back to consciousness. She remembered fragments of the dream – purple teacups, or was it teapots? The details were hazy, but the terrifying vision of the forest remained vivid in her memory.

As she lay there, trying to piece together the dream, a different tapping sound caught her attention. It was coming from her window, more deliberate than the rain. Instinctively, Rosemary shored up her magic, preparing for any potential threat.

"Rosemary, are you alright?" Burk's familiar voice called softly from outside. "I don't want to wake you if you're sleeping. Just let me know if you're awake."

She pulled back the heavy velvet curtains to reveal Perseus Burk clinging effortlessly to the edge of her second-story window, his vampire abilities on full display. Rosemary couldn't help but smile at the sight.

"Oh, to be a vampire," she said as she opened the window for him. "You don't want to use the door like a normal person?"

Burk grinned. "Nice to see you too," he replied, gracefully entering the room.

He had been busy dealing with vampire politics and bureaucracy for the past couple of days, trying to figure out how best to communicate about his very particular situation. The council's help had been minimal; they were still analysing the data from the experiments with Rosemary in Scotland. So far, they hadn't uncovered anything particularly interesting, other than something to do with Rosemary and Burk's unique connection.

As they lay in bed together, watching the lightening sky outside through the now-open curtains, Rosemary confided, "I keep having these weird dreams. There's something terrible happening in the forest."

Burk's brow furrowed with concern. "I know," he said, his voice low and serious. "The vampire authorities are concerned, but they don't know what's going on."

"Neither do we," said Rosemary, absently twirling a strand of her hair. "Maybe we should get Athena's grandmother on the case too. She'll probably have a potion for that." The sarcasm in her voice was thinly veiled.

Burk chuckled, his chest rumbling against Rosemary's back. "I don't envy you being entangled with the fae in your family."

"Well, we can't all be vampires, I suppose," said Rosemary. A thought struck her. "In fact, isn't it prohibited for witches to be vampires?"

Burk nodded, his expression turning serious. "Occasionally, somebody with some level of witchy power has been turned into a vampire throughout history. The council now has protocols in place. If somebody has too much power, it can react rather badly with the vampire transformation and result in unintended consequences. Athena practically begged me to turn her into a vampire at the Winter Solstice when you were trapped in the underworld. I had to decline – for multiple reasons of course. If a witch's powers haven't fully come in yet, there can be a waiver, especially if it's just some subtle folk magic. After all, most people have some kind of magical heritage if you go back far enough. But for truly powerful witches, it's expressly prohibited for them to become vampires."

"What do the authorities do to them?" Rosemary asked, her curiosity piqued. "Do they just get destroyed?"

Burk's face darkened. "That might be the best outcome, at times."

Rosemary sat up, shocked. "How is that the best outcome?"

Burk sighed, sitting up as well. "If I may be blunt, Rosemary, the vampire authorities that you've interacted with so far are relatively benign compared to some of the higher-ups in the global scheme of things, and several renegades that have amassed enough power to defy the authorities at every turn and never be held to account," he explained. "They would love to get their hands on a super-powerful witch-vampire, just to study what it does to our magic combined with yours, or to use that power in devious ways."

A chill ran down Rosemary's spine. "That doesn't sound very good," she murmured.

"If people are actively seeking that kind of thing, I bet there'd be somebody Machiavellian enough to actually turn a powerful witch into a vampire," Rosemary mused, her mind racing with the implications.

Burk shook his head firmly. "The vampire penalties for such an act wouldn't be worth reckoning with, I don't think," he said. "And it's not a simple thing to create a vampire. The rituals are complex. Besides, powerful witches are not without their defences. But you're right, it is a risk. Some people make irrational choices just because they thrive on chaos. After all, my brother was like that."

Rosemary felt a pang of guilt at the mention of Burk's brother. "I feel guilty every time you mention him," she admitted softly.

Burk's arms tightened around her. "Don't," he said gently. "Sometimes I think you did him a favour. His whole existence was one of misery, and it had been for over a thousand years. You set him free. And I don't know whether there's any part of his soul that's still intact, but if it is, he has a lot of healing to do."

"I suppose that's a nice way to think of it," said Rosemary, though the weight of her actions still hung heavy on her heart.

They lay there in comfortable silence, Burk's cool arms around Rosemary, until the morning light had fully descended and it was time to get ready for the day. The smell of pancakes wafted up from downstairs, and Rosemary's stomach growled in response.

In the kitchen, they found Athena already up and busy at the stove. "Pancakes again! You're up bright and early," Rosemary observed. "Ready for school?"

Athena flipped a pancake with practiced ease. "Couldn't sleep very well," she admitted. "I had the weirdest dream. You were in it."

A memory tickled at the back of Rosemary's mind. "Was there anything purple?" she asked, a hint of excitement in her voice.

Athena's eyes lit up. "Aha!" she exclaimed. "It worked!"

"What?" Rosemary asked, confused.

"In the dream, you suggested we envision purple teapots to see if we were really dreaming the same thing," Athena explained.

Rosemary's eyebrows shot up. "Oh, did I? I can barely remember. Dream me must have been onto something."

Athena nodded eagerly. "And we were – we were dreaming the same thing. That means, to my mind..." Her voice trailed off as she looked into Rosemary's eyes. "...that what we saw was actually what's there. The creatures," Athena continued, her voice barely above a whisper. "The creatures in the forest."

Rosemary gasped, the gravity of the situation hitting her anew. "Do you think they were forest animals? Do you think they've been turned into monsters through whatever malevolent thing was happening there?"

"Something tells me you're right about that," Athena replied, her face grim. "There was something so tragic about them. They were suffering, starving, screaming out for nourishment that can never be satisfied. That is more frightening than any Irish monster itself, far more terrifying than just a fear gorta."

A heavy silence fell over the kitchen, broken only by the sizzle of pancakes on the griddle.

"We have to tell Neve," Rosemary said. "I'll pop into the station, see if she's there when I'm at work."

"Keep me updated," Athena requested, glancing at the clock. "I've got to go to school, although with everything that's going on, I don't know how I'm going to concentrate."

Rosemary reached out and squeezed her daughter's hand. "I believe in you," she said warmly. "You can do this."

As Athena gathered her things and headed out, Rosemary couldn't shake the feeling that they were on the precipice of something big and terrifying. But as she watched her daughter walk down the path, head held high despite the weight on her shoulders, Rosemary felt a surge of pride.

47

ATHENA

The corridors of Myrtlewood Academy hummed with magical energy. Athena clutched her astrology project to her chest, ducking under a floating chandelier that seemed to have a mind of its own. The brass doorknob of Dr Stella Ceres' classroom wiggled excitedly as Athena approached, as if recognising her magical signature.

Inside, star charts adorned the ceiling, constellations twinkling softly. A model of the solar system rotated lazily in the corner, planets occasionally emitting puffs of colourful dust. Athena slid into her seat, a carved wooden chair that adjusted itself to her posture.

Dr Ceres glided in, her robes shimmering like starlight. Graded projects from the previous week floated through the air. Athena's landed on her desk, revealing a glowing 'A' and a note praising her 'exceptional insight into the influence of the North Node and Dark Star Lilith'.

"Hey," Beryl whispered, her voice barely audible over the gentle chiming of a nearby astrolabe. "Can we talk?"

Athena nodded, curiosity piqued.

"I've been thinking," Beryl began, fidgeting with her pen. "Maybe we could call a truce? I know things have been...well, about as pleasant as a misfired tickling charm between us, but I enjoyed our potions practice. It seems I misjudged you, Athena Thorn. I know people don't like me, but—"

Athena studied Beryl, noting the absence of her usual sneer. Making a split-second decision, she said, "Actually, I was planning to invite everyone to Thorn Manor for study sessions. Would you like to come? I could help you more with Automancy."

Surprise flashed across Beryl's face, her eyebrows rising. "Really? I'd...I'd like that."

"Great," Athena replied. "Just one condition."

"What's that?"

"We both have to try communicating without hexing or vexing each other!"

Beryl let out a small laugh, the tension visibly leaving her shoulders. "Fair enough. I know I can be prickly. I'm trying to be better, it's just...well, let's just say I don't have the best role models."

Athena nodded. "You've already come a long way, Beryl. I'm happy to attempt...to be your friend."

Beryl smiled. "Thank you. I know that for all my magic, I'm not exactly a charming person."

"But I am!" Felix's cheerful voice interrupted.

Athena rolled her eyes good-naturedly. "That's true. Felix can be charming when he's not turning everything into chaos. Sam and Ash are lovely too, and so is Derron. I'm sure they'd all be friendly with you if you gave them a chance."

Sam turned and eyed Beryl warily. "What's brewing here?" they asked.

Athena took a deep breath. "I'm inviting everyone, including Beryl, to study at Thorn Manor. What do you think?"

A moment of silence stretched between them. Finally, Ash shrugged. "Sounds good to me. As long as no one ends up as a toad."

Sam looked uncertain. "Are you sure about this, Athena?"

Beryl's face fell. "Look, I get it if you don't want me there. I know I haven't always been...kind."

"Hey," Felix chimed in. "You don't have to be nice. They put up with me, don't they?"

Athena smiled.

As the lesson progressed, Liliana, the new Irish student with long dark plaits, answered a particularly challenging question about celestial alignments.

"Impressive, Liliana," Dr Ceres remarked. "How did you know to read an ephemeris if your last school didn't offer advanced Astrology?"

Liliana shrugged, smiling. "Luck of the Irish, I suppose."

Athena's eyes narrowed. Something about Liliana's casual remark triggered a connection in her mind to the fear gorta creature lurking in the forest. Could Liliana's sudden arrival at Myrtlewood be more than coincidence?

After class, Athena approached Liliana. "Hey, I was wondering... have you ever heard of a fear gorta?"

Liliana's eyes widened slightly. "Of course. They're part of Irish folklore. Why do you ask?"

"We've had some...issues in the forest lately," Athena said cautiously. "The magical signature of a fear gorta was picked up, around there – you must have heard about the damage – something is devouring all the life from the ecosystem. I thought maybe, since you're from Ireland..."

Liliana shook her head. "Fear gorta aren't like that. They don't destroy forests; they're part of the magical ecosystem. Is that what's happening here?"

Athena studied Liliana's face, searching for signs of deception.

The Irish girl seemed genuinely confused, but Athena couldn't shake the feeling that there was more to the story.

∼

THE DAYS BEGAN to blur together as Athena threw herself into preparations for the Imbolc ritual and her studies. The kitchen table at Thorn Manor continued to be a sea of textbooks and Marjie's special focus-enhancing tea. The study sessions with her friends became regular occurrences as they all supported each other to learn. Beryl had a wonderful time exploring the deep automancy of Thorn Manor, and had become reasonably adept at using the magical dynamo devices the school expected them to practice on.

Athena invited Liliana to join their study group, to keep a closer eye on her. As they pored over their books, Athena noticed how Liliana's knowledge seemed to go far beyond what was taught in class. She spoke of ancient Irish myths and magic with an unsettlingly ancient familiarity. When questioned about it, Liliana simply shrugged and said, "My mum's work exposes me to a lot of lore." But Athena couldn't help her suspicions growing.

The threat in the forest loomed. Athena's nights were haunted by vivid dreams – twisted trees with faces reaching out with gnarled branches, creatures howling in pain and hunger. She'd wake gasping, her sheets tangled around her legs and faintly glowing with residual magic.

If this isn't a normal fear gorta, what is it?

She continued to wonder, and to research, to no avail. But with each passing day, and with each weekly session with Azalea, Athena felt herself growing stronger. The vampire therapist's gentle guidance helped her navigate the tumultuous sea of her emotions. "Feel it all," Azalea would say. "Let it wash over you like a charm."

As Imbolc approached, Athena found her magic humming. The

nightmares still came, but they no longer left her writhing with fear. Instead, she channelled that energy into her preparations, determined to face whatever darkness awaited them in the forest.

Marjie returned from her travels a week before the festival, bustling around the kitchen of Thorn Manor with a whirlwind of energy and a trunk full of magical artifacts. The kitchen filled with the scent of freshly baked bread as she taught them the traditional foods of Imbolc, conducting a symphony of self-kneading dough and perfectly timed ovens.

"It's a time of purification and renewal," Marjie explained one evening as they all gathered around the hearth, which crackled with enchanted flames that changed colour to match the mood of the room. "We're welcoming back the light, but we must also acknowledge the darkness we're emerging from."

Athena nodded, thinking of the looming threat in the forest. "It feels fitting, doesn't it? That we're facing this...whatever it is...at Imbolc?"

Rosemary squeezed her daughter's hand, a faint protective glow emanating from where their skin touched. "We'll face it together, love. All of us."

The final days before Imbolc passed in a flurry of magical activity. Athena and her friends wove Brigid's crosses from enchanted rushes that hummed softly as they were braided. They crafted candles infused with phoenix tears and unicorn hair, their flames dancing with images of their hopes for the coming spring.

On the eve of Imbolc, as Athena put the finishing touches on her ritual space, drawing the last symbols with a hand that trembled with anticipation, a bone-chilling howl echoed from the forest. The sound was filled with such pain and hunger that it made her blood run cold and the magical wards around Thorn Manor flare visibly.

Something big was coming. Athena knew it. But all she could do was prepare as best she could.

48

ROSEMARY

Rosemary was just settling in for the night when an urgent knock at the door startled her. She opened it to find Dr Drake from the vampire research facility, his eyes glowing unnaturally in the darkness.

"Ms Thorn, you must come with me immediately. You're in grave danger," he insisted, reaching for her arm.

Rosemary stepped back, confused and alarmed. She reached for her phone, only to find her pocket empty. "I need to call Burk—"

"There's no time," Dr Drake interrupted. "Your security is at stake. We must leave now."

Something felt off, but Rosemary didn't want to show her fear. She took a deep breath, trying to think of a way to stall. "Before we go anywhere, I have some questions about your research. I've been wondering about the effects of moonlight on vampire physiology..."

As she rambled on with increasingly ridiculous queries, Rosemary reached out mentally.

Athena...

Mum?

I need help. Dr Drake is here, acting strange. Call Burk.

On it, Mum, came Athena's swift reply.

Dr Drake grew increasingly agitated as Rosemary stalled. "We don't have time for this! We must go now!"

Suddenly, there was a rush of air. Burk, Charles, and Azalea materialised, surrounding Dr Drake.

"What did you do?" Burk demanded, his voice low and dangerous.

Dr Drake's eyes darted wildly between them. He lunged for Rosemary, but Charles intercepted him, grappling with the rogue researcher. Azalea joined the fray, her movements a blur as she helped restrain Dr Drake.

Burk placed himself protectively in front of Rosemary as the others subdued Dr Drake. The struggle subsided with Dr Drake pinned to the ground.

"I need Rosemary to love me," Dr Drake confessed, his voice breaking. "I need to take her away somewhere. I need to taste the sunlight again, to feel it on my skin. I'll go mad without it."

"A bit late for that," Rosemary quipped, her heart still racing. "I'm sure you are already entirely mad."

Dr Drake's shoulders slumped. "I didn't mean to do it...I had no choice."

"Do what?" Charles demanded.

"The creature...in the forest," Dr Drake admitted. "I brought it here. The fear gorta...it seemed fitting for the season. And I understood its hunger."

Rosemary gaped. "You're responsible for the havoc in the forest?"

"I wanted to distract you...to frighten you so you'd come willingly...I designed the container for the creature myself and spent months in Ireland. I did it all for you, Rosemary...for us."

Rosemary squinted at the vampire. "You did this all for you and it was a very silly idea, wasn't it?"

Dr Drake nodded miserably as Charles and Azalea hauled him to his feet.

"The council will deal with this," Charles said grimly.

As they prepared to take Dr Drake away, Burk reached for Rosemary. "Are you alright?"

Rosemary nodded, still processing. "I am now. Thank you."

Athena had joined them on the doorstep and was deep in thought. "It doesn't make sense though, does it?" she said. "One fear gorta spirit set loose in the forest surely couldn't cause so much havoc."

Burk shook his head. "I've seen this kind of thing before, a lonely spirit far from home can seek out strange companions. Whatever is going on in there"—he gestured over to the forest—"I'm sure it's not one simple thing but a complex combination of forces."

Rosemary shivered. The air was cool, but so too was the prospect of facing that complicated darkness.

49

ATHENA

The town circle buzzed with activity as Athena and her friends put the finishing touches on the Imbolc ritual preparations.

Beryl carefully arranged candles in an intricate pattern, her brow furrowed in concentration. Sam and Felix argued good-naturedly about the proper placement of the altar, while Ash and Derron arranged the delicate Brigid's crosses they'd woven from fresh rushes.

The air hummed with anticipation, making cobblestones beneath their feet subtly hum. Athena's hands trembled slightly as she adjusted the offerings, her mind racing with everything that could go wrong. She'd been preparing for weeks, but now that the moment was here, doubt gnawed at her insides.

Sam paused in arranging candles, their nose twitching. "Does anyone else smell that? It's like...decay, but not quite."

Ash sniffed the air, frowning. "Now that you mention it...it's faint, but it's there. Coming from the forest, maybe?"

Athena felt a shiver run down her spine. "Let's just focus on the preparations," she said, pushing away a nagging sense of unease. But the scent lingered, a constant reminder of the darkness that lurked just beyond the town's borders.

"A little to the left, Felix," Athena called out, gesturing to the altar. "We need to align it with the cardinal points."

Felix grunted as he shifted the heavy stone slab. "You know, a levitation spell would make this a lot easier."

"And risk messing up the energies we've been cultivating all day? Not a chance," Sam retorted, earning an eye roll from Felix.

Athena smiled at their banter, but it felt forced. Her eyes kept darting to the forest's edge, where shadows seemed to move of their own accord. The sun was sinking lower, painting the sky in hues of orange and purple, but the beauty was marred by an oppressive feeling of dread. She couldn't shake the fear that her own actions, her desperate attempts to numb her pain, might have played a part in whatever was coming.

"Do you think we're ready?" Beryl asked, her voice uncharacteristically small. The usually confident girl looked pale, her eyes wide with worry.

Athena swallowed hard, forcing a reassuring smile. "We have to be," she said, hoping her voice didn't betray her own doubts. "We've done everything we can."

Athena's attention was quickly drawn to the approach of Ferg. His polished shoes clicked against the cobblestones as he made his way towards her.

"Ah, young Athena," Ferg greeted her, his voice as pompous as ever. "I must say, I'm quite impressed with your dedication to tradition. It's heartening to see the youth taking an interest in our time-honoured customs."

Athena nodded respectfully. "Thank you. We've put a lot of thought into the ritual."

Ferg's eyes narrowed as he surveyed the setup. "Yes, well, some of these elements seem a bit...unconventional. Are you quite sure about the placement of the—"

"The extra protective circle of black salt?" Athena interjected smoothly. "Given the current threats to our town, with the forest protections weakening and those ominous creatures, we needed some extra safeguards."

Ferg's bushy eyebrows shot up, a flicker of fear passing through his eyes. "Ah, yes, quite right. Very sensible indeed." He leaned in closer, lowering his voice. "Between you and me, my dear, I've been having the most unsettling dreams lately. Visions of hunger, of a darkness that consumes everything in its path. You haven't...seen anything like that, have you?"

Athena's heart raced. Of course she'd had similar dreams but didn't wanted to worry him. "I...I'm sure it's just pre-ritual jitters," she said, trying to sound more confident than she felt. "We're all a bit on edge."

Ferg's gaze fell on a beautifully crafted statue of Brigid. "Oh my, is that—"

"A tribute to the goddess Brigid," Athena confirmed, unable to keep a hint of pride from her voice. "We wanted to honour her properly."

Ferg beamed. "Splendid. Absolutely splendid!"

As the mayor moved on to inspect other aspects of the ritual space, Athena caught her mother's eye. Rosemary approached with excitement and apprehension.

"This is going to be interesting if Ferg's around when the goddesses show up," Athena murmured. "Assuming they do show up."

Rosemary sighed. "I'm really not sure if they will. Yes, I finally got up the nerve to invite the Morrigan, but I honestly don't know what's going to happen. Do goddesses actually have a sense of time? I'm not sure of anything at the moment."

"If they come, do you think they'll come to the ritual as well?" Athena asked, her voice hushed.

Rosemary merely shrugged in response.

"Mum," Athena said hesitantly, "have you been feeling...off lately? Like something's not quite right?"

"Are you looking for a clever way to insult my outfit?" said Rosemary. "Because now's hardly the time."

"No, I'm serious."

Rosemary's brow furrowed. "You mean besides the obvious threat looming over us?" She studied her daughter's face. "Athena, what aren't you telling me?"

Before Athena could respond, a cold wind whipped through the square, extinguishing several candles and sending a shower of sparks into the air. The crowd gasped, and Athena felt a surge of panic. She rushed to relight the candles, her hands shaking so badly she could barely hold the matches.

Marjie burst into the square with an armful of shimmering decorations. "The town hall is nearly ready for the cocktail party," she announced breathlessly. "I've been trying to come up with decorations fit for both the season and the goddesses. It's no easy task, let me tell you!"

As if on cue, Detective Neve appeared, her face grave. "I've just heard from Juniper," she said without preamble. "She's been monitoring the protections around the forest that the witching authorities put in place. It's...not looking good."

A tense silence fell over the group.

"How bad is it?" Athena asked, her voice barely above a whisper.

Neve's expression was grim. "The barriers are weakening faster than we anticipated. Whatever's in there...it's getting stronger."

A murmur of fear rippled through the crowd. Athena felt the weight of their expectations pressing down on her. She was supposed to lead this ritual, to protect them all, but how could she when she couldn't even control her own life?

The moment was shattered when a glowing half-moon sliced into the air above the town circle, through which Dain and a dazzling group of extremely shiny fae guards tumbled out.

Athena blinked in surprise. "Don't you think this might be a little bit distracting?" she asked Dain, gesturing to the glittering fae. "They're all so...shiny."

Dain grinned. "They'll just be in the background, rather than enjoying the festivities. Think of them as very attractive security."

But Athena noticed the tension in Dain's jaw, the way his eyes kept darting to the forest. The fae weren't just here for show – they were prepared for battle.

Burk appeared as well, and his sparkling ability to walk in daylight stirred wonder among the crowd. He hadn't been out in public in the daytime very much, sure his luck would run out. Athena smiled at his growing confidence.

Athena she spotted Liliana among the crowd, standing next to several tall women, one of whom might have been her mother. The Irish girl's eyes stared out towards the forest at the edge of the village with an intensity that sent a shiver down Athena's spine. For a moment, Athena could have sworn she saw Liliana's pendant glow faintly, the raven's eye seeming to wink in the fading light.

Athena shook her head, trying to focus on the task at hand.

Soon, more helpers arrived. Cedar and Finnegan pitched in, helping Marjie to set up for the cocktails and feast to be held after the ritual.

"When darkness falls, Charles and I have rallied some vampires to come along," Burk informed them. "Though I'm not sure how useful we'll be, given that we can't be outside until nightfall. We take responsibility for one of our own going rogue and letting this spirit loose on Myrtlewood."

Athena nodded. "The ritual should all be over by then, and the feasting too, but I'm grateful for any support."

She was about to respond when she noticed several of her teachers approaching. Her stomach clenched with nervousness.

Ms Twigg, sensing Athena's anxiety, stepped forward. "We're here to help, dear," she said warmly. "You're doing a marvellous job."

The praise eased the tension in Athena's shoulders, if only slightly. As she continued to prepare the ritual space, she found her thoughts drifting to Elise. A part of her longed for her friend to be there, sharing this moment. But as she looked around at all the people who had come to support her, she felt a sense of peace wash over her. She knew that if Elise were here, she'd be proud. And for now, that was enough.

"It's time," she announced, her voice carrying across the hushed crowd. As she spoke the first words of the ritual, candles flared to life around her, their flames burning unnaturally bright. The air grew thick with the scent of incense and magic, and Athena felt power surging through her veins.

But beneath the exhilaration was a current of fear. Because as the ritual began in earnest, she could have sworn she heard something moving in the forest – something large, and hungry, and drawing ever closer.

More and more people started to arrive for the ritual. Athena's gaze was drawn to a group of women she didn't recognise. There was something unusual about them – an otherworldly grace to their movements, a shimmer in their eyes that seemed more than human.

The one with blonde hair caught Athena staring and smiled, warm and slightly unnerving. Athena felt a shiver run down her spine. The ritual was about to begin, and she had a feeling it was going to be unlike anything they had planned for.

Athena stood at the centre of the circle, her heart pounding with a mixture of excitement and trepidation. Around her, the faces of friends, family, and townspeople glowed in the warm light of dozens of candles.

50

ROSEMARY

As Athena began to speak the sacred words to honour Brigid, Rosemary's gaze wandered over the assembled crowd. Rosemary's brow furrowed as she noticed several unfamiliar faces. One woman in particular caught her attention, with striking raven hair and eyes that seemed to glint unnaturally in the candlelight. Rosemary nudged Burk, whispering, "Do you recognise her? I thought I knew everyone in town."

Burk shook his head. "There's something...different about her. About all of them," he murmured back.

The ritual continued, the air thick with the scent of incense and the buzz of magic. Athena's voice rose and fell in a mesmerising cadence as she recited a chant to Brigid:

In the depth of winter's night,
Brigid's flame burns fierce and bright.
From darkness springs new life anew,
As we honour the old and welcome the new.

. . .

The sound of breaking glass echoed through the square.

Neve, standing near Rosemary, gasped as Juniper materialised beside them in her usual purple pin-striped suit. Her plum coloured hair was a mess, her face ashen.

"The protections," Juniper panted, "they've been broken. The energy of the festival is amplifying everything, including the dark forces stirring in the forest."

As if summoned by her words, a seeping darkness began to creep into the air.

Rosemary felt it before she saw it – a gnawing hunger in her chest, an insatiable emptiness that threatened to consume her from within. Around her, people groaned and sagged forward, as if suddenly drained of all energy.

An unnatural stillness descended upon the square. The flames of ritual candles flickered and dimmed, as if cowering from an unseen threat. A bone-chilling wind swept through the gathering, carrying the acrid stench of decay, a whispering ancient malevolence...

Rosemary clutched at her chest, gasping, and looked around to see others mirroring her actions. Faces contorted in agony and bewilderment as this alien sensation took hold, draining the vitality from their bodies.

"We need to cast the circle!" Athena called out. "Ashwyn!"

Ashwyn thumped her staff on the ground; she buckled over slightly, her blonde hair tangled in the unearthly breeze that swept over the town. Clearly struggling with the same gnawing hunger as the others around her, but experienced enough in magic to press on, Ashwyn thumped her staff once more, and golden magic emanated from it, encasing her. She lifted it up, pointing towards the edge of the circle, and moved quickly, encasing the entire gathering in a protective barrier.

. . .

THE CIRCLE IS CAST
We are between the worlds
Beyond the bounds of time
Where light and dark meet, together as one.

ROSEMARY SIGHED in relief as the hunger dissipated, but while the circle was safe for now, the danger was far from over.

From the forest's edge, darkness began to seep. This was no gentle twilight, but a living shadow that devoured light and warmth as it advanced with terrifying speed.

An oily, black ooze poured down the streets, engulfing everything in its path. Trees withered and twisted as it passed, their bark splitting to reveal pulsing, corrupt veins beneath. Leaves turned to ash, scattering on the wind like the remnants of hope.

*It's okay...*Rosemary told herself as a favourite elder tree was corrupted. *Marjie has a plan for restoring the trees...we just need to get out of this in one piece.*

The spring blossoms ties to the trees outside the circle wilted and crumbled, their petals dissolving into nothingness. Even cobblestones began to crack, the very foundations of the town groaning under the weight of this encroaching malevolence. The air grew thick and oppressive, each breath a struggle against the suffocating miasma of despair.

As the darkness reached the square's edge, it paused, roiling and bubbling like a sentient tar pit. Then, with agonising slowness, something began to emerge from its depths. At first, just a shape, a deeper shadow within the writhing mass. But as it rose, Rosemary's mind recoiled from the horror before her.

The creature that crawled forward defied all natural laws, its body a nightmarish fusion of corrupted forest life and tortured souls. It stood taller than the surrounding buildings, its form constantly shifting and changing. Countless legs – some like twisted tree roots, others chitinous and segmented – supported its massive bulk. Arms, too numerous to count, ended in hands with elongated fingers that looked like gnarled branches, tipped with sharp, dripping mandibles.

Its torso was a patchwork of bark, exoskeleton, and twisted human flesh. Moss and fungi grew in patches, pulsing with an unholy life of their own. But it was the face – or rather, faces – that truly horrified Rosemary. It barely resembled human or animal, contorted in agony, eyes of various colours and sizes blinking independently, darting around in panic or staring blankly. Mouths opened in silent screams or gnashed teeth that were far too sharp to be natural.

The stench was overwhelming – rotting vegetation mixed with the coppery tang of blood and the putrid odour of decay. It was the smell of a forest floor corrupted, of life perverted into something unspeakable.

The encroaching darkness pulsed and throbbed. Shadows danced and writhed with the shapes of tortured beings, the poor forest animals who were dragged into this mess.

Rosemary's heart went out to them, but reached for the hope Marjie had provided that magic could restore the forest. The most pressing issue right now was stopping the entire town from being devoured by this beast of insatiable hunger.

From the forest, more horrors emerged. Trees uprooted themselves, their branches contorting into grasping limbs, leaves withering and falling. The rustling of their approach sounded like the rattling of countless bones. Birds with too many wings and eyes that glowed an eerie green circled overhead, their cries a cacophony of tortured souls.

Small animals skittered at the edges of the shadow, their forms warped beyond recognition. Squirrels with spider-like limbs chittered madly, their ravenous eyes seeking out prey to feast upon.

The villagers stood frozen in terror, their faces pale and drawn in the sickly light. Children clung to their parents, whimpering. Even the bravest among them felt their courage waver in the face of this unimaginable horror.

The creature before them was an affront to nature itself, a being of such twisted malevolence that its very existence seemed to tear at the fabric of reality.

As the monstrous entity turned its attention to the gathered crowd, Rosemary felt a wave of hopelessness wash over her.

The creature's many mouths opened in unison, and when it spoke, its voice was a cacophony of screams, whispers, and inhuman growls that seemed to come from everywhere at once. It was the sound of a hundred forests crying out in pain, of countless souls begging for release.

I AM THE DEVOURER!

THE WORDS ECHOED with an otherworldly resonance that shook the very ground.

Zade reached for Rosemary's arm. "It's Don in there. I know it is. He's broken and hungry and trapped by his own weaknesses, but it's him."

Athena looked at him, sadly. "We'll see what we can do."

But Rosemary had doubts as to whether anything within the former mayor was salvageable.

I AM HUNGER INCARNATE, CORRUPTED AND AMPLIFIED. YOUR WORLD, YOUR LIVES, YOUR VERY ESSENCE – ALL SHALL BE MY FEAST.

. . .

THE DARKNESS CONTINUED to seep from the woods, no longer just an oily black ooze, but a living shadow that whispered promises of oblivion. It crept up walls and slithered across the ground, extinguishing candles and torches in its wake. Where it touched, colours faded, leaving behind a world of ashen grey.

Athena's friends and Marjie shepherded the vulnerable among them to the opposite side of the circle, along with Ferg. The unfamiliar women stayed put – there was no time to worry about that now.

Desperately, Rosemary reached for her magic, one hand pressed against the side of the circle, creating an opening so that she could send out a defensive blow. A beam of fiery energy shot from her hands towards the Devourer. "Don't come any closer!" she shouted. The spell crackled through the air, leaving the scent of ozone in its wake.

To her horror, the creature simply opened its maw and swallowed the energy whole.

"Have you got any more?" it asked, its voice dripping with malicious glee. "That was delicious."

Its eyes glowed with an unholy light, pulsing with the power it had just consumed. The creature grew larger.

Rosemary felt her hope falter. How could they fight something that fed on their very defences? She glanced around frantically, seeing the fear mirrored in the eyes of her companions. The weight of their impending doom pressed down on them all.

"Your magic only makes me stronger," the Devourer gloated, its voice a dissonant chorus of countless consumed souls. "Every spell, every prayer, every desperate hope – I will feast on them all."

As if to emphasise its point, more tendrils of darkness shot out from the Devourer's form.

Zade staggered forward, his face a mask of horror and disbelief.

"This...this is beyond belief," he whispered, his voice barely audible over the cacophony of destruction.

Burk, usually so steadfast, trembled. "It's like standing before an avalanche, knowing there's no way to stop it. In all my years here...I've never seen anything like this. Once night properly falls the vampires will descend, but what if he just eats them?"

Neve clung to Nesta, tears streaming down her face. "Is this how it ends?" Nesta whispered, cradling their baby. "Everything we've built – just...consumed?"

Athena raised her voice in defiance. "No. This is not how is ends!"

"Your world ends here," the Devourer proclaimed. "And in its place, only hunger will remain."

Rosemary glanced around frantically, seeing the fear mirrored in the eyes of her companions.

As the Devourer loomed over the terrified crowd, its grotesque form blocking out the sky, a laugh suddenly rang out – rich, powerful, and utterly fearless. The sound cut through the miasma of terror like a blade of pure light.

One of the women Rosemary hadn't recognised threw back her hood, her raven-black hair billowing out around her as if caught in a preternatural gust of wind. Before the stunned onlookers, she began to grow, her form shifting and expanding until she towered over even the monstrous Devourer. Her transformation was awe-inspiring and terrifying in equal measure as she shed her mortal form.

The Morrigan was beautiful, wild, deadly and devastatingly powerful in every inch of her being.

The air crackled with raw energy, the scent of rain-soaked battlefields filling the area. Lightning danced in her eyes, and the shadows at her feet came alive, taking the shapes of ravens and wolves that circled her restlessly. Her very presence seemed to push back the encroaching darkness.

The Devourer hesitated, its countless eyes widening in recognition. "You...I know you. The Morrigan. You were darkness. You were like me. Join me, and we'll be unstoppable."

The Morrigan threw back her head and laughed again, the sound echoing with the cries of a thousand ravens. The earth trembled, and several nearby windows shattered. "You can't be serious," she said, her voice resonating with ancient power. "I've got my own mischief to get up to, thank you. Besides"—she wrinkled her nose, waving a hand dramatically in front of her face—"you need a bath. Badly."

"Stop playing with your food, sister," came another voice, rich with amusement. The blonde woman Rosemary had noticed earlier stepped forward, growing in stature to match the Morrigan. As she transformed, the air around her shimmered with golden light, and the scent of fresh grass and blooming flowers overpowered the Devourer's stench.

Where her feet touched the ground, lush grass and wildflowers sprouted instantly. The withered trees nearest to her suddenly burst into bloom, their leaves a vibrant green that exemplified the coming spring.

"O great Goddess, Brigid," Ferg breathed in awe, falling to his knees. "The maiden of spring." His eyes were wide with wonder, and a tear rolled down his cheek. "We are unfit for your divine light, but humbly offer you anything you desire."

Rosemary's mind reeled as the truth dawned on her. "We invited goddesses," she muttered, her voice a mix of awe and panic. "We're not prepared for this."

Brigid's laughter was like the tinkling of crystal streams. "Don't worry, dear one," she said, her voice warm and soothing. "We're just here for cocktails. Though I must say, your hospitality leaves something to be desired." She gestured at the Devourer with a wry smile.

Rosemary felt overwhelmed by the sheer power radiating from the divine beings, her mortal senses struggling to comprehend what she was witnessing.

As if on cue, Ferg's panicked voice rose above the chaos. "I should have booked catering!" he wailed. "Do goddesses eat canapés? What about dietary restrictions? Oh gods, do gods have allergies?"

His fretting was interrupted as two more women stepped forward, their forms shimmering as they revealed their true natures. The temperature plummeted as one transformed, frost spreading from her feet in intricate patterns. Her face wrinkled like a landscape painting, her hair turned white as snow twisted with bones and treasures, and her eyes gleamed with the cold light of distant stars.

"The Cailleach," someone in the crowd whispered, their breath visible in the suddenly frigid air.

The other woman's transformation brought with it the scent of herbs and the sound of bubbling cauldrons. Her hair grew longer, greyer and untamed, and her eyes held the wisdom of ages.

"Cerridwen," Athena breathed.

The Devourer, momentarily cowed but quickly regaining its bravado, growled, "You are no match for me!" Its voice shook the ground, and tendrils of darkness began to spread from its form, threatening to engulf everything in their path.

The Cailleach's eyes glinted mischievously, like sunlight on icicles. "Oh really? You are rather large, aren't you? Perhaps there's something that can be done to remedy that situation." With a casual snap of her fingers, a sound like cracking ice echoed through the square.

Before anyone could blink, the Devourer began to shrink. Its booming voice rose in pitch as it dwindled, the process both fascinating and horrifying to watch. The creature's form twisted and contorted, its howls of rage turning to squeaks of indignation. In moments, the terrifying monstrosity that had threatened to devour the world was reduced to the size of a large, particularly ugly rat.

"That's better." Rosemary sighed in relief, feeling light-headed from the rapid turn of events. "Thank you for that. Though I think I might faint now."

"Oh no, you don't," the Morrigan said, her piercing gaze falling on Rosemary. "You, human, have some explaining to do. You were supposed to invite me for cocktails, but something tells me you deliberately invited us here to clean up your mess." Her eyes burned with the intensity of a thousand battlefields, and Rosemary felt as if her very soul was being laid bare.

Rosemary gulped.

As the goddesses loomed over her, their power palpable in the air, Rosemary couldn't help but think that facing the Devourer might have been the easy part of her evening. The real challenge, it seemed, was explaining herself to a group of mildly annoyed deities who had been promised a party and gotten an apocalypse instead.

"Rosemary Thorn," the Morrigan growled, advancing on the witch. "You never really wanted to have cocktails with us, did you? You invited us here as an insurance plan, didn't you?"

Rosemary felt the colour drain from her face as rage flared in the goddess's eyes. "Uhh, no, that's not entirely the case – we are all set up for cocktails in the hall. Marjie did the decorations like I said. It was just…convenient."

"Convenient?" the Cailleach asked drily.

"What I mean to say is…" Rosemary continued. "The seasonal festivals around here are always strange, so inviting you at this time was a calculated risk, yes. I didn't know what was going on in the forest, and having powerful fr—erm, powerful allies around seemed like a good idea."

"You really expect us to be allies when you trick us like this?" The Morrigan scowled.

"Well, I don't invite my enemies for cocktails, do I?" Rosemary blurted out before covering her mouth.

Not helping! Athena hissed in Rosemary's mind.

The Morrigan approached her, slowly. This was it. Rosemary had a moment of realisation that this could be her end – at the hands of an angry deity because she'd been too clever for her own good.

The Morrigan raised her hand. "You...seem like you need to be taught a lesson by the gods and I'm only too happy to step in and grant this for you. What will it be? Perhaps I could turn you into a raven for a few years..."

"Please don't," said Rosemary. "Parenting and running a chocolate shop are hard enough as it is!"

The Morrigan narrowed her eyes. "I demand tribute."

Just then, a brilliant golden light erupted from nearby. Everyone turned to see Neve and Nesta's baby glowing like a miniature sun.

The Morrigan's anger dissipated instantly, replaced by delighted surprise. She dropped her stance and turned her full attention towards little Gwyn, forgetting Rosemary entirely. "Ooh! A magic baby! This place really does have everything!"

51

ATHENA

Athena panted in relief as the Morrigan turned away from her mother and cast doting glances at baby Gwyn. Their divine presence settled at the sight of the small divine child. "A god-child," they muttered. And as they cooed at the baby they shrunk themselves down to a size not much bigger than mortal humans, though no-longer in disguise, and perhaps only so that Nesta would let them have a cuddle.

Small mercies... Athena been trying to think of a way to step in that wouldn't just get them all killed.

Soon, the Morrigan's attention had shifted again, back to the tiny shouting cockroach of a creature that had caused this whole mess and gotten in the way of her festival.

She breathed in deeply and the tiny devourer trembled.

"How about I take him back to the underworld with me, along with all this mess?" the Morrigan asked, sniffing the air. "Make sure he has a bath in the river first."

Athena stepped forward, pale and determined. "Wait!" she cried, placing herself between the Devourer and the assembled goddesses. "I...I recognise his suffering. I've seen it in my dreams."

Rosemary joined her daughter, understanding dawning on her face. "You're right. This isn't just evil, for Don. It's pain."

The Morrigan's lip curled in disappointment. "Spare me your mortal sympathies. He's chosen his path."

But Athena stood her ground. "No. It can't be so cut and dried. There has to be another way. Don," she addressed the creature directly, "I understand now. You've become this...this thing because of hunger. An eternal, insatiable hunger."

The Devourer's many eyes fixed on Athena, a flicker of recognition passing through them. "You," it hissed in its tiny shrunken voice. "I recognise your pain, your hunger. We are alike, you and I."

Athena's breath caught in her throat. "You're right," she admitted, her voice barely above a whisper. "I was addicted. To power, to magic... to wanting. But Don, it's time to let go. This pursuit...it's destroying you. It's destroying everything."

As Athena spoke, the Morrigan's gaze shifted to Rosemary, her eyes narrowing dangerously. "I want to keep it as a pet."

"No, Mother." Liliana stepped forward, grasping the Morrigan's hand and tugging it as if to get her attention.

"Mother?" Athena gasped, her eyes darting between Liliana and the Morrigan. The air seemed to crackle with tension, the residual magic from their recent battle still hanging heavy in the atmosphere.

The dark goddess smirked, her eyes glinting with mischief. Shadows danced around her feet, taking the shapes of small animals before dissipating. "Oh, did she forget to mention that little detail?" Her voice carried the echo of a thousand whispers.

Rosemary shook her head. "Wait a minute. Didn't we just set you free last Mabon?" she asked the Morrigan. "Weren't you stuck in some kind of pocket dimension for centuries?"

The Morrigan threw back her head and laughed, the sound like a murder of crows taking flight. The sky seemed to darken momentarily. "Oh, Rosemary Thorn, you mortals and your linear thinking. Time works differently for us gods. Your 'last Mabon' could be any number of my yesterdays or tomorrows. Besides, I always work in the world through those who worship me, and at times, we bear children together."

She looked dotingly at Liliana who shifted uncomfortably. "I wanted to tell you, but..."

Athena frowned. "You told me your mother was a researcher and a diplomat."

Before Liliana could respond, a woman stepped forward from the crowd. She was tall and elegant, with streaks of silver in her dark hair and eyes that held a fierce intelligence. Her robes were adorned with intricate raven designs.

"That would be me," the woman said, her voice carrying authority and a hint of an accent Athena couldn't quite place. "I am Professor Morgane. I believe I can explain."

Athena blinked, taken aback. She had never met this woman before, yet there was something familiar about her presence.

Professor Morgane gazed at the Morrigan. "I am a devoted follower of the great dark goddess, the Morrigan." She bowed in reverence. "As well as a researcher specialising in ancient Irish magic and diplomacy. Something was detected here in Myrtlewood, weeks ago, and I was sent here... but I digress. Liliana is both my mortal daughter and a child of the Morrigan. In her divine wisdom, my Goddess gifted me with Liliana to raise in the mortal realm."

The Morrigan rolled her eyes. "Yes, yes, you did fine. She's mine now, though. I'm taking her with me."

Professor Morgane bowed deeply, adoration still shining in her eyes. "As you divinely will it, my Goddess. It has been my greatest honour to serve as Liliana's guardian these past years."

Athena and Rosemary exchanged a concerned glance.

Liliana looked torn, her eyes darting between her classmates and the imposing figure of the Morrigan. "I...I didn't mean to deceive anyone," she said softly, her Irish lilt more pronounced in her distress. "I told you that my mother moved around a lot for work, didn't I?"

"You said she was a diplomat," said Ash. "And I suppose that's true too..."

"It was easier than saying she's an ancient goddess of darkness, don't you think?"

"Lily," the Morrigan said gently. "Let Mammy do her work now. I'm bringing us home a wee pet."

She returned her attention to the Devourer. A pained groan cut through the air as he writhed on the ground.

"Let Athena handle this, mother," said Liliana. "And for goodness' sake, make him human-looking again."

The Morrigan shrugged and nodded to the Cailleach. "Do your worst."

The Cailleach snapped her fingers and the Devourer rose up again, back to the size of his former human stature, losing many of the bulges and extra eyes and mouths, but retaining the dark gooey state he'd acquired.

Athena stepped forward, her heart thundering like a storm contained within her chest. The Devourer towered before her, a writhing mass of darkness and hunger that seemed to devour the very light around it. She took a deep breath, drawing on her inner strength and the lessons learned recently.

"Don," she called out, her voice carrying an unexpected resonance that echoed through the air. "I know you're in there, buried beneath layers of pain and hunger. I understand. I've felt that void too."

The Devourer roared, its cry shaking the earth beneath their feet.

. . .

YOU KNOW NOTHING, CHILD! I AM BEYOND YOUR MORTAL COMPREHENSION!

The air crackled with divine energy. The Morrigan stepped forward. "Careful, creature," she warned, her voice a symphony of battle cries. "This 'child' has more power than you know."

Brigid joined her, sunlight streaming from her hair and flowers blooming in her footsteps. "Indeed," she agreed, her voice as warm as spring's first day. "Athena, show him what lies within you."

Empowered by the goddesses' words, Athena felt a surge of magic course through her veins. She raised her hands, and to her amazement, glowing strands of golden light emerged from her fingertips, weaving intricate patterns in the air.

"Remember who you were, Don," she pleaded, sending the tendrils of light towards the Devourer. "Remember the man who loved, who dreamed, who hoped."

The creature howled as the light touched it, its form rippling like a disturbed pond. "That man was weak!" it shrieked, but there was a note of uncertainty in its voice.

Rosemary stepped forward, her eyes blazing with maternal fury and love. "No, Don. That man was strong. Strong enough to feel, to care, to connect. He only became weak when he could crave nothing but power..." As she spoke, the air around her shimmered with protective magic, bolstering Athena's light.

The Cailleach raised her staff, and a whirlwind of snow and ice swirled around the Devourer, containing its thrashing form. "Winter teaches us to find warmth within," she intoned, her voice as ancient as the mountains. "Find that spark, Don June, before the cold consumes you entirely."

Cerridwen approached, summoning a cauldron to float before her, bubbling with a potion that smelled of rebirth and renewal. "The choice is yours," she said, her eyes reflecting the wisdom of ages. "Remain as you are, or step into the cauldron of transformation."

The Devourer writhed, eyes frantically darting between the assembled goddesses and mortals. Athena's golden light continued to weave through its form, illuminating the man trapped within the monster.

Brigid stepped forward, an ornate mirror materialising in her hands. "Don June," she called, her voice ringing with the power of spring's awakening. "Look upon yourself and see the truth of your soul."

As the Devourer gazed into the mirror, a shock wave of energy pulsed outward. The assembled crowd gasped as they saw not the monster but Don's life spread out before them, memories and feelings swimming in the air - his joys, his sorrows, his loves, and his losses.

"You have shut yourself off from all light and goodness," Brigid said gently. "Your pursuit of power was an attempt to fill an unfillable void. But see now the richness of the life you've forgotten."

The Devourer trembled, its form flickering between monster and man. Black tears like liquid obsidian streamed from its eyes, sizzling where they hit the ground. "I...I see it now," it wailed, its voice a chorus of regret. "The power of my mind to turn all things to rotting deprivation. I'm...I'm a hungry ghost."

"Then choose," the goddesses said in unison, their voices merging into a symphony of power that shook the very foundations of reality.

The Devourer turned its grotesque visage towards the mirror. In its reflection, it saw not the monster it had become, but the man it once was – and all the choices that had led him to this moment.

Brigid smiled, benevolently. "Little man, your singular pursuit of power and revenge was an attempt to satisfy the insatiable. You merged with ravenous spirits because your hunger was akin. But to what end? You can never be satisfied, not through your pursuit of the suffering of others. Desires can lead to misery if we are always in the gap – always wanting, never content."

She reached out, touching the creature's temple with a glowing hand. "The choice is yours. Continue on this path of darkness, or reclaim your place in the world of light."

"I see it now…" he said, his voice like that of a young child.

"Then choose," Brigid urged.

For a moment that seemed to stretch into eternity, the creature was still. Then, with a gut-wrenching cry, it began to convulse. Black goo poured from its mouths, splattering on the ground.

Then, with a cry that echoed across dimensions, Don made his choice.

The transformation was cataclysmic.

The Devourer's form erupted in a geyser of darkness, but where the ichor touched the earth, it blossomed into a riot of magical growth.

Flowers of every description burst forth – snowdrops, crocuses, roses, and blooms that had never been seen in the mortal realm. The air filled with butterflies and birds born from the darkness, their wings shimmering with otherworldly iridescence.

As the last of the tarry substance left him, Don June collapsed to the ground, once again in human form. But he was changed – his hair streaked with silver, his eyes holding a depth of wisdom born from his ordeal. He wept openly, each tear transforming into a small, glowing crystal as it hit the ground.

"You did it," Athena whispered.

Don looked at her, his eyes clear for the first time in years. "Thank you," he said, his voice raw with emotion. "For seeing me. For not giving up."

The Morrigan approached, a rare smile on her face. "Well fought, mortals," she said, her voice carrying the cry of ravens. "You've proven yourselves worthy of our attention…"

"The ritual," Athena said. "We only just got started...it won't take long. Would you all mind?"

On one hand it seemed trivial now to complete the Imbolc festival. On the other hand, Athena had put so much work in, and it seemed an appropriate way to honour the goddesses present.

Zade sat comforting Don on the footpath as the ritual continued and was completed almost as planned if the messy interlude could be ignored.

It was traditional and beautiful and everything Athena had hoped for, especially since now the ground was covered in flowers not black goo.

As the circle was finally opened, Athena looked over at Don, seeing not the monster he had been, but the man he could become.

"You always get what you want with magic," she mused to her mother. "But the journey to get there changes you. It changes what you want."

Rosemary nodded. "That sounds incredibly wise, so I'm just going to agree."

As they joined the others, the air thrummed with possibility.

The Morrigan turned back to Rosemary, an amused glint in her eye. "Well, well. You invited me here to clean up your mess, but you know, I can't even be mad. That's exactly the kind of scheme I'd pull."

Rosemary, emboldened by the turn of events, grinned back at the goddess. "And I wouldn't hesitate to invite you again."

With a wave of the Morrigan's hand, the remaining darkness around the outskirts of the town and forest vanished, leaving behind only the sweet scent of spring flowers, regenerating trees, and wildlife.

"Right...Who's coming for cocktails?" Rosemary asked.

52

ROSEMARY

Rosemary stepped into the town hall and felt her breath catch in her throat. Marjie had outdone herself. The ceiling rippled with the illusion of a starry night sky, constellations shifting and rearranging themselves into mythical creatures that danced overhead. Ethereal trees sprouted from the corners, their branches laden with glowing fruit that pulsed in time with the soft music filling the air. Butterflies made of pure light flitted around, leaving trails of shimmering stardust in their wake.

"Marjie," Rosemary breathed, spotting her friend expertly manoeuvring through the crowd of newly arrived villagers and goddesses with a tray of drinks that seemed to change colour with each step. "This is...incredible."

Marjie beamed, her eyes twinkling almost as brightly as the stars above. "Well, we don't host goddesses every day, do we? Speaking of which, you might want to check on Ferg. He's about to wear a hole in the floor pacing in front of the buffet table."

Rosemary followed Marjie's gaze to see the mayor, looking more flustered than she'd ever seen him, frantically rearranging a platter of what appeared to be golden apples. As Rosemary made her way over, she caught some of Athena's conversation.

"You didn't tell me your mother was a goddess," Athena said to Liliana.

"I suppose it's not the sort of thing people go around bragging about," said Liliana. "It tends to just get me in trouble when other kids want me to prove it! Especially where Mammy is concerned."

"I agree," said Athena. "Your mother is terrifying, but in a good way."

"Ferg," Rosemary called as she drew near. "Everything alright?"

He spun to face her, his usually impeccable hair slightly dishevelled. "Rosemary! Do you think the ambrosia should go next to the nectar, or should I keep them separated? And the unicorn milk pudding – is it too presumptuous? I mean, it's more a themed thing than real unicorns, isn't it?"

"Ferg," Rosemary cut him off gently, placing a hand on his arm. "Take a deep breath. Everything looks wonderful. I'm sure the goddesses will be impressed."

As if summoned by her words, the Morrigan materialised beside them, eyeing the spread with interest. "Ooh, is that unicorn milk pudding? Haven't had that in centuries." She snatched up a bowl, downing it in one gulp before turning her piercing gaze on Ferg. "You, mortal. This spread is...adequate. Well done."

Ferg looked like he might faint from the faint praise. Rosemary steadied him as the Morrigan sauntered away, her dark gown seeming to absorb the light around her.

"See?" Rosemary said. "Nothing to worry about."

Across the room, Rosemary spotted Athena deep in conversation with Brigid. Her daughter's face was alight with curiosity as the goddess gestured, tiny flames dancing between her fingertips. Rosemary felt a surge of pride mixed with a twinge of worry. Athena had shown such strength and compassion during the confrontation with

Don, but Rosemary knew the road to recovery from addiction was never easy.

Her musings were interrupted by a dry chuckle beside her. The Cailleach had appeared, her ancient eyes fixed on Athena and Brigid. "Your daughter," she croaked, "she has a strong spirit. Reminds me of someone I knew...oh, a few millennia ago."

Rosemary wasn't quite sure how to respond to that. "Thank you... err I think? She's been through a lot, but she's resilient."

The Cailleach nodded sagely. "The strongest trees grow in the harshest winds, dearie. Keep nurturing that spark in her." With that cryptic advice, she shuffled off towards a group of wide-eyed townspeople, martini in hand.

Rosemary's gaze drifted to where Dain stood, deep in conversation with Cerridwen. The worry lines on his forehead had deepened, and Rosemary felt a flutter of anxiety in her stomach. Whatever was happening in the fae realm, it couldn't be good if it had Dain this concerned.

She was about to make her way over to them when a commotion near the entrance caught her attention. Burk had just arrived with a group of vampires. Among them was Azalea, who immediately made a beeline for Athena.

Rosemary watched as Azalea and Brigid exchanged a look of mutual respect before turning their attention back to Athena. It was a strange sight – a vampire therapist and a goddess, both invested in her daughter's wellbeing.

"Quite the gathering you've orchestrated," a voice purred in her ear. Rosemary turned to find the Morrigan at her elbow, a wry smile playing on her lips. "Vampires, fae, goddesses, and a town full of witches. You do like to keep things interesting, don't you, Rosemary Thorn?"

Rosemary felt her cheeks flush. "I suppose I do. Though I'll admit, this evening took a few more interesting turns than I had anticipated."

The Morrigan laughed, the sound like distant thunder. "That's the thing about magic. It has a way of taking your plans and turning them on their head. But you handled it well. That bit with Don and your spawn...it was almost impressive."

"Thank you," Rosemary said, surprised by the almost-compliment. "I just hope he's getting the help he needs now."

The goddess's expression softened almost imperceptibly. "Brigid's taking care of that. She has a soft spot for lost souls." Her gaze sharpened again as she fixed Rosemary with a penetrating look. "Now, about these cocktails you promised me..."

As Rosemary led the Morrigan towards the bar, where Marjie was now mixing drinks that sparked and fizzed with magical energy, she caught sight of her reflection in one of the large windows. She looked tired, yes, but also...proud. Proud of Athena, proud of her friends, proud of her community that had faced darkness and emerged stronger.

Moments later, Rosemary raised her glass in a silent toast to new alliances, hard-won victories, and the magic of community. The night was still young, and in Myrtlewood, anything was possible.

The night passed in a blur of laughter, music, and yes, divine cocktails. The Morrigan proved to be an enthusiastic, if terrifying, bartender, mixing drinks that smoked and changed colours. Brigid's presence caused the enchanted flowers to bloom more vigorously, their perfume intoxicating. The Cailleach's frost created intricate patterns on the glasses, while Cerridwen shared tales of ancient magic that left the listeners spellbound.

As the party began to wind down, Rosemary found herself on the balcony, taking a moment to breathe in the cool night air. She leaned against the railing, feeling the weight of the day's events settle on her shoulders. The magic in the air was palpable, a reminder of the thin veil between the mundane and the divine.

A familiar presence joined her. "Quite a night," Dain said, his voice low. There was an otherworldly quality to him now, as if the presence of the goddesses had awakened something fae within him.

Rosemary nodded, too exhausted to speak.

"You know," Dain continued, a strange note in his voice, "things are...changing in the fae realm. I may need your help soon..."

Rosemary turned to him and shook her head. "I'm going to need a lot more sleep and many more cups of tea before I can even begin to contemplate fae politics, especially the way things are going with the vampires. I can't help but feel that something is going to go dreadfully wrong."

Athena came up behind her and rested a hand on her shoulder. "And not to mention, Mum, I'm going to grow up and leave home pretty soon..."

There was a lightness in her that made Rosemary's eyes crinkle and tear up. Athena was feeling better and that was worth all the fae and vampire politics in the world.

"It sounds like you're up for new adventures," Rosemary said, hugging her daughter. "And I'll always be here for you, even when you don't want me to be."

Athena patted her on the back. "I'm counting on it."

A personal message from Iris

Hello lovelies. Thank you so much for joining me on this magical journey. If you enjoyed this book, please leave a rating or review to help other people find it!

I'm not sure when the next Myrtlewood Mysteries book will be written and published, but you can preorder the The Crone of Arcane Cinders, next Myrtlewood Crones book, on Kindle (paperbacks will be out close to the release date in January).

If you're looking for more books set in the same world, you might want to take a look at my Dreamrealm Mysteries series too.

I absolutely love writing these books and sharing them with you. Feel free to join my reader list and follow me on social media to keep up to date with my witchy adventures.

Many blessings,

Iris xx

P.S. You can also subscribe to my Patreon account for extra Myrtlewood stories and new chapters of my books before they're published, as well as real magical content like meditations and spells, and access to my Myrtlewood Discord community. Subscribing supports my writing and other creative work!

For more information, see: www.patreon.com/IrisBeaglehole

ACKNOWLEDGMENTS

A big thank you to all my wonderful Patreon supporters, especially:
- John Stephenson
- Danielle Kinghorn
- Ricky Manthey
- Wingedjewels
- Elizabeth
- Rachel
- and William Winnichuk

ABOUT THE AUTHOR

Iris Beaglehole is many peculiar things, a writer, researcher, analyst, druid, witch, parent, and would-be astrologer. She loves tea, cats, herbs, and writing quirky characters.

facebook.com/IrisBeaglehole
x.com/IrisBeaglehole
instagram.com/irisbeaglehole

Printed in Great Britain
by Amazon